THE JUDAS DILEMMA

ROBERT HEATH

www.robertheathbooks.com

Cover design by Derek Murphy

To my mother, Betty Heath, who always knew that,
one day, I would write this book. And to my wife,
Deborah, and my children Mallory, Brendan and Hayley
who made sure that I did.

And the one called Judas Iscariot went to the chief priests
and said, "What are you willing to give me if I hand him
over to you?" And they paid him thirty pieces of silver, and
from that time on he looked for an opportunity to hand him over.

—Matthew 26: 15–17 NAB

PROLOGUE

Birmingham, Alabama: 2003

She was asleep.

These days, sleep was never a sure thing for Connie Miller. Until two years ago, she'd had an ideal life, full of professional and personal fulfillment, dream vacations, and a million dollar house on the Gulf to escape to. She hadn't regretted her decision to forego law school and support her husband Alan's orthopedic surgery practice, until she'd caught him in bed with a pathologist at a medical conference in New Orleans. The ensuing divorce left her shattered, and her life was now a blur of work, soccer tournaments, and ballet recitals.

Connie dreaded spending a weekend alone in the sprawling house in Riverchase. Her son Adam was away at a soccer tournament in Columbus, GA and Ashley, her teenage daughter, was at a sleepover with several friends from school. Even Paige, her three-year-old shitzu, was unavailable, the victim of eye surgery and a postoperative infection, and was recuperating over the weekend at the vet.

Connie was thrilled when Robin Patterson called and she'd eagerly accepted Robin's invitation for a girl's night out. Connie, Robin and three friends, all divorced women, began with cocktails at Bodega's downtown, followed by dinner, and cocktails, at The Blue Onion. The Robin Williams show at the Civic Center was hilarious, and the women continued to laugh hysterically about it over more drinks back at Bodega's. Eventually, Connie caught a cab home and staggered inside, locking the door behind her but neglecting to arm the security system. She finally fell into bed at 2:00, drained and drunk, and was instantly comatose.

* * *

He watched her for a long while.

He'd been sitting two tables away from her at Bodega's, listening intently to Connie and her friends loudly complain about men in general, and their ex-husbands in particular, while his rage intensified. While they were at the Civic Center, he'd left his pickup at a restaurant, then walked to Riverchase and waited. The lock on the back door was no problem at all, and he was pleased to find the security system disarmed, though he was more than capable of bypassing it.

Now, sitting silently in the darkness of her bedroom, he could hear his own heart beating in his ears so loudly that, for a moment, he feared that it might wake her. So he waited, watching. He'd been here before.

Arising, he smiled slightly as he crossed the room and approached the bed.

He knew she was alone.

He could take his time.

CHAPTER ONE

The face that stared back at Rian Coulter wasn't pretty. In fact, Rian wasn't sure that she'd ever looked worse.

Clad only in panties, she stood in front of the bathroom mirror in her hotel room at the New Orleans Marriott and surveyed herself. Her shoulder length dark brown hair seemed to go in a hundred different directions. She had become fairly adept at spotting the grey ones, which, even at age thirty-one, were beginning to assert themselves regularly, and she pulled the obvious ones out. Her normally crystal blue eyes looked puffy and bloodshot, the aftermath of a weeklong bout with allergies and the foray into the French Quarter last night.

I wish I hadn't agreed to do this, she mumbled to herself. *I feel like shit.*

She washed down two Advil and a Claritin with some sulphur smelling tap water and picked up her iPhone to check the time. It was 8:30, and her speech before the annual meeting of the Southern Defense Lawyers Association was an hour away. She could resurrect herself and be ready to give a lecture on her topic, "Ethical Considerations in Defending Criminal Cases," to a room full of colleagues who were, undoubtedly, more hung over than she was.

While most criminal defense lawyers viewed the annual SDLA meeting as a tax-deductible reason to party in New Orleans, Rian was on a different schedule. It had been a particularly frantic week for her already. She'd been in depositions for three days this week, followed by a hearing on her motion to suppress the evidence in the Gibson case.

Her client, Amari Gibson, was charged with possession of cocaine as the result of a search warrant served at his home two months ago. The search warrant, in describing the premises to be searched, only mentioned the house. The coke had been found in Gibson's car, and Rian had argued to the court that the police had illegally exceeded the search authority authorized by the warrant and, therefore, the evidence should be suppressed.

The judge had taken the case under advisement and had indicated that he would rule on the question by Monday. If the motion was granted, the case was over as there was no other evidence to prosecute Gibson. If not, the case would be one more trial on Rian's already overflowing calendar.

Ordinarily, this sort of routine felony case would be handled by one of the Assistant Public Defenders assigned to the trial division. As the Chief Assistant, Rian normally handled the more high profile, serious cases such as murders, rapes, and major drug trafficking defenses.

Several of her assistants had left the office for private practice, and the abysmal budget appropriation for the Public Defender's Office had left her boss, Jack Brown, unable to replace them.

Since there was little hope that the Florida legislature would increase their funding any time in the near future, Rian had to pitch in and take on more cases in addition to her administrative duties.

Money for defending criminals wasn't a popular topic in a Republican dominated legislature, and this was an election year.

As she continued to get dressed, Rian's mind drifted to Sean Rowan. He was charged with manslaughter arising from an auto accident in which Sean, nineteen, was accused of drag racing with another teenager in Pensacola. The roads were wet and Sean had lost control of his car when he rounded a curve and slammed on his brakes to avoid another car stopped in the middle of the road. The other driver had stopped to talk with some girls standing on the side of the road, and Sean's car had hit a drainage culvert and flipped, killing one of the girls instantly. Both Sean and his passenger, Paul Sansom, had been injured, Paul seriously when he was thrown into the dashboard and suffered a closed head injury.

Rian had learned from the deposition of the toxicologist this week that Sean had no alcohol nor illegal substances in his blood and that the driver of the stopped car had a blood alcohol level of .12, well over the legal limit of .08. The prosecution's expert witness had made a good impression in his deposition this week and although Rian had managed to score a few points, she was unsure whether she could poke enough holes in his testimony for the jury to disbelieve him.

Paul's deposition had been heartbreaking, the effects of his head injury still lingering.

Sean had no previous criminal record, and his fate lay squarely in Rian Coulter's hands. The case was weighing on her heavily, and her pretrial nerves were already kicking in. The trial was three weeks away.

Rian's phone blared Frank Sinatra singing it his way, her father's ringtone.

"Hi, Dad," Rian said when she answered. "Everything okay?"

"Everything's fine, Peanut," her father replied, using the nickname he'd called her by since she was a little girl. "We're about to get on the road and I just wanted to check in with you. Your mother's running a little behind schedule."

Rian smiled, picturing her father in the car in the driveway ready to go and waiting impatiently while her mother puttered around the house, checking again to make sure the doors were still locked and the stove was still turned off.

Rian's father Craig was a Tallahassee dentist. He'd insisted on naming her Rian, with the unusual spelling, as a nod to his Irish heritage, and Rian had always enjoyed the looks on everyone's faces when she was introduced and they realized she was most definitely not the male they had anticipated. Her mother Beverly retired from the Leon County school system last year after a breast cancer scare.

The Coulters had a vacation house at St. Teresa, south of Tallahassee near the little hamlet of Panacea, and they were headed there for a couple of weeks. Rian spent many summers there in the large log cabin house lounging in the hammock on the back porch and eating fried grouper at Angelina's. She hadn't seen the house in years.

"Patience is a virtue, Dad," Rian chided him. "Call me when you get there and say hey to Angie for me."

"I will. Good luck with the speech, and remember to smell the roses. Love you." Whenever Dr. Coulter thought that his ambitious oldest child was working too hard, he would remind her to "stop and smell the roses." There just weren't any roses in her garden right now.

"Love you," Rian replied and clicked off.

In the seven years since she'd graduated from law school at Vanderbilt University, Rian had risen quickly in the legal profession. She excelled at Vanderbilt under the tutelage of Professor Charles Eastan, who had drafted the Model Evidence Code that many states had adopted as their own. He fueled Rian's passion to be a trial lawyer, and she had been a powerhouse on Eastan's moot court team in school, winning the southern regional trial competition twice and losing only to Stanford in the nationals.

Upon graduation, she accepted a position with a competitive salary at the Birmingham, AL firm of Ashton, Baker, Pennington & Moring, a blue blood civil litigation firm that represented corporate, oil and gas, and insurance clients. Rian soon realized that, although she was required to bill 2,400 hours a year, she would only see the inside of a courtroom if she were setting up an exhibit for one of the partners and that it would be years before she would ever be allowed to try a case of her own. It was impossible to bill forty-five hours a week without either working twice as many or cheating, something Rian was unwilling to do.

After little more than a year, she left and accepted an entry-level position in the Public Defender's Office in the First Judicial Circuit of Florida. The office was based in Pensacola, a quiet, mid-sized town on the Gulf Coast in northwest Florida less than fifty miles from the Alabama border. Her salary was a fraction of what she had earned at Ashton, Baker but she had all of the trial work she wanted.

Rian invigorated the office and voraciously tried cases throughout the circuit from Pensacola to the eastern edge of the circuit in Walton County, trying over seventy jury trials in six years. As court appointed counsel, public defenders had virtually no choice in selecting their clients, many of whom were guilty of the offenses with which they were charged. The success rate in trial for public defenders was usually low, but Rian had distinguished herself as a gifted trial lawyer. She never ventured into a courtroom without being thoroughly prepared and she quickly established a reputation as a formidable adversary in trial. Prosecutors regularly reevaluated their plea offers when she was assigned to a case.

None of this went unnoticed by Jack Brown, the elected Public Defender who quickly promoted her to the Felony Division, then to Chief Assistant. Rian's name was already being bandied about town as Brown's successor should he decide not to seek reelection.

At 9:20, Rian strode down the hotel hallway, transformed from her earlier self and now wearing a navy blue suit, tailored perfectly to accentuate the athletic body that she worked hard to maintain. Her silk blouse and Antonio Melani pumps gave her a feminine, yet professional look, a balance essential to maintain for female lawyers. She strode confidently into the hotel ballroom, ignoring the not-so-subtle glances in her direction, and took her place at the end of the table on the stage. Five minutes later, she gave her colleagues a big, bright smile and told them how to effectively represent their clients while avoiding the ethical pitfalls along the way.

CHAPTER TWO

"And I'd like some attention paid to . . . just a minute," the woman said, turning and resuming her conversation with the device attached to her right ear. She walked away, leaving him standing in the driveway like an idiot while she shrieked and swore at the person who had drawn her ire.

"No, Danny, I *cannot* wait. These buyers are highly motivated, and if I don't show this listing within the hour, they're going to go with someone else. He's an executive with Alabama Power, for Christ's sake, and he's only here for the day. They can probably pay cash for the goddamn house."

Apparently, Danny still hadn't seen the light because she began to pace back and forth in the street, her high heels beating a staccato rhythm on the pavement and gesturing with her hands.

"Tell the fucking bank I'll call them back, then have the buyers meet me at the property in twenty minutes," she said, punctuating the air with her finger. "It's in Oak Ridge, that new gated community in Pelham near the Galleria. Tell them to take the Oxmoor Valley exit," she commanded. "The address is 3214 Valley Ridge Road."

She touched her ear, disconnecting the call, and marched arrogantly to her Mercedes parked in the driveway.

She completely ignored the man standing there quietly leaning on his rake, and was already on another call by the time she roared past him, taking a right out of her driveway and accelerating down the street.

* * *

He watched her disappear in the distance, then smiled to himself.

Taking the pruning shears from his truck, he busied himself for a few minutes in the shrubs near the east window, which he learned led to a laundry room. Noting the utility box was unlocked, he opened it using the shears, studied it briefly, and closed it, again using the shears.

He climbed back into his truck and slowly backed out of the driveway, then proceeded in the same direction that the woman had shortly before. He drove deliberately to the I-65 entrance ramp and headed south, taking the Oxmoor Valley exit near Valley Ridge Road in the Oak Ridge subdivision.

CHAPTER THREE

Judge Terrell Carson strode up the ramp toward the bench, his black robe flowing behind him as the court security officer called court to order.

"All rise," the uniformed officer announced. "The Circuit Court in and for Escambia County, Florida is now in session. The Honorable Terrell C. Carson, presiding."

The judge took his seat on the bench and welcomed everyone, inviting them all to sit as well. Carson was a large man, athletically built, and looked much younger than his sixty-four years. He still had a military demeanor, although it had been decades since he'd last flown a Navy fighter and retired at the rank of captain. Carson had been the first African-American judge in Escambia County history, appointed by Governor Lawton Chiles in 1992 and re-elected without opposition since. A former prosecutor, Judge Carson was widely regarded by the lawyers who practiced before him as a tough, no nonsense, yet fair judge.

The courtroom wasn't large, but was impressive nonetheless. Rich oak paneling on the walls surrounded them, and there were rows of church pews on either side of an aisle behind the ornately carved oak bar about three feet high that bisected the room. A hinged gate in the wall allowed admittance to the area where the trials were conducted.

The jury box contained two rows of seats and extended down one wall of the courtroom. In the center was the judge's bench, on a raised platform that placed him well above anyone else in the room. The Great Seal of the State of Florida glimmered on the wall behind him, between flag stands bearing the American flag on one side and the flag of the State of Florida on the other.

To one side and below the bench, only a few feet from the jury, was the witness stand, a small box and seat where the witnesses would sit while testifying during a trial. The clerk of court sat in an identical box on the other side of the bench.

The lawyers sat at the two oak conference tables arranged in front of the bench about eight feet apart. A court reporter sat directly in front of the bench, straddling a computerized stenographic machine, awaiting the judge's signal and primed to record every word uttered during the court proceedings. This whole area was set a few feet below the rest of the courtroom, giving it a theater- like quality.

Judge Carson gazed down at the lawyers and asked, "Is the State ready to proceed?"

Alan Banning, the prosecutor rose from his seat and said, "The State is ready."

"Is the defense ready?" asked the judge.

"We are, Your Honor," said Rian, placing a reassuring hand on Sean Rowan's shoulder.

"Mr. Banning, you may make your opening statement," instructed Carson.

Banning stood and cast a smug, self-confident look at Rian as he strode to the podium to outline the State's case for the jury. She gave him a smile and, without the jury seeing it, a slight wink that caught Banning off guard.

Banning, you cocky son of a bitch. You have no idea what's coming.

Banning gave the jury an overview of what he expected the State's evidence to show and reminded them that their verdict was to be based solely upon the evidence, not on any feeling of sympathy.

Both he and the judge looked startled when Rian waived her opening statement, choosing to present her version of the case after the State rested theirs. This was an unusual move and somewhat risky since the jury would only hear the initial evidence in the case through the prism of the prosecution's viewpoint. The jury might conclude that Rian didn't have an alternative theory to present and might be inclined to lean the State's way before ever hearing evidence from the defense. On the contrary, veteran defense lawyers like Rian Coulter could poke holes in the State's case through cross examination, then snatch the momentum away by giving a powerful and detailed opening statement before presenting the defense's case.

Banning spent the rest of the afternoon plodding through a typical prosecution case; the investigating officer, who described the scene upon his arrival, the medical examiner, who testified that the death of the victim was caused by blunt force trauma to the head, shattering her skull and severing her spinal cord.

The driver of the other car that Sean was supposedly racing also testified. On cross-examination, he admitted to Rian that he'd never met Sean and there had been no discussion of or agreement to race that evening. He just assumed that Sean wanted to race him because Sean's tires spun when he left the parking lot of the grocery store that was closed for the evening.

Things got a little more interesting when poor Paul Sansom testified. Rian asked one question on cross; was Sean engaged in a drag race that night?

"I don't know. I have no memory of that night," Paul said.

As court recessed for the day, Sean looked anxiously at Rian.

"Things went pretty much as anticipated today, Sean," Rian said, understanding his anxiety. "Tomorrow is our day. Go get some dinner and try to take your mind off things. I'll see you in the morning."

The fireworks will begin then.

As she left the courtroom and headed back to the office, Rian could already feel the stress and tension of the day closing in on her. She was always spent after a day in trial, even if things had gone well. As she passed through the security door and headed down the hall to her office, her secretary Abby Threadgill emerged from the copy room and they nearly collided.

"Hey," Rian greeted her. "Did we get everything?"

"Every bit of it," Abby responded with a conspiratorial grin. "It's all on your desk except for this last bit that I just copied." She handed Rian a stack of documents.

"And you put the brief on a flash drive so I can edit it tonight, just in case the system crashes?" Rian asked.

"Done. Just email me any changes tonight and I'll finalize it by the time you get here in the morning," Abby said.

"Perfect. I'm out of here then. Thanks, Abby."

Rian threw the papers Abby had given her along with another stack on her desk into a briefcase and left through the door that led to the parking garage. Her black BMW 328i was parked in its reserved space near the door. There were few perks that came with her position in the Public Defender's Office and a BMW was certainly not among them. The car had been a surprise from her father for her thirtieth birthday last year. The parking space was courtesy of the taxpayers.

Rian instinctively looked around for safety reasons, then climbed into the car. She pulled out her phone and checked her emails and text messages. There were the usual interoffice emails, and one from Sam, letting her know that he'd made the flight to Atlanta after all and would arrive in Pensacola around 9:00.

Nothing in Pensacola was far from anything else, and it only took a few minutes for Rian to drive the seven miles from her office to the townhouse she rented in the Historic District. She was too preoccupied on this night to appreciate the beautiful, tree-lined streets, the gas lanterns, and the colonial architecture, but she always had a warm and cozy feeling when she pulled up to her little home nested between the huge oak trees.

It was a warm April evening, and the tulips, petunias and, impatiens that covered the front flower beds were in full bloom.

Inside, Rian quickly changed from her suit into a t-shirt, shorts, and running shoes, pausing only to speak to Mannix, her cat that was loudly demanding attention. She needed a run to relax and clear her mind for the work she still had to do tonight to be ready for court tomorrow.

She dropped some food in the bowl for Mannix, pulled her hair back into a ponytail, slipped in her iPod earphones, and headed out the door.

Pensacola was the westernmost city in Florida, or as the mayor put it, "the Western Gate to the Sunshine State." Founded by Spanish explorers in the sixteenth century, the city sat at the southern tip of Escambia County. The downtown overlooked Pensacola Bay and, just beyond, the Gulf of Mexico.

Cultural life was focused mainly in the Historic District, a sizeable area of two hundred year old homes, churches, and other buildings that had been converted into shops, offices, and restaurants. A few miles to the south was one of the most picturesque beaches in the world, with the typical assortment of beach bars, outdoor restaurants and, in recent years, high rise condominiums. With its laid back style, her adopted hometown suited Rian perfectly.

After the first mile or so, Rian could feel the tension beginning to fade from her body, and by mile two, she was already mapping out her cross examination of Paul Jasinski, the State's accident reconstruction expert who was to testify tomorrow.

She planned to blow Jasinski, and the State's case, out of the water, and she quickened her pace, eager to get back home and look at the materials that Sam's office had gathered on Jasinski.

Rian cruised past the bayside seafood companies and virtually sprinted the last part of her four-mile course. Pouring sweat and breathing heavily, she arrived back at the townhouse tired but ready to work. She called in a delivery order of Greek pasta from Mancini's down the street, which arrived just after she finished her shower. She ate quickly, then settled onto the sunroom couch with Mannix to go through the stack of depositions, financial records, and other impeachment material.

Three hours later she was ready.

* * *

At nine o'clock the next morning, Rian watched impassively as Alan Banning led Jasinski through his qualifications for the jury; undergraduate and master's degrees in civil engineering from SMU and several years of consulting work at his firm named Jasinski Engineering and Analysis in Austin, TX. He droned on for several more minutes describing the field of engineering and his involvement as an expert witness in various courts in the field of accident reconstruction.

Jasinski had conducted tests of the road surface where the accident occurred and Sean's Camaro, ultimately concluding that Sean was traveling at a speed of sixty-six miles per hour when he applied his brakes and slid off the road, killing the unfortunate young lady standing there. Such speed, especially under the conditions, was clearly unsafe, according to Jasinski, and was the major contributing factor to the crash that took the victim's life.

The speed limit was only thirty-five in the area, and Rian knew that if the jury believed his testimony, Sean would be in serious trouble.

Jasinski certainly looked the part, dressed in an expensive gray suit, starched white shirt, and an electric blue tie. His thinning hair and white pocket square in his coat reminded Rian of Joe Biden.

As she rose to cross examine him, Rian gave Jasinski and the jury a warm smile, then approached the witness stand and extended her hand.

"Hello, Mr. Jasinski," she said. "I'm Rian Coulter. It's nice to finally meet you."

Jasinski looked confused, unsure of whether to shake hands with her or not. Banning started to rise to object, then hesitated and sat back down. Jasinski looked at him for some sort of signal and, seeing none, reluctantly shook Rian's hand.

"Uh, hi," was all he could manage with a half smile.

"Sir," Rian continued as she walked back to the counsel table, "when did you reach the conclusion that Sean was traveling at sixty-six miles per hour?"

"After conducting the physical tests on the roadway, determining the weight of Mr. Rowan's vehicle and inspecting the tires," he answered.

"And you were hired by Mr. Banning in this case ten weeks ago?"

"Correct," said Jasinski.

"At a cost of?" Rian asked.

"My initial retainer was $3,500," Jasinski said proudly.

"And you charge $300 per hour from the time you left your office in Austin until you return, correct?" said Rian, hoping the jury was already doing the math.

"Yes, that's correct," said Jasinski.

"It's important for you to examine the road surface so that you can calculate the coefficient of friction of the road and the tires to determine the speed of the vehicle, isn't it?" asked Rian.

"Yes," he said.

"And when did you perform that examination, Mr. Jasinski?" she asked.

"Two days ago," answered Jasinski. Rian could see Banning flinch out of the corner of her eye.

"Was Mr. Banning or anyone from his office with you at the time?" she asked.

"No."

"Then, by any chance, did Mr. Banning show you this?" Rian said as she reached over and pulled a document out of her trial notebook and approached him, handing him the document. Jasinski's face darkened when he read it, and he looked up silently, glancing again at Banning.

"What is that document, sir?" asked Rian, standing halfway between the counsel table and Jasinski.

"Well, it, uh, it appears to be a government report that I'm not familiar with," he said.

"It's a report from the State of Florida Department of Transportation showing that Beal Avenue, the *same* Beal Avenue where this accident happened, was resurfaced over sixty days ago, isn't it, Mr. Jasinski?" Rian said, her voice rising.

"It appears so, yes," said Jasinski, softly.

"And changing the road surface from a gravel road to blacktop would dramatically affect your speed calculations, wouldn't it, sir?"

"No," said Jasinski confidently, regaining his composure.

"You're certain?" she asked with raised eyebrows.

"Yes."

Rian walked back to the counsel table and retrieved a document.

"Sir, do you recall testifying as an expert in the case of *State vs. Arbinger* in the Harris County District Court in Houston in 2002?" she asked.

"I'm not sure . . . I've testified in many different cases," he responded defensively. At this point Banning woke up and protested.

"Objection. We haven't been provided this information," he said.

Before Rian could respond, the judge overruled the objection. Rian handed a bound volume to Jasinski and asked that he turn to page eighty. She handed an identical one to Banning.

"Did you not testify under oath in that case that calculating the coefficient of friction on a road surface changed from gravel to blacktop would render any determination of speed impossible?" she asked.

"Yes, but--" he replied, but Rian was on a roll and already changing directions.

"Since you've testified here that you've made many court appearances, how many times have you testified as an expert for the prosecution in criminal cases in the past five years, Mr. Jasinski?" she asked.

"Three, maybe four," he answered.

Rian walked back to the table and produced two large boxes from underneath, placed there by Abby this morning before court began.

"Sir, I have here trial transcripts from nineteen trials and twenty-two depositions that you've given since 2009 as an expert in accident reconstruction, metal fatigue, and even a gunshot case, all for the prosecution. You've been paid an average over $150,000 a year for the past seven years as the prosecution's expert. Is that true? You're under oath here," Rian said, glancing over at the jury, who was paying close attention.

Banning was on his feet. "Objection," he screamed. "Your Honor, this is outrageous," he pleaded, but the damage had been done already.

"It certainly is," said Judge Carson. "Answer the question, Mr. Jasinski."

Jasinski stared at Rian for a long moment, his shock turning to anger, then resignation.

"Yes," he said quietly. "I don't dispute it."

She handed him another document and he stared down at it.

"Your testimony was stricken in the case of *Commonwealth vs. Prentiss* last year in Boston on the basis of fraud, wasn't it, sir?" Rian continued.

"That was a misunderstanding," Jasinski protested.

"But a fact, nevertheless," Rian said. "I have more. Need I go on?" she asked, satisfied that she had shown Jasinski to be the hired gun that he was.

Now it was Judge Carson who was on his feet. "We'll be in recess. Counsel, in my chambers. Now!" he ordered and stormed off the bench.

When Rian and Banning got to the judge's chambers, they found him with his black robe unzipped, pacing the floor while the court reporter set up her machine. Banning started to speak, but the judge held up his hand, stopping him cold.

"This is all on the record," he said ominously.

When the court reporter nodded, the judge sat on the corner of his desk, crossed his arms, and looked squarely at Banning.

"Mr. Banning," he began, "you have about sixty seconds to convince me that you didn't know about all of this ahead of time."

Banning looked deflated. "Your Honor," he pleaded, "I hope you know me better than that. I swear to you that I didn't know. He came highly recommended, and we vetted him, or at least I thought we did."

No one spoke for a minute. At last, the judge smiled and shook his head.

"I thought I'd seen just about every damn thing possible, but this beats most of it," he said, chuckling. "I assume he's your only witness as to what happened?"

"Unfortunately, yes," Banning replied wearily.

Judge Carson turned to Rian, who thus far hadn't said a word.

"Then I see no reason to keep going. Ms. Coulter, I assume you'll be moving to dismiss?" he asked.

"Yes, Your Honor," Rian replied. The judge cut his eyes to Banning.

"And you won't be opposing the motion?" he said. Banning shook his head.

"The record will reflect that Mr. Banning indicated no. Motion granted. Case dismissed."

Rian felt a surge of relief, but a little sorry for Alan Banning. He was smug and unjustifiably cocky but, overall, not a bad guy. The abuse that he would endure when word of this disaster reached his office would be severe.

They returned to the courtroom, and Rian informed Sean that the case was over and he was free to go. His jaw dropped, then he hugged Rian tightly, then hugged his parents who were seated in the gallery. Rian turned to shake Banning's hand, but his table was cleared and he was nowhere in sight. She suspected that by the time she got back to the office, he would already be at O'Steen's Irish Pub.

Rian turned and was surprised to see Sam sitting in the back of the courtroom. He smiled and slowly clapped his hands, then stood and came toward her.

"Not bad, Counselor," Sam said as he put his arm around her. "You could be a rich woman in private practice."

"How long have you been here?" Rian asked, stepping back so she could look at him.

My God. I've missed you.

"Long enough to see the good stuff," Sam said, smiling. "Let's go. Inform your office that you're gone for the rest of the day."

Rian and Sam locked arms and left the courtroom together.

CHAPTER FOUR

Lieutenant Glenn Palmer gazed at the water as he drove east on Highway 98.

Although the drive along the coastal highway was always scenic, the view from the bridge over the Destin pass was nothing short of spectacular. To his right, Palmer could see the beach surrounding Destin Harbor, a small cove that emptied through the pass directly into the Gulf of Mexico. On a sunny day, the sugar white sand contrasted with the Gulf water which, in this particular spot, was a brilliant emerald green in the shallow harbor area and changed to a sapphire blue as it became deeper. This was why they called this area the Emerald Coast.

Ahead was Destin, once a small fishing village that had been transformed back in the seventies when the developers moved in and began building high rise condominiums on the beach. The sleepy little fishing village was now a busy vacation destination with year-round tourists from all over the world bustling between the beach, the high end outlet shopping malls, and expensive restaurants. Multimillion dollar homes dotted the landscape, and it wasn't unusual to spot some of the rich and famous who occasionally escaped to Destin. It was rumored that Tom Cruise owned one of the houses on the Gulf.

The serenity of the scenery was in stark contrast to the objective of Palmer's trip. The Walton County Sheriff's Department had requested his assistance in the investigation of a homicide at a house just east of Destin.

Although Destin itself, and the high rises, were situated in Okaloosa County, it sat right on the border of Walton County which was much more rural. The county seat, DeFuniak Springs, was thirty miles to the north and was a typical Southern small town with the county courthouse square in the center of town. It bore little resemblance to the southern part of the county on the coast that had become smugly known as South Walton.

From swampy land filled with palmetto plants and occasional small, run-down, flat-roofed cottages developers created beachfront living communities like Seaside and Watercolors. These quaint, self sustaining hamlets contained a mixture of expensive homes, townhouses, shops, restaurants, small grocery stores, and medical facilities, all surrounding interior parks and connected by an interlocking web of narrow streets, pedestrian walkways and boardwalks. Outside of these small communities, South Walton retained much of its rural character. Although much more secluded and quiet than its neighbor Destin to the west, property values here were ridiculously expensive and exclusive.

It was unusual for Escambia County deputies to be called to assist in counties as far away as Walton, but Palmer's experience as an investigator was unique.

He held a master's degree in criminology from Florida State University and spent fifteen years as an investigator with the Florida Department of Law Enforcement in Tallahassee. His reputation as a skilled investigator with a forensics background made him a valued addition to the Sheriff's Department when his old friend Jim Rhodes was elected Sheriff.

Rhodes offered Palmer the position as Chief Deputy, but Palmer declined, preferring instead to accept less money in exchange for the ability to revamp the Crimes Against Persons Unit and the autonomy to run it however he wished. True to his word, Rhodes had stayed out of his way, and Palmer now ran a top notch department of seventeen investigators.

Palmer continued east on U.S. 98 through Destin, past the Sandestin resort, and into Walton County where he turned south onto State Road 30. He drove through Grayton Beach and into the Blue Mountain community, stopping at a yellow one-story house where an unmarked police car and a marked Walton County cruiser were parked in the driveway.

Yellow crime scene tape was strung between the front porch columns and still made an "X" design on the front door, even though the crime had taken place over a week ago and Palmer knew there would be no body present.

As he got out of his car, Palmer saw Sergeant Randy West leaning against the unmarked car along with another officer Palmer didn't recognize. Palmer had worked with West before and considered him to be a good investigator. A uniformed deputy was standing near the front door.

"Sergeant West, I presume," Palmer said as he approached them, eliciting a smile from West. The two men shook hands, and West introduced Brian Proctor, an investigator in his department. Proctor was all business and the two shook hands.

"Thanks for coming, Glenn," West began. "We can go inside and I'll fill you in as we go."

The three officers walked up the stone path to the house where the uniformed officer had unhooked the crime scene tape so they could enter. West produced a small pocket knife and carefully slit the tape at the door and unlocked it with a key.

The door opened into a great room with two cream-colored leather couches aligned perpendicular to each another facing a large plasma television in the corner. An open kitchen to the left overlooked an eat-in bar and the living room.

The tile floor echoed their steps as the three walked in, and Palmer immediately noticed an odor that he had smelled many times, but never grown accustomed to. It was the smell of death, a part sweet, part sour mixture of blood, feces, and other body fluids that escape a body after death. Even after a week, the smell still lingered.

"Bedroom's back this way," Proctor said, motioning to his left down a hallway. Palmer noticed a few drops of blood on the hallway wall and more on the tile floor at the entrance to the bedroom. Stepping inside the bedroom, he noticed that it was sparsely furnished with a cheap wicker dresser and mirror and an inexpensive chair in the corner. The room was dominated by a king-sized bed in the center. The bedcovers were thrown to one side and the pillows were crusted with dried blood. Other stains were apparent on the sheets.

"Obviously, the victim was found in the bed," West began. "She had a deep head wound. The ME thinks she was dead for about two days before she was found due to the amount of decomp. We think she was struck once in the hall, causing the spatter that you saw on the wall, then killed here."

"Tell me about the bindings," said Palmer.

"That's why I called you. She was basically hog tied. Thin rope was looped around her neck, through a slipknot, then around her ankles and tightened. Her head was pulled back almost touching her feet. If she tried to lower her legs, she would increase the pressure on her throat. Her legs would have cramped like hell. Must've been excruciating. I downloaded all of the pictures on a flash drive that I'll send back with you."

"What's her story?" asked Palmer.

"Her name was Monica Jessup, age forty, county comptroller from Baton Rouge. Rented this same house two years ago and had been here for a few days before this happened. A lawyer in Tifton, GA owns the house. He rents it out through a local real estate firm."

"Witnesses?"

"Nothing. We haven't found anyone who interacted with her at all. Nobody saw or heard a damn thing. We don't even know if the murder took place at night or in broad daylight."

"Front door looks clean," Palmer observed. "Any sign of forced entry?"

"Looks like someone tried to force the back door but it didn't work. We aren't sure how he got in."

Palmer looked around the room. The hard surfaces were black with fingerprint dust, and pieces of the sheets and pillow cases had been cut and removed. He walked through the rest of the house, but noticed nothing else significant.

Leaving through the front door, he walked around the house, inspecting the ground, windows, and the back door, noticing gouge marks in the frame as though someone had tried to pry it open. It was a metal door and was slightly bent around the lock. The house sat at three o'clock in a small cul-de-sac, but there were no other houses near it.

It was unlikely that anyone in the nearby houses had heard anything. During the summer, the inhabitants of this community were pretty transient.

The June heat soon had all of them out of their sport coats and loosening their ties despite the breeze blowing in from the Gulf. West locked up the house, and Palmer followed him to the small sheriff's substation that serviced South Walton.

An uneasy feeling had been gnawing at Palmer since West had described the way Monica Jessup had been tied up. Proctor produced some bottles of water and they sat together at a beat-up conference table in the back of the office. West retrieved a file from a briefcase and passed it to Palmer.

"This is the case file so far. We don't have the tox report back yet on Ms. Jessup. That'll probably take another week. Naturally, we got a million prints from the place, so that's been a dead end, too. Everything is on this zip drive," West said, passing Palmer a small USB drive. Palmer slipped it into his shirt pocket and opened the file.

A typed report by the first officer on the scene recounted that a housekeeper who came to the house two days a week had found Ms. Jessup. It was a service offered by the real estate company that rented the house and the cost was built into the rent. The housekeeper entered as usual through the front door at approximately ten o'clock on Friday morning and discovered the victim in the bedroom.

The front door had been locked but not dead bolted. The dead bolt required a key to both lock and unlock. She had last been there on Tuesday morning, leaving about noon.

West's initial report was next, noting the interview with the neighbors and the rental company that turned up nothing. Ms. Jessup's Jeep Cherokee had been processed, then released to her family. Her American Express account indicated that she'd had dinner at a local restaurant named Carmella's on Tuesday night, leading West to conclude she had died either that night or sometime Wednesday since that was the last charge on the card.

No one at Carmella's remembered seeing Monica Jessup that night. She apparently had dined alone but had some drinks and wine on her credit card.

"Not a lot to go on, I know," West observed. "We're still interviewing people, but it seems that when Ms. Jessup wanted to get away, she did just that."

Palmer flipped a file divider over and thumbed through the crime scene photographs. They had obviously been taken with a digital camera because the file copies were little more than thumbnails of the larger photographs. All he could discern from them was that Monica had been face down on the bed with a gaping wound in the back of her head. Her hands and feet had been bound behind her. He would study the pictures more closely when he got back to the office and retrieved the photos from the flash drive. There was no autopsy report or anything else from the medical examiner in the file.

As he closed the file, Palmer noted that the disquieting feeling he'd been having had increased.

He handed the file back to West and asked, "What does the ME say about sexual assault and cause of death?"

"Sexual assault with some form of object as yet undetermined. No semen in Ms. Jessup, and we didn't find any on the bed or any bloody objects at the scene. She'd been hit with something in the throat that caused major bruising. Cause of death was more than likely loss of blood from the blow to the head, but the autopsy report isn't back yet either."

Palmer mulled this over. "Randy, you guys need to keep a tight lid on the media about this. I haven't heard anything about it over in Pensacola, which is good. What about here?"

"Initial news story, but it hit on a Friday evening when nobody was watching. Nothing since."

"Good. I'd suggest no news conferences or updates. I don't think a lot of these details need to be known."

"Agreed."

"I'll start working this and let you know if we come up with anything."

"Okay. I'll let you know when the autopsy and tox reports are back. What's the best way to get those to you?"

"Fax them," said Palmer and handed West his business card.

The men rose and shook hands again as Palmer left. West's department was overworked, understaffed and ill equipped to handle an investigation like this. He knew that if this case was going to be solved, it would be up to his team.

As he turned his car back toward Pensacola, Glenn Palmer could not shake the strange, unsettling feeling that he had.

For some reason, there was something different about this case.

CHAPTER FIVE

Rian's iPhone sprang to life with Carrie Underwood singing "All American Girl," Abby's ringtone. She thought for a moment about letting it go to voicemail, then felt guilty about it. She sat on the bed and punched the button.

"Abby, please tell me you just have a question."

"Hey, Boss. I'm sorry to bother you on your day off, but we have a situation. Barry Sellers's wife went into labor this morning and he has plea day at nine. Jack says he needs you to cover."

Fuck. They never leave me alone.

"Tell Madison or Granger to do it," Rian snapped. "I need a day off."

"Already tried that. Madison's got depositions and Jack says Granger can't handle Judge Axley. He said to find you."

Shit.

Sam stuck his still wet head out of the bathroom and looked at Rian, a toothbrush protruding from the side of his mouth. She looked back at him and shook her head.

"How many cases?"

"Fourteen. He's announcing ready for trial in one, nine have signed plea offers in the file. You'll have to work something out on the other four."

Just perfect.

Rian glanced at the clock radio on the table. It was 8:15. She'd have to break her neck just to get there on time and she didn't want to be late for Judge Axley. She was stuck, and she knew it.

"Pull the files and put the four that I have to work pleas on top. Who's the ASA on these?"

"Brian Lassiter," said Abby.

At least he's reasonable.

Rian sighed. "Okay, I'm on my way."

Sam stepped out in his t-shirt and boxers. "Let me guess," he said sarcastically. "So-and-so's got a hangnail, the supervisor's got a hemorrhoid, and you're the only one who can save the day."

"Pretty close, McKinney," she said. "You know how it is when you're indispensible."

"I'm serious," he said. "You're getting used, Rian, and you know it. You have too much talent and potential to be doing this mundane shit." Rian knew he had a point, but it still pissed her off.

"Look. I have to be in front of Axley in forty-five minutes. I don't have time for this, so spare me the lecture, okay?"

Sam held up his hands in mock surrender and stepped aside so Rian could hop into the shower. She skipped the hair wash and was in and out in five minutes, dressed and downstairs ten minutes later. Rian fortunately didn't need much makeup.

She walked into the kitchen and found Sam leaning against the counter, a mug of coffee in hand. His dark hair was neatly in place and he was dressed in a blue, French-cuffed shirt with gold nugget cufflinks, gray slacks, expensive wine-colored shoes and matching belt. His initials, *SJM*, Samuel Jackson McKinney, were embroidered on his shirt pocket, which held an expensive, onyx-colored fountain pen. His blue blazer was draped over the back of a chair.

She looked at him briefly, then walked over and kissed him softly. "I'm sorry," she whispered. "Sometimes I'm just not fit to be around."

"Already forgotten," Sam replied. "I know you need to go, but I still think you should give it some thought."

"I will," Rian promised. She poured coffee into a stainless steel travel mug. "I'll cook for us tonight, okay?"

"Sounds good to me. I'll call when I leave the office."

As Rian headed out the door, she tried to push down the frustration rising inside her. She had seven years of legal experience now and had already tried as many jury trials as other lawyers twice her age. The reason she had accepted the position with the public defender in the first place was to gain trial experience. She now had that.

While she still enjoyed the high profile cases, she was being called to fill in for her subordinates more and more frequently. She had discussed the situation with Jack Brown, who was sympathetic, at least at first. Her suggestions for reorganizing the office had gone unheeded.

The discussions with Jack had turned to complaints, then arguments. Finally, Jack had told her that it simply didn't matter how much she bitched about it, he saw no change in the foreseeable future. The economy was down and more appropriations from Tallahassee just weren't coming. He had to work within his budget, and there was nothing he could do about it.

Rian wasn't sure how much more of this crap she could, or should, put up with. Her contemporaries in private practice were becoming partners in their firms and drawing salaries and bonuses far in excess of Rian's. Betsey Templer, that obnoxious weasel who was a class ahead of her at Vanderbilt was probably making six figures plus at her firm in Chattanooga. Even pricks like Alan Banning would be in private practice in six months and making far more money than Rian did.

Maybe Sam was right. She had the resume and was marketable. There was a fine line between staying long enough at the PD's office and staying too long. Maybe it was time to consider moving on.

She called Abby when she got into the car and told her to meet her with the files outside the courtroom on the fourth floor. She parked in the garage and took the stairs and the breezeway over to the courthouse. Abby was waiting when Rian got there and they ducked into an empty jury room to look over the files.

As Abby had said, most had written plea offers signed by the defendants, so all Rian had to do was to formally enter the plea and the judge would impose the agreed upon sentence. Those were no brainers. Sellers had one case that was going to trial next week and she would simply announce that fact to the judge.

I hope to hell I don't get stuck trying that case.

Rian would have to quickly meet with the other four to see what offers the State had made and the defendants' willingness to accept them. She glanced at her watch. It was 8:40, meaning she had twenty minutes to arrange pleas in four felony cases with clients she had never met. She scribbled their names on a Post-It note and opened the door to the courtroom. It was already crowded with the prosecution team, private attorneys, defendants, probation officers, and other courthouse personnel. Rian caught the eye of the court security officer, Vince Peters, and raised her eyebrows, holding up the note and wiggling it in the air. When he walked over, Rian smiled and said, "Vince, would you mind seeing if these people are here yet?"

"Sure, Ms. Coulter," Vince replied. "Anything I need to know about?"

"No security concerns. I'm just covering for Barry Sellers and need to talk with them for a second," Rian said.

"No problem," said Vince, taking the Post-It note from Rian.

"Thank you, Vincent," she said giving him a smile. Vince blushed and turned to call the names as Rian ducked back into the jury room.

"What do you know about these other four?" she asked Abby.

"I checked with Jennifer to see if Barry left her any information. Nelson is a first-time possession of pot over twenty grams. Should be standard probation. Dollerson is an aggravated assault, but the weapon was his bare hands. Lassiter will probably let him plead to simple assault and probation. Prince is a forgery, but a weak case. Barry says they'd probably do a worthless check on that one and give him sixty days to pay the money back."

"What about Duncan?" asked Rian.

"Nothing on him. Jennifer didn't even know who he was." Rian pulled the file and looked through it. Duncan was charged with attempted burglary and possession of burglary tools. The file contained a bare bones arrest report, an intake sheet where Sellers had initially interviewed Duncan and the pleadings that consisted of the formal charges. There was no criminal history in the file. That was unusual and could mean either that it was missing or that Duncan had no previous criminal record. It appeared that Sellers had done little to prepare the case.

That's strange. How could Barry have let a case get this far without more information?

There was a knock at the door, and Vince stuck his head in.

"I have Dollerson, Prince, and Nelson waiting outside. Duncan didn't answer the bell," he said. "I'll keep trying. Who do you want first?"

"Doesn't matter," said Ryan. "Let me know if Duncan shows up."

In just a few minutes, Rian had met with Vivian Nelson, Anthony Dollerson, and Deshonte Prince and secured their agreements to enter pleas of no contest if the state would go along with the deals that Rian proposed.

She could understand why Dollerson had been charged with aggravated assault. He was about six-seven and his fingers seemed to reach Rian's elbow when they shook hands.

While she was meeting with them, she heard Vince call court to order and knew that Judge Axley had begun the court session. There were always a few private defense attorneys there with their clients and she knew that Axley would take them first so they wouldn't be delayed unnecessarily from their lucrative practices. This would give her a few extra minutes.

She got the three defendants to sign plea agreements, then grabbed the files and entered the courtroom.

Judge Clement Axley was a diminutive man with nearly white hair, a matching beard, and round wire-rimmed glasses. He made up for his lack of stature with an oversized ego and ruled his courtroom with an iron fist.

Axley was convinced that his intelligence was far superior to his fellow judges, and he frequently let them know it. They allowed him to be Chief Judge because no one else wanted the job, and he presided over his fiefdom with the arrogance of a king. No mere attorney could match his brilliance, and he considered his position on the circuit bench to be beneath him.

When Rian entered through the side door, the judge was in the middle of one of his usual condemnations of a defendant and, probably, his attorney as well. He took note of her presence, but didn't break stride. Rian gave Vince a look to see if Henry Duncan had shown up yet. Vince shook his head.

The private attorneys finished, and Rian began working through Barry Sellers's docket without incident. After each client's case was disposed, she would glance back at Vince to see if Duncan was there because she'd never met him and wouldn't recognize him even if he was. She wasn't particularly concerned.

If he didn't show up, Judge Axley would revoke his bond and issue a bench warrant for his arrest. Duncan would then have both the cops and the bail bondsman looking for him.

About halfway through the docket, Vince handed Rian a note to let her know that Duncan had arrived. When she had the chance, Rian looked back to see a man who looked to be in his mid-thirties with longish, sandy blond hair sitting in the back of the courtroom. He was wearing jeans and a work shirt of some kind. He didn't react when Rian looked at him.

Nice of you to show, asshole.

When Rian had finished with the others, she addressed Judge Axley. "Your Honor," she began, "I see that my last client has arrived. I didn't have a chance to meet with him. May I have a brief recess?"

Axley peered at her over his glasses with an irritated look. "Ms. Coulter," he said, "we've been here all morning and have just one case left. Surely you have *some* idea of what you want to do with this case?" the judge said, the word "some" dripping with sarcasm.

"Actually, judge, I don't. I've never met this man before," Rian shot back, not the least bit intimidated.

"Well, in *that* case," the judge said, the sarcasm even worse this time, "I guess we'll just all stand by and wait while you do. Court will be in recess for five minutes. Nobody leaves the courtroom," he ordered and left the bench.

Rian turned and addressed Duncan from a distance. "Mr. Duncan, please come with me," she said and walked toward the jury room again, holding the door open for him to go in ahead of her. She noticed Vince was standing nearby. Duncan was of average height and build, but now that she was closer, she noticed that he had striking blue eyes. The name "All Seasons Landscaping" was embroidered in yellow cursive letters on the left side of his shirt. She introduced herself and was surprised when Duncan flashed her a bright, white smile. There was something vaguely familiar about him.

"I'm sorry to have delayed you, Ms. Coulter," he said. "I apologize for causing you to be chastised by the Judge."

"Chastised" is not a word used by most maintenance people.

"You're here now," said Rian, ignoring his apology entirely. "I'm filling in today for Mr. Sellers, and I'm afraid that there's little in your file to go on. What can you tell me? We don't have much time and I doubt Judge Axley would be agreeable to a continuance of your case."

"I assure you that this is all a misunderstanding," Duncan said. "I was landscaping a lady's yard and she must have thought that I was trying to enter through the back to steal from her or something. I was simply trying to locate her to find out where she wanted me to locate the fruit trees. The police didn't want to listen to my side of the story."

There was something a little strange about Duncan, but Rian brushed it off.

"The court file indicates that you posted a cash bond of $2,000. Why didn't you hire an attorney?" Rian asked.

"It was all the money I had," said Duncan. He could have paid a bail bondsman ten percent and saved the rest.

"Doesn't matter," Rian continued. "What burglary tools did you have in your possession?"

"None," answered Duncan. "I merely possessed the tools of my trade. I suppose that just about anything could be a 'burglary tool,' depending upon your viewpoint."

"Were they seized?" asked Rian. "I don't see them listed in the report."

"No. I turned them over to Mr. Sellers in the event they were needed."

"I don't see a criminal history in the file either," she continued. "Have you been in trouble before?"

"Never. I just moved to the area recently, but I have no previous violations of the law. I've never even had a traffic citation."

There was something about this guy that Rian instinctively didn't like, but her time was up. "I think I can bargain this down to a misdemeanor trespass and get the judge to not adjudicate you guilty and put you on probation for six months if you want to enter a plea."

Duncan shook his head. "I would prefer not to be on probation. I would find that too . . . limiting."

What a winner this guy is, Rian thought.

"They might agree to waive the probation if you forfeit the bond," she said. "Or you could go to trial next week, take your chances with Mr. Sellers, and run the risk of going to jail."

Now maybe I have your attention.

"I can live with that," he said simply. Rian thought so.

Vince knocked on the door. "The judge is on his way down," he said. Rian grabbed Duncan's file and went back into the courtroom. She heard the back elevator used by the judges chime as she leaned over and spoke softly to Brian Lassiter. "Can we do a withheld adjudication of guilt on a simple trespass if he forfeits the cash bond?" she asked. Lassiter thought for a second before answering.

"No probation?"

"No. He finds it limiting." Lassiter laughed as Axley took the bench again, then nodded his agreement.

"Ms. Coulter, are we ready to proceed?" asked Axley with less sarcasm than before.

"Yes, Your Honor. The State and defense have reached an agreement. In exchange for Mr. Duncan's plea of nolo contendere to a charge of trespass, the State will dismiss the charges of burglary and possession of burglary tools and require that he forfeit his cash bond of $2,000." The judge cut his eyes over to Lassiter.

"Mr. Lassiter?"

"The State agrees, Your Honor," Lassiter said.

"Very well, then," said Axley. "Mr. Duncan, is this how you want your case to be disposed of?"

"Yes, sir," said Duncan.

The judge announced the sentence on the record, then recessed court again and left the bench. Rian started to gather her files and noticed that Duncan was still standing next to her. He had a wry smile and she turned to face him.

"Is there something else I can do for you, Mr. Duncan?" she asked, her voice betraying her annoyance.

"No. I wanted to compliment you on your performance," he said and turned to leave.

"You're welcome," said Rian. "Goodbye."

And good riddance.

CHAPTER SIX

J. T. Spencer sat at the head of the table in the private back room at O'Steen's Irish Pub surrounded by most of the movers and shakers of Northwest Florida. Real estate developers, bankers, corporate executives, local and state politicians, and Republican party leaders all told stories of conquest and triumph, laughed at each other's jokes, and discussed their plans for continued dominance, all over local microbrews.

Ordinarily, it would be impossible for a city councilman to assemble such a group, but they were here with a common objective: electing J.T. Spencer the next state senator from District 4. The general election wasn't until next November, over a year away, but the Republican primary was in March.

If Spencer could build up a sufficient war chest, he might scare off any serious opposition and win the election at the primary. He doubted that anyone would be foolish enough to run as a Democrat. If they did, his fundraising efforts would bury them.

Spencer's tenure on the Pensacola City Council had been relatively tame and, as a result, his name recognition wasn't what it should be for someone who had held public office for the last eight years. The agenda for the meeting tonight, in addition to fundraising, was to discuss ways that Spencer could raise his profile in the public's mind. A few hand-picked representatives of the media who were sympathetic to the cause were also in attendance.

At the other end of the table sat tonight's other special guest. Senator Arden Chambers was the incumbent senator from District 4 and Chairman of the powerful Senate Governmental Affairs Committee. Through three terms in the House of Representatives and now four terms in the Senate, Chambers had never lost an election since his first campaign in the eighth grade, although even then there had been questions that he had compensated his classmates in return for their votes. He was a consummate politician who never forgot a name, or a favor, and was either a powerful ally or a formidable opponent.

Chambers was walking away from likely the safest seat in Florida, where he'd last been reelected with seventy-seven percent of the vote, to throw his hat into the ring for governor. Early polling showed Chambers with a commanding lead over his opponent, a trial lawyer from Jacksonville.

Chambers had presided over a discussion this evening that centered on one of his campaign issues; the legal profession, although he rarely referred to it as a profession. Chambers hated lawyers; all lawyers. Even when he'd been sued and forced to hire legal counsel, he detested even his own lawyers, who billed too much, accomplished too little, and nagged him incessantly about settling. Arden Chambers was not a settler.

In Florida, lawyers are regulated by the Florida Bar, an organization that all lawyers practicing in the state are required to belong to upon admission to practice. Ethical and disciplinary matters are handled by the Bar and overseen by the Supreme Court who are, of course, lawyers.

Chambers had long held the opinion that this was tantamount to the fox guarding the henhouse and allowed lawyers to run unchecked and wreak havoc in society. He intended to campaign for governor on the promise that, when he was elected, he would see to it that the legislature wrested the power of regulating lawyers from the Bar and put it where it belonged, in the hands of the people and their elected representatives.

The powerbrokers in attendance tonight all supported that idea, and Spencer was urged to get on board. It would raise his public recognition level, be popular in his district, and be of assistance to Chambers as well. The Governor-to-be assured Spencer that he had enough clout with his colleagues to get Spencer appointed to the right committees next November when they were elected.

"These goddamn bloodsuckers answer to no one," Chambers was railing. "They'll sue your ass at the drop of a damn hat with no consequences for the lives they destroy. Hell, they even sue each other." The powerbrokers all laughed at that.

Spencer was taking it all in, but feeling a little uneasy about it. He actually knew some pretty nice lawyers whom he considered friends. They had supported him in his previous campaigns. His wife Eleanor knew their wives and, while they weren't exactly close friends, they did socialize with them at charity functions and Old Pensacola events. He'd been paired with Jack Brown, the Public Defender, last spring in a golf tournament and they'd gotten along well.

Spencer was wondering if this attack was really necessary when he noticed the room had fallen silent and everyone was looking at him.

"You seem to have checked out on us there, son," Senator Chambers said, chuckling.

"I -- I'm sorry . . . I, uh, guess I was just thinking ahead," ventured Spencer.

"I was saying that we ought to get out in front on this lawyer thing early. You know, present a united front and all," said Chambers. "That's real important. I'm going to call a press conference for next week and wanted to know if you wanted to appear with me J.T. It'd help you, too."

Spencer's skin began to crawl. He didn't like being put on the spot like this and was second guessing the wisdom of pushing for this meeting tonight. Perhaps he wasn't suited for the type of politics that went on at the state level and he should reconsider just being a full-time accountant again.

The President of the Chamber of Commerce leaned over and gave Spencer a reassuring slap on the shoulder and murmurs of encouragement from the others followed. He wanted to stall for time and have the chance to talk with Eleanor about all of this. She had a nephew in law school and would probably be as uncomfortable with all of this as he was.

"Well, I wasn't aware that we were going to stake out such a position this evening. I'd like to think about all of this for a day or two." Before he even finished the sentence, Spencer knew that he'd just given the wrong answer. The faces before him confirmed it.

"Councilman," Chambers said derisively. "What is there to think about? Is there a bigger boil on the butt of mankind than a bunch of lawyers?" A few of the powerbrokers chuckled nervously, but most sat impassively looking at Spencer. He hoped that they couldn't see the beads of sweat forming on his forehead.

Chambers pounced again. "Look, J.T. If you don't have the stomach for this, let us know now. If you don't want to get in the boat with us, we still have time to find someone who does." Spencer detected slight nods from the others in the room. Another awkward silence followed and Spencer had to make his decision. He had to sell his soul to the Devil.

"Senator," he said with as much confidence as he could muster. "It would be my honor to appear with you anytime and anywhere. You can count on my full support."

Cheers erupted in the room, and everyone's glasses were refilled. When this was done, the Chamber president rose from his seat and immediately all eyes were on him. He raised his pint and looked at Chambers, then at Spencer.

"Governor Chambers, Senator Spencer, here's to you. I just have one thing to say," he said, pausing for effect. Then, taking the quote from Shakespeare's *Henry VI* completely out of context, he said with mock seriousness, "The first thing we do is kill all the lawyers." The powerbrokers howled with laughter and everyone clinked glasses in the center.

CHAPTER SEVEN

Palmer clicked the mouse periodically as he scrolled through the pictures that documented Monica Jessup's murder that flashed onto his computer screen, casting an eerie glow around his darkened office. His shift had ended hours before, but Palmer wanted to look at these when he wouldn't be interrupted by the phone or by other investigators.

These weren't images he wanted to take home. He clicked through the exterior shots quickly, pausing momentarily to look at the photographs of the back door that supposedly had been an attempted point of entry into the house where Monica was killed. In the close up shots, there appeared to be some evidence of rust where a tool of some sort had been used to pry the door open, leaving some scratches and a couple of small dents around the lock.

Even in the humid, salty beach air rust wouldn't form that quickly, and Palmer concluded that these marks had nothing to do with Monica Jessup's murder. He scribbled a note on a legal pad to ask Randy West to check with the rental company to see if there had been a report of any previous attempted break in at the house. Since this attempt, whenever it was, had clearly failed, the question that remained was how the killer had gained access to the house.

Palmer suspected that the murderer must be someone that Monica Jessup knew, or at least trusted, to let into the house. The investigation so far had turned up no one in the immediate area who knew Monica or even interacted with her so the likelihood that she knew her killer seemed remote to Palmer. Did someone follow her to Blue Mountain?

He next scrolled through the shots taken in the great room and of the blood spatter on the wall that he'd noticed on his inspection. Monica had received an injury to the back of her head, and the blood on the wall to the right would indicate that the blow came from left to right and that the killer was likely left-handed. Palmer made a note of that on his pad. There was no blood on the floor at that point, which was unusual.

Scrolling through to the pictures taken of Monica at the scene, Palmer studied these closely, paying particular attention to the manner in which she was tied up.

Monica was in good physical condition at age forty. She had muscular, toned legs with arms, shoulders, and abdominals that indicated a woman who exercised regularly. She was face-down on the bed, nude and leaning slightly to her right as though looking toward the doorway. Her eyes were open and slightly bulged, and her tongue protruded slightly from the front of her mouth. Her blonde hair was caked with dried blood that had poured out of the head wound and drained down her face and onto the pillow that was also drenched in blood.

Palmer knew that head wounds bled profusely and many times looked worse than they were, so he didn't automatically assume this to be the cause of death. Her skin was discolored because gravity had caused her blood to pool toward the front of her body.

The ligatures were more interesting. The killer had looped half inch nylon rope around Monica's neck, fed it back through a slip knot behind her to her ankles, wrapping around them, and then drawing them up behind her tightly. When done, Monica's feet would be drawn toward her head. If she tried to lower her legs, the rope would tighten around her neck, choking her. Her hands were tied together with the same rope, but were under her body with the rope extending back between her legs, through a similar slip knot, then wrapped around her ankles and secured. By having her arms bound in front, any attempt to raise them would pull down on her legs, choking her as well.

Hogtied, just as Randy West had said.

Palmer studied the close ups and noticed that there was a large bruise on the front of Monica's neck, halfway between the base of her neck and her chin. It was round and larger than the rope, but he needed a full frontal view to get a better look. Additional pictures should accompany the autopsy report, and he made additional notes.

Palmer pulled off his reading glasses and pinched the bridge of his nose. Staring at the pictures had given him a headache, and he had the same feeling of discomfort that he'd had in Blue Mountain a few days ago. He needed caffeine and grabbed his coffee mug off the desk and headed to the door. Just then, his desk phone buzzed and the voice of one of his investigators came over the speaker.

"Hey, L.T.," the voice said, using his interoffice nickname, "You still here?"

"Not for long but, yeah, I'm still here," Palmer replied.

"Autopsy report from the Walton County thing just came in over the fax. Want me to run it up to you?"

"Nah. I'm coming down for coffee anyway. I'll come get it."

"Okay. It's at my desk."

Palmer took the stairs down one floor, emerging near the break room that served the Crimes Against Persons division. He poured some coffee, frowned when he noticed that there were no Equal packets in the container, and headed down the hall to the CAP unit. The investigator who had buzzed him, a young man named Sanchez, saw him come in and met him halfway, carrying the report.

"I couldn't help but peek at it, L.T.," he said. "Sounds pretty gross."

Palmer nodded, but didn't reply. Taking the report, he took the stairs back to his office and settled in behind his desk to read it. He had met the author, Dr. Benjamin Crawford, a few times, but didn't know him well. He was an experienced medical examiner and had a good reputation with local law enforcement and the State Attorney's Office over in Walton County.

The report was marked "preliminary" and initially detailed the circumstances of the case as it was known and was information that Palmer already knew, so he skipped over to the section that described the examination of Monica Jessup's body.

> The subject is a well developed, well nourished white female who appears to be her stated age of forty years. Height is 66 inches, weight is 131 lbs. A rose tattoo is present on the left scapula and the body is otherwise devoid of distinguishing marks. A blood sample was drawn and transported to the laboratory for toxicological analysis. Fingernail scrapings were also obtained and turned over to law enforcement. Small hemorrhages were present in both eyes. Wounds consistent with bite marks were present bilaterally on the subject's tongue.
>
> Exterior examination revealed a 2 cm by .27 cm posterior wound on the crown of the head. The skull was not displaced, and x-ray examination showed no evidence of fracture or hematoma at the wound location. MRI examination of the brain was deferred due to budgetary concerns; however, it is unlikely that the trauma resulting in the wound was sufficiently severe to cause injury to the brain. A 4.3 cm by 4 cm slightly oval bruise was present on the anterior neck. Further examination revealed that the subject had suffered a fracture of the larynx consistent with the exterior bruising. X-ray examination also revealed a non-displaced fracture of the hyoid. No exterior wound was present at that location. Additional linear bruising consistent with cervical ligatures was also present.

> There was extensive linear bruising around the wrists and ankles, also consistent with ligatures. No defensive wounds were noted.
>
> The subject had extensive damage to the tissues in the vaginal and rectal area indicating forceful penetration with an object. Bruising was extensive in both areas. Wood splinters were extracted from both areas; however, further indications of the nature of the object used was prevented due to the extent of the tissue damage. No semen was present in either the vaginal or rectal area.

Palmer paused to digest what he had read so far. Monica had apparently been initially attacked from behind and struck in the back of the head with some object, presumably by a left-handed person. This would explain the spatter of blood on the right side wall of the hallway.

Apparently, the wound wasn't severe and he didn't know whether the blow rendered Monica unconscious.

Someone, or something, had struck Monica in the throat, possibly fracturing her larynx and the hyoid bone in her neck. Palmer had to consider the possibility that the ligatures could have caused these injuries as well.

She'd also been violated with some sort of wooden object. The evidence of extensive bruising in the area indicated that Monica had still been alive when this occurred.

Palmer read through the report of Dr. Crawford's examination of Monica Jessup's internal organs which were normal except that her lungs revealed that she'd apparently been a smoker at some point in her life. Eventually, he reached the doctor's conclusions based upon the autopsy examination:

> Preliminary cause of death is determined to be strangulation as evidenced by the hemorrhaging in the anterior neck and eyes, lacerations of the tongue and fracture of the larynx and hyoid. Secondary cause is felt to be blood loss from head wound and trauma to the vaginal and rectal tissues, when combined with the extreme stress imposed upon the subject, possibly led to shock and death onset. Cause of death is considered preliminary pending results of toxicology analysis.

Palmer sat back in his chair and looked up at the ceiling for a long time. He'd handled cases where the victim had been tied up before, but never one like this. He'd been involved in strangulation cases, too, but not like this. Monica Jessup wasn't this killer's first victim, he felt certain.

The possibility that he'd fought to keep in his subconscious since he visited the crime scene now came bursting through into the forefront of his mind, offering an explanation for his increasing feeling of dread.

Surely not, he thought. If this was an isolated event, that possibility would not exist. However, if another victim showed up, Palmer would have to consider the possibility.

He turned back to his computer and navigated back to the beginning of the file on the flash drive to find the image of

Monica Jessup's Louisiana driver's license. He cropped her photo and printed a color copy. He removed everything that he'd attached to the bulletin board hanging on the wall near his desk and, as was his custom, placed Monica's photograph by itself in the center with a pushpin; a custom reserved only for the victims of serial killers.

CHAPTER EIGHT

"Happy birthday to you, happy birthday to you, happy birthday to Ri—an, happy birthday to you. Sorry I missed you. Have a great day."

Rian laughed out loud at the voicemail left by her younger brother, Brian. Rian and Brian. Their names were so similar that when someone called out to one of them, they both turned around. Very funny, Mom and Dad, she thought for the thousandth time.

Brian was seven years younger than Rian, but they were much closer than the age difference between them would otherwise allow. Where Rian had been a disciplined student, Brian had partied his way through Lowndes High, then through college and fraternity life at Birmingham Southern.

Their lives had briefly overlapped in Birmingham when Brian was a freshman and Rian was working at Ashton, Baker. The time demands on them both, and the fact that Brian was a typical college freshman, didn't allow them to spend a great deal of time together, but they both enjoyed being there together away from home.

Rian thoroughly enjoyed the times that she cooked dinner for Brian and his fraternity brothers, several of whom were gorgeous and lavished attention on Rian. There was no mistaking that they were brother and sister. Brian had the same dark brown hair and crystal blue eyes as Rian, both gifts from their mother. Like Rian, he was lean and athletic and had been a soccer star in both high school and college. He still played club soccer in Birmingham, although a recent ankle injury had sidelined him for a while. Brian managed to get through college with a respectable enough grade point average to land a position with Colony Bank in Birmingham and had survived Colony's takeover by a larger bank earlier in the year.

Rian dialed his number and was surprised that he answered on the second ring.

"Hello there, old lady," he said cheerily.

"Old, my ass," Rian said. "Get your sorry butt down here for the Bridge Run and I'll show you who's old." They both laughed and chatted for a while catching up with each other's lives. Brian had a new girlfriend named Amanda, who was a paralegal. They had been dating for a few months, but nothing was serious.

"How's Sam?" Brian asked. "Any news?"

"Sam's great. We're great. There's no news really; we're just taking it slow."

"Figures. You let me know when I need to come down there and kick his ass."

"Yeah, I'll be sure to do that."

The longer Rian's relationship with Sam went on without any sort of permanent commitment, the greater the possibility it would stagnate and eventually die on the vine. She knew Brian didn't want to see her heart broken.

Although she thought Brian was a little dramatic about it, Rian had to admit that she wondered deep down where she and Sam were heading eventually. She was crazy about him, and he seemed to feel the same way about her. They'd been together for over two years, starting as colleagues, then friends, then whatever they were now. They both had seemed to avoid any specific discussion of their future together.

Maybe Sam felt the same, but they never talked about it specifically. Rian didn't press the issue. Life was pretty good right now, and she didn't want to jinx it.

"So, what are the big plans today?" Brian asked. It was a beautiful Saturday morning, and Rian was determined not to work that day.

"There's a concert in the park and the seafood festival's going on this weekend. We might hang out there for a while. Sam said not to make any evening plans, but he won't tell me why." Rian reached across the bed and playfully slapped the sleeping Sam on the butt, eliciting a groan from somewhere deep in the pillow.

"Sounds promising," said Brian. "I'll let you go, Ri. Have a wonderful day. I love you and miss you."

"I love you, too, Bri," she responded, her voice catching just a little. "Keep me posted on the Amanda situation."

Rian clicked off and walked downstairs, leaving Sam still crashed in the bed. She almost stepped on Mannix as he ran between her legs, and she found him sitting on the counter waiting for her to pour him some milk in a bowl when she entered the kitchen. She gathered him up and he laid on his back in her arms while she rubbed his tummy, a blissful look on his face and his motor running at full speed.

Rian poured coffee and booted up her laptop to read the online version of the paper. The physical version of the paper struggled to survive like so many others and had become so thin that it was almost not worth the effort.

Rian subscribed to the online version, though she felt a little guilty about it. Some of her fondest memories from her childhood had been sitting in her father's lap while they read the newspaper together.

She clicked through the major headlines relating the latest political and economic news, all of which was depressing. She noted that Senator Chambers still held a commanding lead in the race for governor and made a mental note to send a contribution to his opponent, not that it would do much good. Both Sam and her dad thought it was a bad idea to show up on such a list when Chambers was sure to win, but Rian just couldn't stand the guy. He was a pompous, arrogant ass, and this anti-lawyer thing he'd started was complete bullshit in her opinion.

She skimmed over the local news, stopping to check the arrest logs to see if any familiar names appeared. There was a small story on page three noting no new leads in a Walton County homicide, but she breezed past it.

A few minutes later, Sam ambled downstairs looking for the coffee.

"How's my birthday girl?" he said as he walked up behind her and slid his arms around her waist.

"Fine," she said, leaning back into him. "What do you know about this Spencer guy who's running for Chambers's seat?"

"Decent guy. Hasn't made many waves on the council. The firm's supported him in the past. Why?"

"I see that he's been campaigning with Chambers pretty regularly, and it looks like he's starting to buy into this lawyer regulation shit of his."

"There you go again. Look, I told you, it's not your fight, and you don't want to make an enemy out of the next governor."

"You sound like Dad. I don't understand why you guys aren't all over it. Can you even imagine being regulated by the damned legislature?"

"Come on. Let's table this discussion for now. It's a gorgeous day and I'm hungry. Let's go get breakfast."

It irritated Rian when Sam blew her off like this, as though her opinions didn't matter. Maybe she was too opinionated and strong-willed for him. Or maybe he had a problem with women who disagreed with him. Either way, it could be a problem in the long-run.

Having announced that it was breakfast time, Sam had gone back upstairs, leaving Rian and Mannix alone in the kitchen. She filled his bowl and headed upstairs herself.

They showered, dressed, and walked down to Julie's for breakfast. They had bagels on the front porch facing the park, then walked over to browse through the booths set up there for the festival. The park was crowded with vendors selling all sorts of seafood, gumbo, crawfish, and draft beer which a surprising number of people were drinking, even at this hour. Rian and Sam strolled through the tents displaying beach art and other local crafts, finally succumbing to a bowl of gumbo and a beer at the end.

"Okay, McKinney, time to spill," said Rian as they sat at a picnic table near the old restored church. "What's the plan for tonight?"

Sam suddenly looked at his watch and feigned an emergency.

"Oh, wow, I almost forgot," he said, his half smile giving him away. "Gotta go. I've got, uh, a thing. Be ready at seven." He kissed her and took off, disappearing into the crowd.

* * *

He watched them from a distance, feeling invisible in crowds like these. To prove his invulnerability, he tested that notion by walking right past them twice in the park without the slightest glimmer of recognition on her part. He watched the man trot away from the picnic table, immediately dismissing him. He was insignificant. She was the important one, and he now knew much more about her. He could, and would, watch her closely.

Just in case things changed.

CHAPTER NINE

Mike Donovan's desk phone rang and he answered it without pausing from the story he was pounding out on his desktop.

"Donovan," he said, tucking the receiver between his jaw and his shoulder.

"Mike. Meet me in my office in ten," said Emmett Bayer, his editor.

"What's up? I'm trying to finish the piece on the crime statistics."

"That may have to wait. I have something I need you to follow up on. Meet me in ten." He hung up.

Donovan punched the keys until he reached a stopping point, then saved the file. He looked at his watch and decided that he had enough time to grab a Diet Coke before meeting Bayer in his office. He picked up his notepad and smartphone, turned off his computer monitor, and headed to the vending machine.

Donovan had been with the *Escambia Herald* for a little over six years. In that time, he had migrated through various duty stations to the crime desk, which had merged with the court desk last year so that the paper could eliminate Ann Winston's position and double Donovan's workload. Although the work was demanding, he liked the fast pace and the freedom to follow a story from the commission of the crime through the court process. He had worked hard to develop a good rapport with law enforcement, prosecutors, and defense attorneys alike.

Donovan was waiting when Bayer stepped off the elevator. Bayer had been the Executive Editor of the *Herald* for as long as anyone could remember. He was an old style newspaperman, well known for both his acerbic personality and his scathing editorials that centered on politics and local government issues. As usual, Bayer was on his cell phone and breezed past Donovan without breaking his conversation, motioning Donovan to follow him into his office. He sat dutifully while Bayer finished his call. When he did, he leaned back in his chair, clasping his hands behind his head.

"What do you know about one of our sheriff's investigators being called in on a homicide in Walton County?" Bayer asked.

"Nothing," Donovan said. "What homicide and what investigator?"

"That's all I know. Bill Prentiss over in DeFuniak Springs asked me about it this morning. I need you to run that down and see if there's anything to it."

"Did he say anything about the homicide? When it was or where?"

"Apparently some tourist on the beach not long ago. Check with the archives to see if we ran anything at all about it."

"I think I would have gotten wind of it if we had," Donovan said. "But I'll check."

"Get back to me on this by Friday," Bayer ordered.

"What about the crime stat piece?"

"It can wait." Bayer signaled the end of their discussion by picking up his phone and placing a call to someone else.

Donovan walked back to his office and turned on his monitor. He pulled up the website for the *Walton County Tribune* to see if there were any stories that mentioned a recent murder. He found none. The *Tribune* had a small circulation and its website was rudimentary, only saving stories in the archives for a few days. Satisfied the search was a dead end, he buzzed Bobby Hamilton at the sports desk. Bobby covered sports throughout the Florida Panhandle and was frequently in DeFuniak Springs during football season.

"Hey, Bobby," he asked when Hamilton answered, "do you have any contacts with the *Trib* over in Walton County?"

"Yeah, several. Why?"

"Bayer wants me to follow up on something. It's probably a black hole, but I need to talk to someone over there who might have some intel on a recent homicide. Probably at the beach if I had to guess."

"Your best bet's Alex Parsons. I know he used to live down in South Walton, but if anybody'd know about it, Alex would. Hang on and I can give you his cell number."

Donovan thanked him for the number and placed a call to Parsons's phone, leaving a message when his voicemail picked up. He was just about to go back to the story on crime statistics when Parsons called him back.

"Thanks for calling me back," said Donovan. "I'm looking for any information that you might have on a homicide over there within the last month or two. I don't know much other than the victim was supposedly a tourist, so I assume it happened down at the beach."

"Monica Jessup," said Parsons immediately.

"Wow. That was fast. Can you tell me anything?

"Unfortunately, not much. She was a public official in the Comptroller's Office in Baton Rouge. It happened back in June. They haven't said much since."

"Do you know anything about one of our investigators being called in for some reason?"

"Scuttlebutt only. She was killed in a house down in Blue Mountain, but they pulled the lid down on it immediately. Rumor has it that they called in an investigator from Escambia County, but that's not been confirmed."

"Who's the lead in the investigation down there?"

"A guy named Randy West. He's a sergeant and normally a straight shooter, but he's not talking."

"Thanks, Alex. I'll let you know if I pick up anything."

"Is there really anything going on? I just figured it was an unsolved."

"It's probably a cold case. Thanks," Donovan said and hung up.

Donovan knew that the investigator called in from Escambia County had to be Glenn Palmer. His history with the FDLE made him the only logical choice. He decided to take a chance and dialed the sheriff's office subdivision in South Walton and asked for Randy West, explaining that he was calling from the State Attorney's Office when questioned. West picked up on the second ring.

"Investigations, West," he said.

"Sergeant West, this is Mike Donovan with the *Escambia Herald*."

Silence.

"I'm calling to confirm the fact that you've called in Lieutenant Glenn Palmer from the Escambia County Sheriff's Office to assist in the investigation of the death of Monica Jessup."

West hung up.

After he got over the initial shock of what had just happened, Donovan reached over and closed the crime statistics story on his computer.

He wouldn't get back to that story for a long time.

CHAPTER TEN

The neighborhood twinkled with Christmas lights as Marie Pettigrew walked the last of her guests out to their cars. The party had gone perfectly and Marie was quite proud of herself. It was too bad that Frank wasn't here to enjoy it, but it was more important for him to make the trip to the home office now so that he could take the time to be with Angie and Eddie and that grandbaby.

As her friends drove away, she took in the streetscape and the decorations at the houses around her. It was an unwritten rule in Kingston Estates that each house had to be decorated for Christmas. While it was permissible to install the lights at any time, it was considered improper to turn them on before Thanksgiving. On November 26, however, the neighborhood suddenly transformed, turning nighttime into day. Each year the decorations got more and more elaborate. The custom had turned into such a competition that the homeowner's association now gave out first, second, and third place awards, complete with signs erected in the yards of the lucky winners.

As she looked around, Marie chuckled to herself. Even the Jewish family down the street had gotten into the act this year, and the blue Hanukkah lights that covered their house offered a nice contrast to the thousands of white, red, and green around them. The Gobles had hired a local company with a bucket truck to put lights all the way to the top of the huge oak tree in their yard as well as to the very peak of their roof. This year, Marie had finally succumbed and hired a landscaping company to do her house.

As she completed her visual tour, she paused and looked at her own house and nodded her approval. They had been expensive, but she decided that it was worth it. As she walked up the driveway, she felt unsteady, probably from too much wine, and decided that she'd clean up a little tonight and leave the rest for the morning.

Kingston Estates was in Cantonment, an unincorporated section of Escambia County twenty miles north of Pensacola. It was a quiet, middle class subdivision with large lots that bordered dense pine woods owned by the nearby paper mill. Frank and Marie Pettigrew had a nice, ranch style home with a large back yard and nothing but woods behind them.

* * *

From his vantage point just beyond the tree line, he had a clear view of the house and the party. It was a cool night, not cold, even though it was December. He watched and waited; patience was one of his virtues. After everyone left, he could clearly see Marie through the sliding glass doors picking up dishes and bringing them into the kitchen. Eventually, she walked through the house, turning out the lights except for the bedroom, its location giving him the last bit of information that he needed. Soon, that light went out, too. Still, he waited as the crickets chirped and the night deepened around him.

At 2:00, the lights on the Pettigrew house, and several others, suddenly went dark, obviously on timers. These lights wouldn't be coming on again, he thought as he clutched the extension cord he'd just removed from the display and stepped silently across the back yard. He approached the sliding glass door and touched it gently. It was unlocked, just as he thought. Sliding it open carefully, he slipped into the house.

CHAPTER ELEVEN

Palmer's cell phone rang and he stabbed at it as he was wiping shaving cream from his face. Glancing at the alarm clock on the bedside table, he noted the time was seven o'clock.

"Palmer," he said.

"L.T., it's Sanchez." Since giving him the autopsy report from the Jessup case several months ago, Palmer had worked a couple of cases with the young investigator and thought he had great potential.

"Call just came in," Sanchez continued. "Homicide out in Kingston Estates in Cantonment. Apparently a pretty sick one. Units are on the scene and the M.E.'s office is on the way. Who do you want to send?"

"You take it. I can be there in about fifteen minutes. Make sure the house is secure and no one gets in but the M.E. people. Make sure the body's not moved until I get there. What's the address?"

Palmer jotted down the address Sanchez gave him and finished dressing quickly. In minutes, he was speeding north on Highway 29 toward Cantonment. He turned into Kingston

Estates, passing the cheerfully decorated entrance sign, and followed the gently curving streets of the subdivision until he reached the Pettigrew home. Several marked sheriff's cars were parked in the streets, blue lights flashing. The Medical Examiner's van was parked on the side and yellow crime scene tape had been strung around the entire perimeter of the property. One uniformed deputy stood at the end of the walkway leading to the house, and he acknowledged Palmer as he ducked under the crime scene tape.

"Lot of onlookers, Lieutenant," he said.

Palmer looked around and noticed that nearly every house on the block had people standing in front, some clustered together in groups. All of them looked stunned and were staring at the Pettigrew house. He glanced at the deputy's name plate and addressed him by name.

"No one gets past the tape, Sanderson. I don't care who they are. If family shows up, come get me. Clear?"

"Yes, sir."

Palmer started up the walkway when a news truck from Channel 4 pulled up and he could see the young girl who anchored the morning news jump out. He turned back to Deputy Sanderson.

"Especially these fuckers," he said.

"Understood, Lieutenant," Sanderson replied. "No problem."

Palmer walked toward the house, ignoring the cries of "Lieutenant, Lieutenant," coming from Miss Anchorperson behind him. Another uniformed deputy nodded to him at the front door.

"Where's Sanchez?" Palmer asked.

"He's in the back bedroom. It's to the right, Lieutenant."

Palmer thanked him and stepped into the house. There was a small entrance area with a study to the left and a dining room to the right. The table was decorated with a green table cloth and a large red centerpiece of flowers. Crumbs were still on the table and the chairs were slightly askew as though the family had just eaten and hadn't finished cleaning up.

Palmer stepped though the dining room and into the kitchen. Plates were stacked in the sink and several wine glasses, some with wine still in them, were lined up on the counter. Coffee cups and serving dishes were collected on the kitchen table. He could see beyond the kitchen into the living room where a female officer whom he recognized as the victim advocate was speaking in a low voice to a woman seated on the couch. The woman was dabbing at her eyes with a napkin.

Sanchez stepped into the kitchen and caught Palmer's eye.

"You ain't gonna believe this shit, L.T.," he said ominously.

Sanchez made a motion with his head for Palmer to follow and lead him into the master bedroom just down a short hall from the kitchen. The room was moderate in size and was crowded with the crime scene unit collecting evidence and the medical examiner people. As he stepped into the room, Palmer froze as he looked at the bed. Marie Pettigrew was lying face-down on the bed. Her face and head was covered in blood that soaked the pillows and sheets beneath her. A green electrical extension cord was wrapped around her neck, then fed through a loop around her ankles. Her hands were bound in front of her and the cord wrapped around her ankles a second time.

Hogtied.

For a long moment, Palmer stared down at Marie Pettigrew, unable to say a thing. He and Sanchez looked at each other, then back at the bed.

"Christ," Palmer muttered under his breath.

"It's exactly like the one --" Sanchez started to say, but Palmer cut him off with a stern look and an almost imperceptible shake of his head. At that moment, Dr. Crawford walked in and stood silently next to Palmer and Sanchez.

"Could you fellas give us a minute?" Palmer asked the crime scene officers. They stopped what they were doing. The technicians from the Medical Examiner's Office stopped, too, and looked at Crawford. He nodded and they all left the room. Palmer shut the door.

"Tell me I'm imagining things, Doctor," he said to Crawford.

"We'll do a full autopsy, of course Glenn, but you know as well as I do what we're looking at." The extension cords that bound Marie Pettigrew weren't as taut as the rope that had tied up Monica Jessup, but the similarities were inescapable. Sanchez looked from Palmer to Crawford and back again as though he was watching a tennis match.

"Does she have a contusion to her throat and a fractured larynx?" Palmer asked.

"I don't know yet. There's too much blood, and I didn't want to clean her neck off before the photos were taken and you'd had a chance to see her." They looked at each other for a moment. "But I'd put money on it."

"Shit," was all Palmer could manage. He was already thinking of how he would get Marie Pettigrew out of her house and keep the media from going nuts over this.

"Listen to me, both of you," said Palmer. "This is a routine homicide. A tragic, awful, fucking sick one, but it's a *routine homicide*. It has no similarity to any other homicide, got it?" Crawford and Sanchez just looked at him. Obviously, the command approach wasn't going to work.

"Look," he said, lowering his voice almost to a whisper. "I need you with me on this. If this gets out, this town will go ape shit and we'll never catch this fucker." That seemed to resonate with them, and they both nodded.

"Just process the scene normally. Dr. Crawford, get me your report as soon as you can." Palmer already knew what it would say.

He turned and left the bedroom. As he headed toward the living room, Sanchez caught him by the arm, stopping him. Sanchez nodded toward the living room where the victim advocate and the woman were still seated on the couch.

"That's Peggy Stanton," he said. "A neighbor. She's the one who found her."

"Do you already have her statement?"

"Yeah. Her husband left his cell phone here at the party last night and she came back this morning early to get it because he had to go to work. She let herself in and found her."

Palmer took a couple of steps toward the living room, then changed his mind. Ms. Stanton looked at him through red, puffy eyes, pleading with him silently to say that this was all a mistake or a dream. He looked at her for a moment, then glanced at the victim advocate before returning his eyes to Ms. Stanton. He had nothing to say. He simply nodded at her and walked out of the house. He could hear Peggy Stanton's wails behind him.

There is no fucking way I'm going to contain this, he thought.

Donovan waited with the crowd that had gathered in front of the Pettigrew home. He moved among them, listening to their whispered conversations about last night's party, the Pettigrew family who lived there, and their speculation about what had happened. It must be bad, they said.

Donovan saw Palmer step through the front door. He looked grim, and Donovan instantly thought of the murder of that woman near Destin back in the summer. He'd gotten nowhere with the Walton County cops about the case or why Palmer had supposedly been called in to assist. He eventually learned that the woman had been tied up and murdered in her bed, but that the authorities had no leads or suspects. There wasn't enough to do a story on, and Palmer had never returned any of his calls. His editor lost interest and Donovan thought the matter was closed.

Until now.

Palmer scanned the crowd as he stood on the front porch of the Pettigrew's house, and Donovan thought that Palmer sought his eyes in the crowd. They looked at each other for an instant, then Palmer headed to his car, cutting a wide swath to avoid the crowd.

Holy shit, thought Donovan.

His instinct told him that these two murders were related somehow. He tried not to let his mind go there, but it did anyway.

Do we have a serial killer here?

CHAPTER TWELVE

Rian sat at her desk furiously putting the finishing touches on a brief that had to be filed before five o'clock. Pausing, she rummaged through the papers next to her computer, then the stack on the credenza behind her.

"Abby," she called out the door, "I can't find the Jensen case. Do you have it?"

Abby came in and, seconds later, pulled the case from the stack at Rian's left elbow and handed it to her.

"Did anybody ever tell you that your desk is a black hole?" she teased.

"Yeah," Rian said, laughing because Abby had told her at least a thousand times. "I think you mentioned it once or twice."

She glanced at the case, extracted the quote she was looking for, and resumed typing. A minute passed before Rian noticed that Abby was still standing there.

"What?" she said.

"You haven't said a word about it all day," said Abby.

Rian gave her a puzzled look. "A word about what?"

"That poor woman who was killed in Cantonment yesterday. Haven't you seen the news today?"

"No. I didn't read the paper this morning and I've been swamped." Rian really didn't have the time to get into a discussion about a case that didn't concern her, but she could tell the normally unflappable Abby was upset.

"They say that that poor woman was tied up like some sort of animal that had been slaughtered."

"That was in the news?" Rian asked.

"No. That's just the rumor going around in the courthouse."

Rian knew about these rumors, and they were often exaggerations if not outright distortions of the truth. The facts that later developed were always more mundane.

"Abby, I'm sure that it's nothing like that, but I really have to finish --" she said, but Abby interrupted her.

"I talked to Tammy, Alan Banning's secretary. Banning was called to the scene this morning."

"Banning?" *What the hell would Banning be doing there?*

"Yeah. The word in the State Attorney's office is that this was really gruesome and a unique way of doing it, you know like a, uh . . ."

"Signature," Rian said, completing her thought.

Great. I'll probably have to represent the sick son of a bitch.

"Yeah, a signature. Doesn't that mean a serial killer?"

Rian wasn't about to add to the rumor mill. Although some serial killers did have a signature, many did not. What sometimes appeared to be a signature more often than not turned out to be an isolated case. This gossip train needed to be stopped quickly.

"Abby, look. I'm busy right now, but I assure you that we don't have a serial killer in little old Pensacola. You don't need to be a part of that speculation. But right now, I need to finish this brief, okay?"

Abby gave her a face that told Rian that she had hurt her feelings by blowing her off. Before she could say anything else, Abby spun around on her heels and left without another word.

Rian shook her head in frustration and returned to the brief. She finished it fifteen minutes later, spell checked it, then sent it to the printer at Abby's desk. Glancing at her watch, she saw that it was 4:45. She would need to walk it across to the clerk's office herself at this late hour.

Abby was pulling the brief out of the printer when Rian walked out and stopped at her desk.

"Abby, I'm sorry. I know you're upset. You just caught me at the wrong moment."

"It's okay. It's just that when you live by yourself, this kind of stuff scares you."

"I know. I live alone, too, but we can't let our lives be ruled by fear, you know?"

Abby stood and handed Rian the brief. She had tears in her eyes and Rian hugged her.

"It'll all be okay. I promise. Want me to see what I can find out?" Abby nodded.

"Okay. Tell you what, why don't you slip out early and beat the traffic? I'll walk this over to the clerk's office."

"I'm okay. I'll do it," Abby protested.

"No, you go ahead. I'll take care of it." That produced a small smile from Abby, who then grabbed her coat and purse and switched off her monitor.

Rian noticed Barry Sellers walking by.

"Hey, Barry," she called out, stopping him. "Would you mind walking Abby out to the garage?" Barry agreed, and Abby thanked her with her eyes and left.

* * *

Rian dropped off the brief and made it home in time for the local newscast at six o'clock. She and Mannix sat together on the couch as Rian switched on the television. In a few minutes, the Channel 4 Eyewitness News began with a somber looking anchorman seated in front of a digital graphic that screamed, "Murder in Cantonment."

"Police today were called to the scene of a shocking homicide in Cantonment," he began, and the scene changed to a street view of the Pettigrew house. There was video footage of the house with the crime scene tape all around, a quick shot of the blue lights flashing on the police cars, then a longer shot of the Medical Examiner's van. The anchor went on to identify the victim as Marie Pettigrew, a thirty-nine-year-old office worker, and a picture of Marie appeared on the screen.

How awful that this happened at Christmas, Rian thought.

The video switched back to the Pettigrew house, and Rian noticed Glenn Palmer walk out of the house. The story closed with videotape of Marie Pettigrew's covered body on a stretcher being wheeled to an ambulance. There was no mention of the victim being tied up or any hint that this was the work of some sort of serial killer.

Rian relaxed a little and picked up her iPhone to call Sam.

"Hey, babe," he answered. "You still at the office?"

"Nope, I'm home. What about you?"

"Still at it, unfortunately. We have the Booker closing tomorrow and all sorts of fires burning."

"Did you hear anything about this homicide out in Cantonment?"

"Just that there was one; why?"

"Nothing, other than Abby said that Banning was called to the scene and the courthouse gossip was that the woman was tied up like some sort of animal. Rumors are starting to fly that it's not the killer's first rodeo."

"Well, you know how that stuff goes. Usually turns out to be nothing."

"Yeah, I know. The six o'clock news didn't mention either of those things."

"And your point is?"

"Remember me telling you about those murders in Birmingham when I was working with Ashton, Baker?"

"What about them?"

"I don't know. It's just that . . ."

Sam felt the tension in Rian's voice. "Rian," he said, "what about the murders in Birmingham? What's wrong?"

"The word was that those women were tied up in a special way. Like, you know, hogtied."

"But that was years ago."

"I know. But they stopped all of a sudden for no apparent reason and they never caught the killer."

"You're letting your imagination get to you, Rian. First, you don't even know if there is any similarity at all between this thing in Cantonment and those murders. Even if there is, that was six or seven years ago and unlikely to be related."

"I guess so. I'm just being paranoid," she said, beginning to feel better.

"I gotta run. We're still on for tomorrow night?"

Rian could hear voices in the background. "Still on," she said. "Good luck with the fires."

She tossed the phone onto the coffee table and switched the television to something other than the news. Leaving Mannix curled up on the pillow, she went to the kitchen and took stock of the refrigerator, then the pantry. Rian shook her head. As usual, she hadn't had time to get to the store and there was nothing worth eating in the house. She contemplated this for a moment, considered calling someone to meet her for dinner, then grabbed the portable telephone and hit the speed dial number for Mancini's.

CHAPTER THIRTEEN

The New Year dawned and Senator Arden Chambers strode into his district office in Crestview carrying a thick roll of newspapers under his arm. He passed his secretary's desk and walked directly into the office of his chief legislative aide, Walter "Skip" Sullivan.

As the county seat of Okaloosa County and Chambers's hometown, the nondescript nature of Crestview belied the strong political power based there. It had produced political powerbrokers of both the official and unofficial type and Chambers was the latest incarnation. After a successful start in the House of Representatives, he maneuvered his way to being elected Speaker by his colleagues. He managed to deliver on enough political promises to be elected overwhelmingly to the Senate and now, eight years later, was poised to bring Crestview something that no one else had; a governor.

Chambers dropped the stack of papers on Sullivan's desk with a loud thud.

"What's this?" Sullivan asked.

"This," said Chambers virtually shouting, "is the latest legal abomination in this state, that's what it is."

Sullivan began looking through the stack of papers and saw that Chambers had brought a copy of every major newspaper in the state, Miami, Tampa, Orlando, Jacksonville, and Tallahassee, all of which had a bold, above the fold headline relating to the state's latest class action case.

Twenty years before, a group of private lawyers had teamed with the state to bring a lawsuit against the tobacco companies to recover costs that the state had paid for medical treatment provided to patients with smoking-related illnesses. The lawsuit was quickly settled and the state recovered billions from which the group of twelve lawyers were paid over two hundred million dollars.

This latest class action involved a complex allegation of insurance premium overcharges that the suit sought to recover on behalf of the state. If successful, the state could potentially receive a windfall of millions of dollars. The lawyers would once again be paid handsomely as well.

"These bastards are using taxpayer dollars to line their own pockets again," Chambers bellowed. "It's a goddamn outrage, and we're going to stop these motherfuckers this time."

"I'm telling you, Skip, now is the time. In hard times like this, the people will not sit still for this kind of bullshit." Chambers always knew what The People would and would not sit still for.

"I want you to make some calls to the Caucus," Chambers continued, referring to the majority group of Republican senators who met frequently and usually voted together in a block. "Tell them that I'm putting the bill in and I want to go to press with it. Tell them I want them to reach across and drag everyone they can from the other side. I'll make it worth their while."

"Yes, sir," was all that Sullivan could get out before Chambers issued another order.

"Once you have those commitments, call the news editors and schedule a press conference. We'll do it at the Capitol." Chambers turned and walked back to his office.

"Give them a short fuse on this, Skip," he said over his shoulder.

"Okay, Senator."

* * *

The Florida Senate was composed of forty members, twenty-seven of whom were Republicans. With that majority, the Republicans could pass any legislation they desired, if they all voted together as a block. It took the vote of twenty-seven senators to defeat a filibuster by the Democrats. If any one of them waivered, the other side could kill a particular piece of legislation.

Like all groups, especially political ones, some Republican senators were more conservative than others and didn't always see eye to eye on every bill proposed. The Democrats in the minority had successfully exploited these differences over the years and managed to persuade a few Republicans to vote with them and stop some bills from being passed.

This was the purpose of The Caucus. Only Republican senators were members, and it met regularly, even several times a week during the legislative session, to keep everyone in the fold.

In recent years, The Caucus was chaired by Arden Chambers. Since his committee controlled much of what reached the Senate floor for a vote, he was an important man to please. Chambers rewarded those who supported him with easy passage of their pet legislative projects. As his campaign for governor became more likely, he used The Caucus to threaten his colleagues if they didn't support his agenda.

Skip Sullivan began placing calls to the caucus members, leaving messages with his counterparts in their offices that Senator Chambers had an urgent matter for their consideration. He did reach Senator Lincoln Phillips from Melbourne who wanted to speak directly with Chambers. Sullivan put the call through to Chambers in his office.

"How are you, my friend?" Chambers greeted him.

"Pretty fair, Arden," Phillips replied. "What's the urgent matter?"

"The goddamn lawyers are at it again. Have you seen this latest bullshit class action?"

"I have, and I'm not sure it's bullshit. What about it? It's small potatoes compared to the tobacco thing."

"It's the last straw. I've had it. I've talked to people and the public is pissed. If I'm ever going to get this bill passed, now is the time. I'm putting it in this session and I want you and The Caucus to support it." Chambers's voice was rising and, with it, his emotions.

"Look, Arden. Take a breath for a second. Nobody likes lawyers, I'll give you that. But this is a big year for all of us. I'm not so sure this is the time to wake the sleeping giant."

"They're the only profession that regulates themselves, Link. Think of what it would be like if the doctors or the hospitals had to answer to no one but themselves. Or any other industry for that matter. Why should the lawyers be so fucking special?"

"I don't necessarily disagree with you. I'm just saying that there's a lot of other stuff on the plate this year."

"I don't give a shit, Link. It's the right thing to do. The people are on my side."

"I realize it could be a good campaign issue for your race, Arden, but it doesn't play as well in everyone else's. The legal lobby will mobilize in force, a shitload of money will be spent, and it'll be an all-out war."

"I don't care. I'm putting in the bill. Are you with me or not on this?"

"I need to think about it," Phillips said, stalling for time.

"Time's up," said Chambers. "Either get on the train or not. Either way, the train's leaving the station."

"The session is six weeks away, Arden," said Phillips. "Just give me a little time to think, okay?"

"While you're thinking," Chambers said, "think about what committee you may, or may not, be sitting on next year. The funding for the university branch might not get to the floor, you know."

There it was. Chambers had planted the bomb under Phillips's seat, only this time with less tact than usual. Typically,

Chambers would sidle up to him as they were walking in the Senate building and grab him around the shoulders, saying, "Let's get that funding bill of yours passed." This was different and more uncomfortable. The walls starting to close in around Phillips and he'd have to play ball.

"You wouldn't do that," said Phillips, knowing that Chambers would indeed do exactly that.

"I want this bill passed, Lincoln. I will do what I have to do."

"I'll make some calls," Phillips said after a long pause.

Chambers smiled broadly. "I knew you'd come to a reasonable decision, Link," he said.

When the call ended, Chambers buzzed Skip Sullivan's desk.

"Schedule the press conference," he said when Sullivan answered.

"But I'm still calling senators," Sullivan protested. "I'm only about halfway through the list."

"Go ahead and make the calls," said Chambers. "But set up the press conference immediately. Do it now."

CHAPTER FOURTEEN

Mike Donovan pulled into Oscar's Restaurant in DeFuniak Springs and parked in the lot the restaurant shared with a Family Dollar store and a building that had once been a K-Mart. Although the restaurant was in downtown, that term was more than a little misleading. Downtown consisted mostly of the Walton County Courthouse, the usual businesses that were in close proximity to it, lawyer's offices and bail bondsmen, a few fast food places, and auto parts stores. If you caught all of the lights, you could be through downtown in less than three minutes.

Donovan got out and approached the restaurant. Across the street was a two-story, non-descript, battleship gray building with a sign indicating that it was the office of the *Walton County Tribune*. Oscar's was a popular local restaurant, but the parking lot was virtually empty. It was ten-thirty in the morning, too late for the breakfast crowd and too early for the lunch one.

Donovan walked in and sat in a booth. A waitress walked over as soon as he did.

"Hi, I'm Gloria, I'll be takin' care of you. You by yourself, hon?"

"Uh, no, actually I'm waiting on someone," said Donovan.

"What can I bring you to drink?" she asked.

"Just some tea, please. Unsweet." In places like DeFuniak Springs, unsweet tea was a specialty order and this elicited a puzzled look from Gloria.

"Sure thing, hon," she said, walking away and shaking her head.

Donovan hadn't planned on eating anything, but realized that he was hungrier than he'd thought. He grabbed a laminated menu wedged between the salt and pepper shakers and looked it over. As he did, he heard the bell over the entrance door tingle and looked up to see a man enter the restaurant. Donovan didn't know him, but since there were no other customers there and the man was walking toward him, he assumed it was Alex Parsons.

"Mr. Donovan?" he asked as he approached the booth. Donovan slid out and offered his hand.

"It's Mike," he said. "You must be Alex Parsons." The two men shook hands and Donovan invited Parsons to join him in the booth.

Gloria returned with Donovan's unsweet tea and another glass for Parsons. "Hey, Alex," she said. "Missed you this morning. You havin' breakfast or lunch?"

"As long as Miss Ida's meat loaf is ready, I'm having it for breakfast and lunch," said Parsons, who didn't look like he had missed too many of either.

"How 'bout you, hon?" Gloria asked Donovan.

"It's not too early for lunch?" he asked.

"Ain't never too early," she said, smiling. Donovan ordered a BLT on wheat toast, without fries. Gloria jotted it down, then walked away, shaking her head again.

When they were alone again, Donovan spoke first.

"I appreciate your meeting me, Alex. You've heard about our deal?"

"Yeah, I heard about it. How similar was it to the thing over here?"

"Well, that's what I'm trying to find out. So far, all I know is that both victims were about the same age, both were killed in their houses, although I know the Jessup lady was in a rental house, and that both of them were supposedly tied up."

"I got a buddy who's a bail bondsman here. He knows some of the guys at the Sheriff's Office, and he says that Jessup was trussed up like a pig about to be sent to slaughter."

"What do you mean?"

"She had rope around her neck looped through a slip knot, then tied around her ankles. If she struggles, it only increases the pressure of the noose around your neck. They call it being hogtied."

"Do they have any suspects, leads, anything?"

"My buddy says they don't have jack shit. No prints, no witnesses, no motive. Nothing."

"What about the Escambia County investigator they called in? I assume it's a lieutenant named Palmer," asked Donovan.

"Didn't know his name, but they definitely called him in. Don't think he offered much help, though." Their food arrived and Donovan realized that his appetite was now only a fraction of what it was a few minutes before. Parsons dove into his meatloaf, green beans, and mashed potatoes. Donovan nibbled at his sandwich while Gloria refilled their glasses with tea.

"What about the other guy who used to work in uniform patrol? Where is he now?" Donovan asked when Parsons, slowed down on the plate.

"He got laid off from the Sheriff's Office. He's a process server now."

"Is he willing to meet?"

"Said he was. Let me call my buddy and see if I can get ahold of him. I'm going to step out because the cell reception in here sucks."

"Sure," Donovan said and sipped his tea while Parsons walked outside. Another customer came in and sat in a booth at the other end of the restaurant, paying no attention to Donovan.

A few minutes later, Parsons re-entered the restaurant and climbed back into the booth.

"He's out serving a subpoena or something," he said. "He's gonna try to reach him and call me back in a minute."

"Alex," asked Donovan, "why hasn't your paper done a story on this yet?"

"Couple of reasons. First, I haven't been able to confirm any of this. Second, my editor won't let me."

"Won't let you? Why?"

"Think about it, Mike. The only reason Walton County survives at all is because of the tourism industry in South Walton. How many tourists you think are gonna want to come here and pay big money to rent a secluded beach house when we tell 'em about poor old Ms. Jessup being hogtied and killed down there. And, of course, the killer's still on the loose."

Donovan could see the wisdom behind what Parsons was saying, even if he disagreed with it.

"So the story gets buried?"

"Probably. Unless something else happens."

Parsons's cell phone rang and he answered it. He listened for a minute, then hung up and looked at Donovan.

"Your lucky day, Mike. The process server was actually one of the uniforms on the scene of the Jessup murder. He'll talk to you, off the record, though, only if you'll come to him. He still has friends at the Sheriff's Office who refer him business."

"Fair enough," Donovan said. "Where and when?"

"In fifteen minutes. Come on, I'll take you. You'd never find it on your own."

They stood and climbed out of the booth. Donovan pulled out a twenty and laid it on the table. They waved goodbye to Gloria from a distance and headed out into the parking lot.

"We'll take my car. He won't recognize yours," Parsons said and they headed across the street to the *Tribune* parking lot.

* * *

Twenty minutes later, Donovan and Parsons sat in Parsons's Chevy Lumina parked along the side of County Road 280 East. Donovan noticed a dark Ford pickup pass them once, then again a few minutes later. After another two minutes, it pulled off the road in front of them. A tall, slender man got out of the truck and Parsons got out to meet him.

"Wait here," he said.

The two men talked at the front of the Lumina. After a minute, Parsons looked at Donovan through the Lumina's windshield and tipped his head backwards, a signal to Donovan to come and meet them. When he did, Parsons made the introductions.

"Mike Donovan, this is Billy Dodson." The two shook hands silently.

Parsons continued, "As I told you, Billy here used to be a uniformed deputy with Walton County, but got himself laid off due to the budget cuts."

"I'm hoping to get back on one day," Dodson said. "So this conversation has to be off the record. Okay?"

"Sure, I understand," said Donovan. Suddenly, Dodson stepped toward him and patted him down, even reaching inside Donovan's windbreaker.

"Is that really necessary?" asked Donovan. "I didn't come here armed."

"I ain't worried about no gun. I don't want this conversation recorded, even if you're the only one who'll hear it."

"There's no tape rolling," Donovan said, wondering now if this had been such a good idea after all.

Having satisfied himself that he was speaking only to those present, Dodson relaxed and leaned back against the tailgate of his truck. He reached into his shirt pocket and pulled out a pack of cigarettes, lit one and inhaled deeply. He folded his arms in front of him and looked at Donovan.

"Alright, what do you want to know?" he asked.

"I understand that you were on the scene of the Monica Jessup homicide in South Walton," said Donovan.

"Yes, sir."

"What can you tell me?"

"I responded to the call initially and was the first unit on the scene. The cleaning lady was standing out in the driveway crying hysterically. I didn't get much out of her at first. She just pointed at the house."

"What did you do?"

"I wasn't sure what was going on, so I made the decision to go ahead inside before my backup arrived. That was against protocol, but I thought the occupant might still be alive or that the suspect might still be in there. When I walked in, there was this horrible smell. I almost puked right then. I cleared the front room and the kitchen, then found the victim on the bed in the back bedroom. That's where the smell was coming from. She was definitely already dead."

"I understand she was tied up," Donovan said. "Not just tied up, but hogtied. Can you tell me anything about that?"

"I can do better than that," said Dodson. He reached inside his jacket and pulled out a cell phone. He clicked a few keys, then handed the phone to Donovan.

What Donovan saw next both shocked and repulsed him. His eyes flew open as he realized that he was looking at a picture of Monica Jessup lying in a pool of blood on the bed.

"Holy shit!" Donovan said. "Where did you get these?"

"I took 'em before backup arrived. Hit the button on the right if you want to scroll through and see the rest."

There were twelve photos in all, from all different angles. In the close ups, Donovan could see Monica's bulging eyes and protruding tongue. He scrolled through the other photos that showed the wound in the back of her head and stopped when he came to the pictures that specifically showed the rope that bound up Monica Jessup.

"What sort of rope was this?" he asked Dodson.

"Green nylon, about an inch in diameter."

Donovan continued through the photographs, paying close attention to the slipknots and the knots securing the rope. When he was finished, he handed the phone back to Dodson, who slipped it back into his jacket.

"Does anyone else know you have these?"

"No. If they did, I'd never get back on at the Sheriff's Office."

"Then why'd you take them?"

"In case I don't."

Donovan saw his point.

* * *

Two hours later, Donovan was at his desk at the *Herald* trying his best to digest what he'd seen. He immediately scribbled notes about the photographs as soon as Dodson left so they would still be fresh in his mind. He looked over the notes again and did a Google search for green nylon twisted rope 1" diameter. As he suspected, there were a million uses for nylon rope, although the search showed that the green variety was commonly used by landscaping contractors. He made a note of it. A separate search for such rope used in homicides, victims bound in nylon rope also proved to be useless. A search of "hogtied crime victims" led him to a number of disturbing porn sites and a link to a metal rock band by the same name.

Donovan didn't need to research any of the *Herald* articles on the Pettigrew murder because he'd written them himself. Like the Jessup case, Marie Pettigrew was found alone inside her house. In both cases, the police gave no statements, held no news conferences, and released no details of the homicides. More importantly, Glenn Palmer was an investigator in both cases. Donovan wondered if these were all the similarities between the two cases.

Donovan had met Glenn Palmer a few times in a professional capacity, but didn't know him well. As far as he could tell, Palmer was a straight shooter who had an impeccable and impressive background. He would play this by the book and not give away anything he didn't have to.

The last time he'd tried a cold call to an investigator, Randy West had hung up on him. He didn't know Randy West, but his only link to both of these cases was Glenn Palmer. All he could do was hang up on him. He would play the straight shooter straight and take his chances.

Donovan walked outside and used his cell phone. After reaching the Crimes Against Persons Unit in investigations, he identified himself and his affiliation with the *Herald* and asked for Lieutenant Palmer. Surprisingly, Palmer took the call.

"Palmer," he said when he answered.

"Lieutenant Palmer, this is Mike Donovan from the *Herald*."

"What can I do for you, Mr. Donovan?"

"I'm calling to discuss the Marie Pettigrew case."

"I cannot comment on an ongoing investigation," Palmer said. Donovan suspected this.

"Lieutenant, I'm calling to see if you care to discuss the relationship between Ms. Pettigrew's death and the death of Monica Jessup in Walton County in June of last year."

"No comment," said Palmer stiffly.

"Can you tell me if there is suspicion that the same killer committed both murders?"

"No comment." This was going nowhere.

"Why were you called in to consult on the Jessup homicide?"

"No comment. Look, Mr. Donovan, I really don't have time to --"

"Just one more question, Lieutenant," Donovan interrupted. "Was Marie Pettigrew hogtied with green rope fed through a slipknot in back of her head and found in her bed, too?"

There was nothing but silence on the other end of the phone.

"What did you just say?" asked Palmer.

"You heard me," said Donovan. "Do you want to comment or not?"

"Where did you get that information?" Palmer demanded.

"Now it's my turn not to comment."

More silence.

"Look, Lieutenant," Donovan said. "You and I both know these murders are connected. I don't want to stir up inaccurate information and neither do you. I know you're a straight arrow. I'm trying to be straight with you."

"Hang on a second," Palmer said, and Donovan could hear a door close in the background. Palmer came back on the line.

"Are you familiar with O'Steen's Irish Pub?"

"Yes."

"Do you know the private room in the back?"

"I know there is one, but I'm not a member."

"I am. Meet me there in half an hour," Palmer said and hung up.

CHAPTER FIFTEEN

Donovan parked his car and walked into O'Steen's exactly thirty minutes later. The hostess greeted him at the door and he told her he was meeting someone in the private room, but didn't know where it was. She gave him some hand signal directions since he could barely hear her over the loud Irish music, and he walked past the bar and down a hallway to his right. After a couple of wrong turns, he eventually came to a heavy wooden door with a brass-plated sign that read "The Powerbrokers Club. Members Only." He opened the door and stepped inside.

The private area was a series of smaller rooms, all paneled in dark, rich wood and dimly lit. Some of the rooms would only accommodate a table for two people. Others were larger, and there was one large room at the end. There was no hostess to greet him and the place appeared to be deserted. Donovan hesitated, unsure of whether to wait for Palmer or to look for him. He decided the latter and found Palmer sitting at one of the smaller rooms in the back corner. There were two glasses of water on the table, and Palmer didn't get up when Donovan approached.

"Have a seat," he said simply, motioning to the other chair. Donovan sat down.

"Are we off the record?" Palmer asked. So much for pleasantries.

"Do we need to be?" replied Donovan.

"We do or we have nothing to discuss."

"Then I guess we're off the record."

Palmer paused for a minute to gather his thoughts, then spoke in a low tone.

"Look, Donovan, you and I don't know each other. Your reputation with my people is that you're good at what you do, you play straight, and don't play any games."

"The same can be said for you, but you didn't bring me here to blow smoke up my ass, I'm sure."

Palmer smiled slightly.

"I need to know that I can trust you."

"Meaning?"

"Meaning that if I tell you something's off the record and just between you and me, I have to know that you'll honor that."

"So all of the cloak and dagger stuff means I'm onto something?" Donovan asked.

Palmer sat back in his chair, a look of disappointment crossing his face.

"You didn't answer my question," he said.

"I didn't hear a question. It sounded more like a command."

This was a potentially sticky situation for Donovan. If Palmer fed him bad information and he reported it, he and the *Herald* would look like idiots. If Palmer swore him to secrecy, then he couldn't print what Palmer told him. He would run the risk of being upstaged by another paper or media outlet and look like an incompetent. Either way, Emmett Bayer would have his head. Alternatively, if Palmer gave him information exclusively and the cops kept as tight a lid on the case in the future as they already had, he could be sitting on a bombshell.

"Here's a question/statement for you then," he said to Palmer. "If I'm privy to information that I can't print until you tell me, I have to know that it's not just some bullshit designed just to throw me off the trail. I need to know that I can trust you too."

"Meaning?"

"Meaning that you can't tell me to sit on this and let someone else beat me to the punch."

Palmer considered this for a moment, then leaned forward, putting his elbows on the table.

"I think we have an understanding," he said.

Donovan relaxed a little and sat back. "Okay," he said. "Where do we go from here?"

"I need to know what you know."

Donovan took a sip of his water, trying to decide how much he should tell Palmer.

"I know that Monica Jessup was found by a housekeeper in the back bedroom of a vacation house in South Walton where there was no evidence of forced entry. I know she'd been dead for several days."

So far, Palmer had shown no visible reaction to what Donovan was telling him. This information wasn't all that earth shattering and could have been obtained by a mediocre reporter.

"I also know that she was hogtied with green nylon rope about an inch in diameter. It was looped around her neck then fed through a slipknot to her ankles that were also bound. She also had a bloody wound on the back of her head."

Donovan saw Palmer flinch just a little as he said this. There was a short intake of breath and just a slight, almost imperceptible flash in his eyes that told Donovan he was right. The reaction was almost unnoticeable and he would have missed it if he hadn't been staring intently at Palmer when he said it. He made a mental note never to play poker with this guy.

"Finally," he began again, "I know that you were called in to consult on the Jessup case and you're the lead investigator on the Pettigrew case. You know I know that because you saw me at the scene the day of the murder."

"And what do you take from all of this?" Palmer asked, having returned to his original stoic self.

"I take that, with your forensics background, the fact that both of these cases involve dead women alone in the house, and the fact that you've been called in on both of them, tells me that they're related and may be similar enough to have been committed by the same person."

He didn't tell Palmer about Dodson's cell phone pictures.

The two men stared at each other and didn't speak for several seconds. Twice, Palmer drew in a long, deep breath and let it out slowly through his nose.

"I don't suppose you're going to tell me how you came by this information," he said.

Donovan made a face. "That's not how this works. You know better than that. Am I accurate?"

"Okay, your intel is pretty good. Both of the women were tied up. Rope was used in Jessup, electrical cords in Pettigrew. Not exactly the same, but the manner in which they were bound is similar enough. Both had wounds on the back of their heads and in the throat area. Both were alone at home at the time. Neither had any signs of forced entry to the homes. Both had been sexually violated with an object of some sort."

"What was the cause of death?"

"Strangulation in both cases."

"Leads? Suspects?"

"We've found no connection at all between the two women. It doesn't appear that they knew each other or had ever crossed paths at all. Their backgrounds were different. Monica Jessup was divorced, Marie Pettigrew was married with grown kids. The situations were different as well. Jessup was on vacation, Pettigrew was a resident. We haven't completely discounted the possibility that they both knew their attacker, but there is no direct evidence that they did."

"Could this be a copycat?"

"I've considered that. I don't think so because we put a lid on the media in Jessup so I'm not aware that any of these details were ever reported. There are no Mike Donovan's over there."

Now it was Donovan's turn to slightly smile. "So," he said. "Where does this leave us?"

"Good question. I'm not willing to say that we have a multiple murderer on our hands. Not by a long shot. But there are enough similarities between the two cases that force me to consider that possibility. We have to keep a lid on the media on this, though. If this gets out, the public will automatically jump to the conclusion that we have a serial killer. That would be bad."

"Where do I fit in all of this?" Donovan asked.

"There are a lot of details that only the person who did this knows. We want to keep those details out of the public's eye. That way we eliminate serial confessors who have nothing to do with it and are just looking for attention, and we have some unknown details if we catch the real killer . . . or killers."

"You still haven't told me what I can and can't print," said Donovan. "I can't just sit on all of this and do nothing."

"For now, I'd ask that you confine your story to the Pettigrew case only. Leave the murder details out. I'll give you some background and a bit of forensics that nobody else has so your story stands out. Don't even mention Jessup. We keep the rest between us."

"And you won't be inviting any of my colleagues to the Big Boys Club to discuss case details, right? When it comes time to go with this, I get a head start."

"No problem."

"I should run this past my editor."

"I'd prefer that you didn't. The fewer people who know about this, the better."

They sat in silence for a minute, sipping their water. Palmer glanced impatiently at his watch.

"What happens if another body turns up?" asked Donovan.

Palmer stared at him.

"We'd both better pray that doesn't happen," he said.

CHAPTER SIXTEEN

Rian pulled off her reading glasses and rubbed her eyes. She was ready for the depositions she was taking tomorrow and was trying to decide whether she could put off the client visits to the jail for another day because of the monstrous headache she had when Abby buzzed her.

"Turn on your TV," Abby said before Rian could answer. "Channel four."

The only real perk that Rian had as Chief Assistant was a cable television feed into her office. Jack Brown in the adjacent office found it necessary to have access to cable news in his office so he could monitor local cases when necessary. She and Jack shared a common office wall, so Rian talked him into letting her put a cable jack on her side as well. She brought her own little nineteen-inch flat screen that was sitting on top of her bookcase.

Rian opened her middle desk drawer, removed the remote, and switched on the television that was already preset to channel four. As the screen flickered to life, she saw a podium supporting a cluster of microphones all identifying various news outlets.

The Florida Capitol stood majestically in the background and the screen graphics indicated that whatever was happening was breaking news and being broadcast live.

This can't be good news.

Senator Arden Chambers stepped to the podium, dressed in his best navy blue suit, his crispest white shirt, a red and blue regimental striped tie, and the ubiquitous lapel pin shaped like the State of Florida in his left lapel. His close-cropped gray hair was perfectly trimmed and his wire-rimmed glasses reflected the setting Tallahassee sun.

"Good afternoon, ladies and gentlemen," he began. "Thank you for coming this afternoon."

Rian's stomach began to churn and her head began to pound.

"As you know, last week's news brought us the latest in a never-ending series of class action lawsuits filed against corporate and business interests in our state," Chambers continued. "This time, the victims are the insurance companies that provide valuable coverage and peace of mind to millions of Florida residents who end each day assured that their homes, automobiles, health, and even their very lives are financially protected."

Rian picked up her iPhone and quickly sent Sam a text message for him to turn on his office television.

"On the surface, this action seems to be in the public interest, as was the tobacco class action brought several years ago," Chambers continued. "While it is true that the state did receive money from that settlement, it was the private attorneys who cut a deal with the Attorney General who reaped the benefits to the tune of hundreds of millions of dollars, taxpayer dollars, after only two months of litigation."

Which is probably the same amount that the insurance industry has put in your pockets, Rian thought.

Rian checked her phone and had a response from Sam.

"Watching it. Pretty slick to come on just before the evening news to get max coverage," said his message. Rian turned her attention back to Chambers.

"I believe that an unregulated, unchecked, and voracious legal industry is a cancer in our state and that the people of this great state are compelling us to take strong action. That is why I, with the full support of my Republican colleagues in the Senate, am introducing legislation today that will end the self-regulation of the legal industry by the Florida Bar and treat this industry equally to doctors, architects, public accountants, and engineers, all of whom are overseen by a specialty board appointed by the Governor with legislative oversight."

Rian turned the television off. She rummaged though her purse and found the bottle of Advil and popped three into her mouth. She washed them down with the last remnant of cold coffee in the mug on her desk, grimacing when she was done.

Sam's ringtone set off her phone.

"Looks like we need to find a new line of work," he said when she picked up.

"What a piece of shit he is," Rian said. "I think he really believes this crap."

"Oh, I think he does, too, but he's just grandstanding. It's an election year, and lawyer bashing is popular. He'll forget all about it once he's Governor."

"I don't know, sometimes I think that waiting tables again wouldn't be such a bad thing," she said.

"Why don't you leave early and swing by my place. We'll have a drink in the hot tub and get an early dinner. How does that sound?"

"Like it'll do wonders for my splitting headache. Except I have to go to the jail to see a couple of clients first."

"Why can't one of the underlings do that?"

"Long story. I just have to go, though. I'll hurry and can be there by six-thirty at the latest. Okay?"

"Do I have a choice in the matter?"

"Nope. See you," she said and hung up.

* * *

Rian pulled the BMW into the parking lot at the Escambia County Jail and parked in one of the spaces reserved for attorneys. As she got out, she noticed that, in addition to hers, there were two other larger BMWs, a Lexus and an Audi also in the reserved spaces. These were definitely not the cars of her co-workers in the Public Defender's Office. If not for her father, she'd probably be driving one of the Tauruses or old Impalas that filled the rest of the parking lot. Once again, the thought of private practice tugged at her, and she heard Sam's voice in her head telling her again how marketable she was.

She entered through the main door and passed through the security checkpoint. She presented her identification to the corrections officer behind the heavy glass window and signed the log indicating which prisoners she was there to see.

Fifteen minutes later, she was making her way through a series of electronically locked doors, the one behind her making a loud crash as it closed before the one in front would open. She walked down the hall toward Interview Room 3, past the holding cell area.

Rian's presence in the hallway produced the usual uproar from the inmates in the holding area, all of whom jumped to the bars and yelled at her to marry them, or worse. Their voices reverberated off the concrete block walls and polished tile floor, reducing them to a loud, continuous roar and, fortunately for Rian, making it hard to hear the individual offers. Rian ignored them and continued down the hall, the tick-tick-tick of her heels on the tile becoming louder as the inmates' voices faded in the distance.

The interview room was open and consisted of a metal table bolted to the floor with a metal chair on each side, also bolted to the floor. Rian put her files on the table and sat in one of the chairs, listening to the yelling and banging sounds that never ceased in the jail.

A few minutes later, a corrections officer brought Anthony Stallworth to the door. Stallworth was a young, large African-American man dressed in a bright orange jumpsuit and wearing dirty white shower shoes. The officer closed the door behind him and Rian could hear the lock engage.

"Mr. Stallworth, I'm Rian Coulter," she said. "Please have a seat." Stallworth sat with a disgusted look.

"You ain't my lawyer. Where's my lawyer?" he said.

"Mr. Peterson has been reassigned. I came to discuss the plea offer in your case."

"What the fuck do you know about my case? I ain't ever seen you before. Peterson only came here once."

"Sir, that's not important right now. You've been charged with aggravated assault and --"

"It God damn sure is important. I got a right to an attorney, not some fancy ass bitch that drops by in her expensive suit to throw my ass to the dogs."

Rian ignored the insult and went ahead.

"Mr. Stallworth, the State has offered to let you enter a plea to simple assault, a misdemeanor, for a sentence of six months with credit for the time you've already served."

"No, I want a trial."

"This is a very good offer for someone with your past criminal record. I think you should consider it."

"No, I want a trial."

"You'll be out of here in sixty days."

"I said I want a trial, *bitch*!"

"If you reject this offer and are convicted of the felony, the judge will have no choice but to sentence you to state prison. It's a huge risk and, frankly, the evidence is pretty strong, so my recommendation as your attorney --"

Stallworth's hands slamming onto the metal table sounded like an explosion. He jumped up and towered over Rian, glaring at her.

"Bitch, did you not hear what I said? I don't want no motherfuckin' plea deal. I want my motherfuckin' *trial*!"

Rian tried not to flinch and held his gaze. She tried to look confident and mask the fear rising inside her. She knew there was a telephone on the wall to her left that she could pick up and call for help, but Stallworth could inflict some serious harm by the time help arrived. She needed to control the situation.

In the calmest voice she could muster, she said quietly, "Sir, I am not your bitch. I'm your lawyer. If you don't want my help, I really don't care. Because whether you take this deal or not, I'm walking out of here. You aren't. You can be a free man in sixty days if you're smart or be in state prison for several years if you're a dumb ass. But I can tell you one thing for sure. If you call me a bitch again, you're going to leave here with your voice a good bit higher than it was before."

The door opened and the corrections officer stepped in, breathing heavily as though he'd been running.

"Everything okay in here, ma'am?" he asked looking at Rian, then at Stallworth, then back at Rian.

Rian stood and picked up her files.

"Sure. Everything's great. I was just leaving. He's all yours."

Lowering her voice, she said to Stallworth, "See you in court, Anthony," and walked out.

They don't pay me enough to put up with this shit.

CHAPTER SEVENTEEN

Christy Price pushed her way through the crowd to the bar and waved her glass at the bartender.

"Another madras please, Dylan," she said, giving him her sweetest smile.

"You got it, babe," replied Dylan.

Christy drained the last of her drink and set her glass down on the heavy oak bar where it was immediately scooped up and sent to the dishwasher. She turned her back to the bar and looked back out into the crowd, swinging her hips and dancing to the music while awaiting her refill. In a minute, Dylan was back with Christy's drink.

"Here you go, sweetheart," he said, holding the drink out to her, but her back was turned and she didn't hear him over the band. She continued to dance in place with her eyes closed, shaking her head and belting out the lyrics to the band's Toby Keith song.

The man sitting at the bar next to her observed all of this, took the drink from the bartender, and got Christy's attention by putting his hand on her shoulder. She stopped dancing and looked at him with a puzzled look at first that disappeared when he held up her drink. Her hips started swaying again immediately and she danced her way back into the crowd, giving Dylan a big, white smile over her shoulder as she went.

Dylan and the man watched her go, impressed by her long blonde hair, her denim shorts, and the pink thong underwear peeking out of the top which barely concealed the tattoo at the small of her back.

The Border Line Lounge was so named because the Alabama-Florida state line ran right through the middle of the place. It was a typical beach bar that had grown in popularity through the years and now had several additions connected to each other through breezeways. There were both indoor and outdoor bars and room for several bands to perform at the same time when necessary.

For ten months out of the year, the Border Line catered to a hard core group of locals and the tourists who rented the condos and beach houses along Perdido Key. The key consisted of a small strip of land that ran along the Gulf of Mexico from just west of Pensacola to Gulf Shores, AL. Orange Beach, on the Alabama side, was packed with high-rise condominiums and trendy beach restaurants. Perdido Key, on the Florida side, had a few high rises, but was mostly filled with two and three-story beach houses, more casual restaurants, and tourist shops.

In March and April of each year the entire key was bombarded by thousands of college students from around the country celebrating spring break. They inundated the rental houses, overwhelmed the restaurants, and partied nonstop for days at a time until they were relieved by the next wave.

The Border Line geared up for spring break and imported some well known country music bands to replace the quirky local bands that normally performed. Operating hours were extended and the lounge put on events like the mullet toss, giving away free beer to the person who could throw a local fish the farthest.

These things, plus the fact that under age students were never refused alcohol, made the Border Line the focus of the students' attention, and they descended on the bar in droves. Every sunrise revealed a fair number of them were found passed out on the beach in various states of undress.

Tonight was no exception. Every room and bar at the Border Line was packed tight with rowdy college students who sang, gyrated to the music, and drank themselves into oblivion.

The man at the bar sipped at his beer, and eventually Christy came bouncing out of the crowd again, headed back to the vacant spot at the bar where she was served the last time. Dylan took her glass and went off to make her refill as the band announced that they were taking a short break.

"So, what's a madras?" asked the man at the bar when Christy arrived.

"It's vodka, orange juice, and cranberry juice," she said. "They're awesome. All my friends drink them. Have you ever had one?"

"No," he said. "I pretty much stick to beer."

"Oh, well then, you simply *have* to try one."

"That's okay," he tried to protest but Christy ignored him.

“Dylan, hey Dy-lan,” she called and got the bartender’s attention. “Can you make me *two* madrases?”

She turned back to the man at the bar.

“I’m Christy,” she said.

“Hi, Christy,” he responded, not giving her his name, but she didn’t notice. Now that he had spoken with her, he could tell that she was pretty drunk.

“Me and my friends are here on bring sprake,” she said, then dissolved into laughter. “I mean spring break.”

“Spring break from where?”

“We go to LSU. I’m not from there, well, I mean I am like from there, kind of, but I go to school there. I’m like *from* Lauderdale.”

“Lauderdale?”

“Fort Lauderdale. You know, like, next to Miami? We call it Lauderdale.”

“I see.”

“Yeah, me and five of my friends came here instead of going to Panama City. That place is a dump. We rented one of the apartments down the street and we’re all piled in together. It’s great.”

“Sounds fun.”

“Yeah. And we can, like, walk here and don’t have to drive.”

The drinks arrived and Christy handed one to the man, who tasted it.

“So, what do you think?” she asked.

“Not bad,” he said. “For my first madras. But I think I’ll stick with my beer for now. You can have mine.”

"Wow, thanks," she said.

"So, where are your friends?" he asked.

"I don't know. Haven't seen 'em in a while. Maybe they went back or passed out or something." She finished first her drink and was now working on the one he had given her.

"I have to pee," she announced. "Will you watch my drink for me?"

"Sure."

"Okay. Thanks. Be right back." She slipped ungracefully off the bar stool, paused for a second to steady herself, and then headed toward the bathrooms. He watched her leave, even more unsteady on her feet than before.

The line for the bathroom was long, and Christy was getting more and more uncomfortable. She danced around for a minute, then decided to try another bathroom. The line there was just as long. On her way to another ladies room she stopped, looked out at the beach and the dark water of the Gulf, then looked around to see if anyone was paying attention. Seeing no one out here, she slipped off her sandals, dropped them into the white sand, and headed for a large sand dune on the beach nearby.

Less than halfway there, she passed beyond the floodlights from the bar and found herself in near pitch black darkness. The sound of the Gulf waves crashing onshore drowned out all other noise from the bar and only made her desire to urinate all the more urgent. She trotted over to the dune and, after looking around once more to make sure that no one was watching, disappeared behind it, dropped her shorts, and peed right on the sand.

When she finished, Christy stood and pulled her shorts back up. As she turned around, she could make out a dark figure standing at the edge of the dune, silhouetted by the lights from the bar behind him. He was holding something. Uneasy and unsure of what to do, Christy just stood there as the figure approached.

"I thought you might need these," said the man from the bar, holding up her sandals. "And this." He held out her drink.

Christy relaxed and took the drink.

"Oh, thanks. You scared me there for a minute," she said.

She drank the entire drink at once, leaning her head back and tipping the cup up and holding it there, making sure she didn't waste a single drop.

With her eyes closed, she never saw the man's fist hit her full force in the throat, shattering her larynx and crushing her trachea. Christy fell straight down in the sand, landing on her butt and falling over onto her back. She was gasping for air and could taste something warm, wet, and salty in her mouth.

Fear gripped her like a vise and she kept clawing at her throat, desperately trying to get air and keep from passing out. It was a losing battle. She was aware that she was being rolled over onto her stomach and that something was wrapping around her neck. She could feel her feet being pulled up behind her, then a heavy weight dropped onto her back, pushing her face down into the sand.

In a panic, Christy tried to raise her head so that she could breathe, but the intense pain in her throat and the weight on the back of her head prevented it. She tried to kick whatever was on top of her, but her legs wouldn't work. Something was holding them together. She vomited, and some of her stomach contents, mostly alcohol, were sucked into her lungs as she desperately tried to take in air, causing an intense, burning pain. She summoned all of her strength for one last effort to free herself, but it was useless.

With her face buried in the sand, Christy finally gave up and let the darkness overtake her.

CHAPTER EIGHTEEN

A large crowd was gathered in front of The Border Line as Palmer drove up. They were mostly college kids. Some of the guys were shirtless and barefoot with uncombed hair and bloodshot eyes indicating that either they had just awakened or had never been to bed the night before. The girls weren't in any better shape. Most were barefoot and in bathing suits with a t-shirt pulled over them.

Palmer scanned the crowd as he slowed and pulled to a quick stop when he saw Sanchez waiting for him.

"This way, L.T.," he said and motioned for Palmer to follow. They walked around the side of the bar to the back, then out to a large dune covered in sea oats. The Gulf was calm this morning, but he could still hear the waves breaking on shore. A couple of squawking seagulls in the air escorted them to the scene on the beach.

Christy Price lay on her side in the sand. She was nude from the waist down and her white tank top had been pushed up to reveal her small breasts. She wasn't wearing a bra. Her skin was pale, and white beach sand covered her face and torso, thicker and matted around her mouth and nose. A man's belt was wrapped around her neck and was pulled through the buckle at the back of her neck. Her legs were pulled up behind her so that her feet nearly touched the back of her head. There was just enough belt left to loop once around her ankles and make a knot. Her arms and hands weren't bound and lay limply in the sand beside her.

"Jesus," Palmer said as he knelt beside the body for a closer look. She appeared to be about twenty and the letters LSU below a purple and gold tiger head on her tank top told Palmer that she was probably a student there. Her tongue protruded from her mouth and was coated with sand. Palmer could see dried blood in her mouth. A large bruise was clearly evident on her throat.

Palmer stood and turned to Sanchez.

"Her name's Christy Price. Originally from Ft. Lauderdale, but currently a junior at LSU," Sanchez said.

"Who found her?" Palmer asked.

"Jogger on the beach found her at about six this morning. He didn't see the belt at first and thought she was just asleep on the beach. His dog wouldn't leave, so he stopped and took a closer look," Sanchez answered.

Palmer looked back up to the bar. The dune would have concealed Christy and her attacker from everyone at the bar, but he knew that people were always milling around on the beach down here. A killer would have to be crazy to do this with so many people close by.

Or that confident.

Surely, someone saw something.

"Who's she here with?" Palmer asked.

"There are five others who came over with her from LSU. They got separated from Christy around midnight and thought she'd left and gone back to the apartment where they were staying. They all got back there about three but she never showed up."

Palmer looked to either side of the bar. The nearest house was on the Alabama side about fifty or sixty yards away. On the Florida side, there had been some houses closer, but they had probably been washed away by the hurricanes because there were only empty sand lots there now.

"Anybody notice her with someone in particular?"

"Not yet, but we're not finished talking with everyone."

Palmer couldn't believe something like this could happen within a few yards of a place packed with a thousand people. He felt certain there were clues here waiting to be discovered, but he was going to need more manpower.

A lot more.

As he considered all of this, Palmer became aware of the sound of a helicopter approaching, not an unusual sound at the beach. At first he didn't pay it any attention, but the sound grew louder and Palmer looked up to see it hovering above them, a large "4" painted on its side indicating it was from the local television station.

"Shit," he said. Turning to the crime scene techs still taking pictures of Christy and the area around her, he yelled, "Somebody get something to cover her up with. Now!"

Turning back to Sanchez, Palmer shouted, "Get on the radio to dispatch and tell them to get that fucking copter out of here. They're interfering with a criminal investigation, and I'm going to arrest every goddamn person on it if they don't get the hell out of here." Sanchez took off in a sprint back toward the bar.

"God *dammit*!" Palmer yelled in frustration to no one in particular as he trudged through the sand back to the bar.

* * *

Sanchez was standing in the main bar area with a young man wearing an LSU football jersey when Palmer walked back in. Two girls were sitting at a nearby table and both were crying.

"Lieutenant," said Sanchez, "this is Peter Ingram. He was part of the group that was here with Miss Price."

Palmer looked at the sunburned, disheveled young man.

"I just can't believe it," he said, staring at the ground and shaking his head. "Not Christy. I mean, we were just with her." Raising his eyes to Palmer, he said, "How in the fuck could this have happened? There were a million people here."

"When did you last see Miss Price?" Palmer asked.

"Shit, man, I don't really know. We all came down in a group. We generally hung around together, but the place was crowded, everybody's getting drinks at different times, going to pee at different times. You meet people, you know."

"So you all got separated."

"Yeah. The deal we had was nobody would leave unless we all left together. Getting separated while we were here wasn't that big of a deal because we'd all hook back up when the place closed down."

"How well did you know Miss Price?"

"I guess pretty well. I mean, we'd hung out a good bit at school and all. Lindsay and Sarah knew her a lot better than I did, though."

Palmer looked at Sanchez, who silently pointed at the two crying girls sitting at the table. Palmer approached the table. One of the girls, a blonde, had her head in her hands. The other girl had dark hair and looked up at him, her face wet with tears.

"I'm Lieutenant Palmer," he said. "I know this is difficult, but I need to ask you a few questions." The girl nodded and Palmer sat down.

"Which one's Lindsay?" he said.

"I'm Lindsay," the brunette said. "Lindsay Farmer." Palmer looked at the blonde and she picked her head up.

"I'm Sarah Walker."

"How well did you all know Miss Price?"

"The three of us were best friends," said Lindsay. "We're sorority sisters at LSU. We do everything together."

"I understand that you all got here as a group, but got separated at some point."

"Yeah. We generally tried to stay in the same area, but the place was really crowded, so it's hard."

"What can you remember about Miss Price last night?"

"I don't know, it was just like a typical night. We were all hanging out, dancing, you know."

"How much did you have to drink?"

The two girls looked at one another, unsure of how to respond.

"Look, I know you're both under age. I don't care about that. I'm interested in finding the person who did this to your friend."

Lindsay spoke first. "I was drinking; we all were. I felt good, but I wasn't wasted," she said.

"Same for me," said Sarah.

"And Christy?"

"She was partying, probably the same as us," said Lindsay.

"She had more than we did," Sarah interjected. "She kinda flirted with the bartender, and I think he liked her so she got served quicker."

"Did you see her with anyone in particular last night?" Both girls shook their heads.

"Was Christy the type who might go off with someone she'd just met and not tell you?"

"No, absolutely not," said Lindsay.

"Definitely not," Sarah said.

"How late were the two of you here?"

"We were here till about 2:00. We walked back to the apartment together."

"Where was the rest of your group?"

"Pete was still down here, I guess," Lindsay said. "Amanda had already gone back before we did because she got sick and started puking. I don't know where Courtney was."

Palmer envisioned a crowded, chaotic beach bar packed with hundreds of young, partying college kids. Attractive, intoxicated young women, wandering around in the dark by themselves would provide a target rich environment for a killer.

"Didn't you worry when you couldn't find Christy?"

Lindsay just looked at him for a long moment. Tears welled in her eyes and spilled down her cheeks.

"I just . . . figured that she was with Pete and Courtney and that she was . . . okay," she said, the sobs starting to come again.

"The thing is," said Sarah, "we didn't really look for her. We just . . ."

"Oh my God, Sarah," Lindsay said. "What am I going to tell her parents?" They both hugged each other and started sobbing uncontrollably. Palmer took that as his cue.

As he stood to leave, he saw Sanchez approaching. He motioned Palmer over.

"L.T., I may have something. There's somebody you should talk to."

Palmer followed him to the bar where they met another young man wearing a Border Line polo shirt. He was standing behind the bar.

"This is Dylan Massey," said Sanchez. "He was the bartender in here last night."

"The manager woke me up and told me what happened," Massey said. "I came out here as quick as I could."

"Tell him what you just told me," Sanchez said.

"I was working this bar last night," Massey began. "I remember the girl real well. She was hot and kinda flirty, but real sweet. We kinda hit it off."

"Was she with anyone?"

"No, that's the thing. She kept coming to me for drinks, then she'd go back out into the crowd and dance, then come back. But she was always by herself."

Palmer gave Sanchez a questioning look.

"Tell him the rest," he said to Massey.

"Well, it may not mean anything but there was this guy sitting at the bar here. He seemed to be interested in the girl."

"How so?

"Well, at one point she came up here and I saw the two of them talking. Then she orders two drinks, one for her and I guess one for him to try. He was drinking beer, but they were drinking other stuff. Anyway, she headed off, I guess to the bathroom or something."

"What did the guy do?"

"See, that's the thing. He'd been sitting here for a couple of hours at the bar. Had one, maybe two beers the whole time he was here. Then she tootled off to the bathroom and I saw him pick up her drink and leave in the same direction. I never saw either one of them again."

Palmer's skin began to tingle. "How did he pay for the drinks? Did he use a credit card?" he asked hopefully.

"No. He paid in cash."

"Can you give us a description?"

"Yeah. About six feet, with sandy blond hair. He had a beard and was tanned, you know, like he works outside or something. Older than these kids. Maybe in his thirties."

"I need you to go downtown and meet with our sketch artist. We may be able to get a composite based on your description," Palmer said. "Detective Sanchez can take you down."

"Do you think this is the guy?" asked Massey. "I mean, you think he was sitting right here at my bar all night?"

"I don't know," Palmer responded. "But, so far, you may be the only living person who's seen him."

CHAPTER NINETEEN

Rian ran at a good pace along Bayview Avenue. Her legs felt strong, her breathing was good, and the endorphins had kicked in giving her a sense of peace and calm. She checked her wristwatch monitor and noted that she was averaging a little over seven minutes a mile. With eight miles down and two to go, she felt she might even have enough left for a little kick at the end. The Bridge Run to the beach was still a couple of weeks away, and Rian was pleased with how her training had progressed.

She turned into the Historic District and the final stretch toward home. She arrived there spent and drenched in sweat and walked around the block once with her hands on her hips to cool down. She bent down to pick up the Saturday *Herald*, such as it was, and let herself in the back door that she'd left unlocked. Grabbing a bottle of water from the refrigerator, she sat at one of the kitchen bar stools and spread the paper out on the counter. She was too sweaty to sit on the couch. Mannix jumped onto the counter and plopped down beside her with an audible thud.

Rian opened the paper and was taken aback at the headline. In bold type normally reserved for major disasters, the paper read,

BRUTAL HOMICIDE AT PERDIDO KEY LOUNGE. A large color photograph of The Border Line Lounge appeared beneath the headline, and Rian quickly read the story. The victim was a young, white female whose name hadn't been released yet because her family hadn't been properly notified. She was apparently found on the beach behind the bar. Other than that, there were few details of the murder itself and nothing at all about any suspects.

Rian was familiar with The Border Line, having represented a number of people on mostly alcohol-related charges that had arisen there. She knew the place would be crawling with college kids on spring break at this time of year and assumed that the victim must have been one of them. Although there were times when the police were called if the partying got out of hand, The Border Line wasn't known for criminal activity, if you didn't count the underage drinking; certainly not for violence like this.

The article recounted the death of the woman in Cantonment who had been murdered back in December. Rian couldn't recall all of the details, but did remember that the crime had been pretty gruesome according to the news reports. Two serious murders in the space of a few months was unusual for this area, and Rian knew this would set off a lot of speculation.

Rian headed upstairs and Mannix assumed his usual spot on the edge of the bed while she climbed into the shower. She stood for a long time with her eyes closed letting the water roll down her back and legs, relaxing her tired muscles. As she did, she let her mind drift back to her brief tenure at the Ashton, Baker firm in Birmingham six years before.

She had liked Birmingham, initially. The city had undergone a revitalization that changed it from a dirty, smoky, steel town in the 1960s to a vibrant, modern community in the 1990s. The area where she had lived reminded her a little of Greenwich Village in New York, with street vendors, artists, and young professionals who lived there. Even though her job at the firm hadn't quite turned out how she had wanted, Rian might have stayed in Birmingham if not for other circumstances.

The town was paralyzed by a series of brutal murders that had begun a year or two before Rian arrived. Seven women had been horribly murdered, and the police believed that a serial killer was responsible for them all. Two of the killings occurred while Rian was there, both young women who lived alone. Both had been bound, gagged, and sexually abused. The killer had struck with machine-like proficiency and then, all of a sudden, the attacks stopped. Speculation ran wild and everyone had their own opinion; the killer had died, the killer was in jail on unrelated charges, the killer had moved to another location.

The police had few leads and fewer suspects and the local news media criticized them on a daily basis. At the time Rian moved to Pensacola, the murders were still unsolved.

Despite the hot water running down her back, Rian felt a cold chill that snapped her back to reality. She remembered the fear in her friends' eyes and how everyone was too afraid to venture out at night, yet too fearful to stay at home alone. Her father had been right to insist that she leave, and she felt much safer in sleepy little Pensacola.

Except that she had the same chill running down her spine now.

* * *

"Hey, Dad," Rian said when her father answered.

"Hey, Peanut," he responded. "I was hoping I'd hear from you today."

"I take it you've heard about our little situation over here?"

"Well, I wouldn't phrase it quite that way but, yes, it's all in our papers over here. Not a lot of specifics, but it sounds damned awful. I can't get that poor girl out of my mind."

"I know. Me, too. I'm sure she was one of the spring breakers over here for the week. Probably went for a walk on the beach or a skinny dip at midnight."

"I remember when you used to do the same stupid thing. Your mother and I worried ourselves sick that something like this would happen to you."

"Well, with age comes wisdom, I guess. Anyway, I just wanted to call and let you know everything's fine. You and Mom are okay?"

"We're fine, honey. How's Sam?"

"Sam's Sam. He's fine."

"Give him a hug from us. Come see us; you know where we live don't you?"

Rian smiled at the good natured dig that her father always gave her when he felt that he hadn't seen enough of her.

"Roses, Dad. I'm smelling roses."

* * *

Donovan tapped the down arrow on his keyboard and read again through the story that scrolled up his monitor screen. Christy Price's unfortunate family in south Florida had been notified of her death and his latest article identified her publicly for the first time. He knew that Channel 4 news would be leading its broadcast with video footage of the scene shot from its helicopter, and he needed his story to at least preempt that in the *Herald's* online version. Everyone else would read it as the lead story in tomorrow's paper.

What Donovan knew that no one else in the media knew was that Christy Price's death was related to Marie Pettigrew's and that both were related to the murder of Monica Jessup. It was only a matter of time before speculation caught up with reality and, if he didn't break the story, someone else would. The story had legs, and the local news outlets, including those from nearby Mobile, AL were all clamoring for an angle to approach it from. He knew that this window of opportunity wouldn't stay open for long.

He read the story again. The headline read *Police Probing Links In Area Murders*, and the story explained the possible link between the two Escambia County killings with the one in Walton County earlier last year. The specific details of the deaths were left out, but the implication was clear; the police believed that one person, a serial killer, was responsible for these terrible crimes. The only thing missing was a quote from the lead investigator, Lieutenant Glenn Palmer. Donovan had called him twice and left messages, but Palmer hadn't returned the calls.

Donovan picked up the telephone and dialed again. He was once again routed to Palmer's desk and reached Palmer's terse voicemail greeting.

"You've reached the desk of Lieutenant Palmer. Leave a message," it said before the beep.

"Lieutenant, this is Mike Donovan calling again. I've left several messages for you already. I'm calling to let you know that we're going with a story in tomorrow's *Herald* that confirms that law enforcement is linking the Price killing to the Pettigrew and Jessup murders. I wanted to give you a chance to comment." He left his number and hung up.

Donovan had called Dr. Crawford and received a brusque "No comment" from the Medical Examiner's Office. He had also tried to reach someone in the State Attorney's Office for a comment, but no one returned that call either. On one hand, Donovan understood their position. They didn't want to alarm the community. On the other hand, the stonewalling would only lead to wild speculation and more intense media scrutiny that was likely to cause even more panic. He was a little aggravated that no one would call him back.

He checked his watch, noting that he still had a few minutes before the deadline to file his story. He got up and walked down the hall to Emmett Bayer's office. Surprisingly, Bayer was not only in the office but wasn't on the telephone. Donovan tapped on the doorframe to get his editor's attention and stuck his head in.

"The story's done. You sure you want me to go with it?" he asked.

"Any comments from Palmer or anyone in the investigation?" Bayer asked.

Donovan shook his head. "No. I got a brush off from Dr. Crawford and have left Lieutenant Palmer three voicemails with no call backs."

Bayer considered this for a moment. "Go with it," he said. "Channel Four is going with theirs, I know. They've had their chance. Fuck 'em."

Donovan headed back to his desk and scrolled to the end of the story.

"The Medical Examiner's Office refused comment and calls to Escambia County Sheriff's investigators were not returned," he typed and hit "Send."

CHAPTER TWENTY

J.T. Spencer slipped on his suit coat, adjusted his tie, and studied himself in the mirror. He wore a charcoal gray suit, a starched white shirt, and a deep burgundy tie. This was an important day for him, and he wanted to look his best. His wife's image appeared in the mirror behind him and he turned to face her.

"Well, how do I look?" he asked.

"Like someone who's about to be elected to the Senate," said Eleanor, brushing some lint off his shoulder.

"Thanks. I'm a little nervous, I have to admit."

"You should be. This is a big day . . . for both of us."

"Who would've thought that I'd, uh, we'd, be in this position? I hope I can do it, El. I mean, this is politics at a whole different level. You have to compromise, cut deals, be ready to --"

Eleanor interrupted him. "John," she said, looking him square in the eyes. "I'm proud of you. We all are. You're a good and honest man, and everyone understands that you have to get elected first to make things change."

"I guess everyone has to dance with the Devil sometimes," he said, laughing.

Eleanor smiled at her husband and placed her hands on his cheeks. "You just go get elected today. Everything else will be fine."

Spencer kissed her and walked out to his car. He was hanging his suit jacket in the back seat when his cell phone rang.

"This is it, Spencer. Crunch time. You ready?" Arden Chambers said, brimming with confidence.

"Ready as I'll ever be, Senator Chambers. Or shall I start calling you Governor-elect?"

Chambers laughed heartily. "Well, there is that small matter of the General Election in November, J.T." At that they both laughed.

"A mere formality, my boy. Today we begin to take back the State of Florida for its people. I just wanted to call and wish you luck; not that you'll need it."

He was right. Once J.T. climbed aboard the Chambers Express, the money poured in as well as the support. His poll numbers skyrocketed, and he was predicted to win today's Republican primary by a wide margin. His Democrat opponent in the November election had only raised a fraction of the funds he had, and everyone expected that the juggernaut would be unstoppable.

"And the best to you, too, sir. Thank you for all you've done for me. I don't know how I'll ever be able to repay you."

"I'll think of a way, J.T. Don't you worry," Chambers said and clicked off.

J.T. wondered what sacrifices he'd have to make and corners he'd have to cut in the future, now that he was beholden to Arden Chambers. He drove the short distance from his house to the little Presbyterian church that he and Eleanor attended. A small sign at the parking lot entrance decorated by American flags advertised that this was the polling place for Precinct 39, and J.T. pulled into the gravel lot and parked. He walked into the community room and greeted the little old ladies sitting behind the tables waiting to check voters in as they arrived. He was the only one there.

They visibly brightened when he approached them. "Good morning, ladies," he said. "Turnout looks heavy today." They all laughed. One of them handed him a computerized ballot form and he stepped behind a partition to fill it in.

It took only a few seconds for J.T. to cast his vote for himself and Arden Chambers.

CHAPTER TWENTY-ONE

Rian and Sam sat quietly at a small, dimly lit table at Mancini's. The restaurant was located at the foot of the bridge that crossed over Jackson Bayou and led to the large Naval Air Station in Pensacola.

Mancini's was an institution in the area and as well known for its quiet, elegant atmosphere overlooking the bayou as for the best Italian food in town. Sam had represented the owner, Dominic Mancini, several years ago when the Navy wanted to build a much larger bridge to the base that would have taken most of Dominic's property and forced the restaurant to close. Sam sued the government successfully and saved Mancini's, earning Dominic's gratitude forever. The first bottle of wine was always on the house whenever Sam and Rian ate dinner there.

Rian swirled the wine in her glass, staring at it absent-mindedly while Sam checked his messages on his smartphone. He stopped and studied her, and she eventually felt his gaze and looked up at him.

"What?" she said.

"I didn't say anything. What's bothering you?" he asked.

"Nothing."

They sat in silence until the food arrived. Sam dug right into his chicken parmagiana. Rian picked at her linguini in clam sauce.

"What's wrong, Rian?" he asked firmly.

"I said it's nothing."

Normally Sam wouldn't push too hard when Rian was in one of these moods, but he did so anyway this time.

"Don't blow me off with that bullshit, Rian. Something's bothering you, and I want to know what it is. I think I'm entitled."

That did it. She slammed her linen napkin down on the table, causing her fork to flip in the air and land loudly on the plate. That got the attention of the older couple at the next table.

"Entitled?" she said, loudly. "Entitled to what, exactly? Do you see a ring on my damn finger?"

"Whoa. Is that what this is about? Rian, we've talked about this and agreed that we'd take things as they came."

"It's not just that, Sam. I'm stressed out. The job I used to love now sucks. All of my peers have moved on to partnerships with benefits and big time practices, and I'm still stuck dealing with assholes at the goddamn jail. And, oh yeah, there's a fucking serial killer in town, I hear." The woman at the next table let out an audible gasp.

"Keep your voice down," Sam said.

"Don't tell me to keep my voice down, damn it," Rian said. "Nothing is going in the right direction for me right now, and on top of that, I have no idea where you and I are headed. My whole life is in the shit."

The waiter approached cautiously and asked if they needed anything. Sam said they were fine.

"I'll have another merlot," Rian said.

"I think maybe you've had . . ." Sam started to say but stopped when Rian gave him the death stare. He shrugged at the waiter, who left hurriedly and headed to the bar. Sam reached across the table and took Rian's hand.

"I'm sorry. Whatever I did, I'm sure it was my fault. I'm sorry." He gave her a half crooked smile. Rian couldn't help herself and started laughing, much to the relief of the couple at the other table.

"Fuck you," she said under her breath.

"Not a bad idea, now that you mention it," he said, and they both laughed.

* * *

Sam pulled his Mercedes into Rian's driveway. She opened the door and got out, but he hesitated, unsure of whether she wanted him to come in or leave.

"Do I dare come in?" he asked in mock fear.

"Of course. Don't be an asshole," she said and started walking to the door. He watched her walk away and noted for the thousandth time the athletic way that she moved, like a panther on the prowl. It never failed to stir an animal-like instinct in him. She was a little unsteady, maybe a little too much wine, and he got out and caught up to her, slipping his arm around her as he did. He was pleasantly surprised that she returned the gesture.

Rian headed straight to the kitchen when they got inside and took some coffee out of the cabinet. As she filled the machine with water, Sam came up behind her and wrapped his arms around her waist, leaning his head down to smell her scent at the back of her neck. He began to lightly kiss the side of her neck. She caught her breath when he did, then made another attempt to make the coffee, despite her lack of concentration. Sam slipped his hands under the front of her shirt and slowly stroked her stomach, feeling her strong abdominal muscles tighten.

Rian abandoned the coffee project and turned to look at him. She said nothing and Sam leaned down and kissed her, softly at first, then more urgently. He pulled back and looked at her, then kissed her again, this time passionately.

"Sam, I'm sorry. I . . ." Rian said when they broke the kiss, but he stopped her by putting his index finger over her lips. She kissed it sensuously; he slowly moved it away, and they kissed again passionately for a long time.

They made love gently at first on the couch, but soon moved to the bedroom and gave in to their mutual passions. Both were athletes, and their sexual encounters frequently became competitive attempts to please one another. When it was over, Rian laid her head on Sam's shoulder while he stroked her hair, both of them exhausted and satisfied. No words were spoken. The only sound was the two of them breathing heavily.

She felt safe with Sam. He was right, they had agreed not to push their relationship, but now Rian wanted a more permanent commitment. She hadn't dated many men and had slept with far fewer. She was starting to imagine herself spending the rest of her life with Sam.

As her eyes got too heavy to hold open and she started to drift off, Rian muttered, "I love you."

"I know," said Sam.

* * *

Something caused Rian to wake with a start, and she sat up and looked around the room. The bedside clock cast a ghostly blue light around the room, and Mannix was curled up at the foot of the bed. She was breathing hard and her heart was pounding as though it would burst right through her chest. She tried to lie back down, but it was pointless; she couldn't go back to sleep. The bedside clock showed that it was three in the morning. Three o'clock. Whenever this kind of thing happened, it was always at three o'clock.

She gave up and slipped silently out of the bed. Sam was on his side facing away from her and sound asleep. She grabbed her laptop off the charger, went downstairs, and curled up on the couch.

She clicked on the laptop and went to the CNN news website. Among the stories about the sinking economy and world terrorism was a blurb that caught her attention: POLICE SEEK LEADS IN TRIPLE FLORIDA PANHANDLE SLAYINGS.

Triple?

Rian clicked over to the *Herald's* website and pulled up the story under the heading BORDER LINE MURDER LINKED TO TWO OTHERS IN PAST YEAR. The story retold the murder of Christy Price, then went into a detailed description of Marie Pettigrew's case. "Police are investigating a link between these homicides and the murder of a Baton Rouge woman in Walton County last year," the story continued. "Monica Jessup, 40, was found dead inside a South Walton beach house on June 23. All three victims had been bound in a similar manner before they were killed, but authorities have refused to comment on whether they believe that a single killer is responsible."

Bound in a similar manner? What the hell does that mean?

She exited the site and went over to Google. A few searches later she located an article from the Birmingham newspaper that followed up on the murders there several years before. The article was a couple of years old and pointed out that, after a series of eight homicides in a two-year period in Birmingham and the surrounding area, there hadn't been another similar case in several years. Many theories had been proposed and, although the police investigation remained open, law enforcement had few clues and the case had been relegated to cold case status.

There was a link to the news coverage at the height of the murders and Rian pulled it up. All of the victims had their arms and legs tied together behind them before they were brutally killed. The police suspected a serial killer, but no description of the killer had ever been reported and no suspect ever questioned or apprehended. This was as she had remembered the situation when she left Birmingham. She was about to click out of the story when she noticed a link at the bottom that said "Update." She clicked on it and what she saw made her blood run cold.

A realtor named Fran Manguson had been found murdered in an unoccupied Oak Ridge home. Another realtor had found her body when she arrived to show the house, and it was believed that Manguson had been killed the day before based on the logs that documented when the house had been shown by other realtors. The body had been found on the floor in one of the bedrooms, the hands and feet bound behind her back and with a large bruised area on her throat. The police were downplaying the notion that Manguson had been a victim of the same killer who had previously terrorized Birmingham.

Rian looked back at the date of the murder; May 14, less than a month before Monica Jessup was killed in Walton County.

This doesn't make any sense.

Mannix suddenly jumped onto Rian's lap and scared her so badly that she nearly dropped the laptop onto the tile floor. She tried to piece all of this together. Why would these killings all of a sudden begin again like this? It was as though the guy was following Rian around.

Get a grip, Rian. That's ridiculous.

Then why was her heart still pounding?

CHAPTER TWENTY-TWO

It was almost ten-thirty when Mike Donovan stepped into the private room at O'Steen's. This was deliberate. Since the restaurant closed at eleven on weekdays, the chances were that The Powerbroker's Club would be deserted, which it was. He looked around just to make sure, then slipped into the last private meeting stall.

"So much for holding your story," Glenn Palmer said, icily.

"Things changed," said Donovan. "I kept my end of the deal. We didn't run with the details of how the victims were tied up or the killer's disabling them by bashing them in the throat. Besides, I tried to call you three times."

"We wanted to keep a lid on this. We don't need to inspire a copycat."

"It's not my damn fault that Channel Four sent a helicopter or that Mindy Franklin wants to take Nancy Grace's place," Donovan said, referring to the attractive blonde local news reporter who was following the story for Channel Four News. She'd been at the scene in the aftermath of Christy Price's murder and had sensationalized the coverage by appearances on Fox News and CNN.

"My editor nearly had a fit over this," Donovan went on. "He insisted that we run with all of the details, but I told him that you and I had a deal and that I would lose you as a source if I did. So don't give me any shit about how I'm not being straight with you."

"Okay, Okay. Calm down and take a breath," Palmer said. "Here," he said, sliding a folder across the table to Donovan, "you're getting this first."

Donovan opened the folder and looked at a police sketch of a white man with sandy hair, pale eyes, and a reddish, blond beard. He looked back at Palmer with his eyebrows raised.

"We have a witness," Palmer said. "You can't use his name, but he works at The Border Line. Said that this guy took a particular interest in Christy Price the night of the murder."

"So it is a serial killer."

"We aren't positive. But, between you and me, yeah. I think we're dealing with a serial killer."

Donovan's skin was tingling and the hair on the back of his neck was standing up.

"There's more," said Palmer. "The sheriff is setting up a task force. I'm heading it up. We want some media on this in the event someone's seen this guy, but we still don't want to publicize the specific details of the crime. Do we still have that understanding?"

Donovan knew that he should run this past Emmett Bayer before he answered, but there wasn't time. He had to grab the opportunity while it was there.

"We still have a deal. Hope this doesn't get me fired."

"It won't," said Palmer.

"I think we should run it on Sunday. That gives me enough time to do what I have to do and we'll get maximum exposure in the Sunday *Herald*."

"That works for me," Palmer said and slid out of the booth. He left the private dining area and turned right, taking the hall down toward the kitchen. He pushed open the kitchen door and walked through the kitchen, exiting through a back door to the parking lot and his unmarked car.

Donovan stared at the police sketch in the folder, already writing the story in his head. After waiting a few moments, he reached inside his jacket and clicked off the recorder in his inside pocket. He closed the folder, slid out of the booth, and left through the main entrance.

CHAPTER TWENTY-THREE

Anthony Arrington was furious. The mayor of Birmingham paced back and forth in his stately office surrounded by mementos of his political career.

The richly paneled walls held a number of framed pictures of Arrington with important business leaders, entertainers, and other politicians. A signed, color photograph of Arrington shaking hands with President George W. Bush in the Oval Office hung near others of him smiling with actor Chuck Norris, Alabama football coach Nick Saban, and even Colin Powell. These had all been rearranged to make space for his latest acquisition, a large photograph of Arrington seated at a table with Sarah Palin, who was leaned over toward him in an apparent hushed conversation. The photo was signed by Palin to "Dearest Tony," thanking him for all of his help and inviting him to "change the world together."

None of that mattered to Arrington at the moment as he paced and mumbled to himself. His tie was loosened and his shirt sleeves rolled up, befitting his anger.

"Trisha!" he yelled. Trisha came running at his command.

"Where the hell is he?" boomed Arrington before she could say anything.

"They said he was on his way, sir. I can try calling again."

"No, dammit," he said, "just send him in as soon as he gets here. Hold everything else."

"Yes, sir," Trisha said meekly. "Uh, that guy from the *Birmingham News* called again."

Arrington stopped and whirled around. His entire balding head was red and his nostrils flared as he struggled to remain civil. He stared at her with his expansive girth rising and falling with each exaggerated breath.

"I do *not* want to talk to that son of a *bitch*," he exploded. Trish disappeared without further comment, leaving Arrington to seethe alone. He looked at the paper in his hands and resumed pacing.

Five minutes later Police Commissioner Aaron Burgess walked in unannounced. Arrington was standing behind his desk, leaning over and reading the article for the third time.

"Have you seen this shit?" he screamed when he saw Burgess come in. "I want to know just what the *fuck* is going on, Aaron," he said, slamming the paper down on his desk.

"Mr. Mayor --" Burgess began formally, but Arrington cut him off.

"Six years. Six fucking years, Aaron. The fucker killed all those women and we never even got a clue. Now he's back and sticking it up our ass again."

Burgess stood silent as Arrington continued his tirade. The mayor's face became redder and the beads of sweat that formed on his forehead began to slide down his cheeks. He stormed around the room, punctuating his comments with a shake of his fist.

"They're calling you incompetent and me impotent," Arrington raged, snatching up the paper and shaking it at Burgess. "*Impotent!* Slanderous bullshit, that's what it is. I swear to God, Aaron, if they take me down over this, I'm pulling you down with me. Do you hear me?"

"First of all," Burgess began, his own anger beginning to rise, "we don't even know if it's the same guy. Not all of the forensics are in and it could be a copycat."

"The goddamn newspaper doesn't seem to share your reluctance. According to them and the rest of humanity, the bastard is back and we're powerless to stop him," Arrington said.

"The *Birmingham News* does not dictate how I run my investigation." Burgess said, carefully keeping his temper in check. "It's one homicide. One. A tragedy, of course, but to automatically link this up as a serial killer is irresponsible. I have my best people on it, but I can't work miracles overnight."

"Then maybe you'd better kick a few butts."

The men and women in Burgess's department had worked tirelessly for years trying to solve the previous homicides, often neglecting themselves and their families in the process. These were good, honest, hard working cops. To insinuate that they were lazy and not doing everything in their power to clear these cases was an insult, one that he wasn't going to take from some fat ass political wannabe.

"With all due respect, Mr. Mayor," he said sarcastically, "perhaps you should worry about the politics and leave the investigation to those who are trained to do it."

Arrington's head looked like it might actually explode. They glared at each other for what seemed like an eternity, then the mayor sat down, leaned back in his expensive leather chair, and put his feet up on his desk. Pulling a cigar from his shirt pocket, he smelled it, then stuck it in his mouth.

"Mr. Commissioner," he said condescendingly, "either you find a solution to this problem or I'll find someone who will. Understand?"

"Are we done here?" Burgess asked.

"We're done."

Burgess turned and left the office, snatching open Arrington's door so hard that it banged the wall behind it as he left.

CHAPTER TWENTY-FOUR

Rian sat on a bar stool at the kitchen counter, sipping coffee from a stoneware mug and reading the Sunday *Herald*. It was a glorious spring day, and the fresh, salty air breezed in from the bay across Rian's deck and through the open doors and windows at the back of the house. It was still a little cool at this time of the morning, and Rian, barefoot and wearing a t-shirt and jogging shorts, felt a chill run down her back. It could have been caused by the breeze or by what she was reading in the paper.

The *Herald* was dominated by the story of Christy Price's murder again, but the police had now released a composite sketch of someone they referred to as a "person of interest," which Rian understood to be synonymous with "suspect." The blond-haired main with the pale eyes and a beard stared out at Rian from the front page above a caption that asked HAVE YOU SEEN THIS MAN? Anyone with information was asked to contact the number to the newly created task force at the Sheriff's Department.

There was something unsettling about the picture as Rian stared at it. She didn't actually recognize the man. Composite sketches weren't meant to be a substitute for a photograph, but she felt there was something vaguely familiar about him that she couldn't quite put her finger on. The description was generic enough to apply to any one of the thousands of people whom Rian had crossed paths with over the years. She had sat face to face with murderers, rapists, and all sorts of other violent criminals as well as untold number of lesser offenders. She'd had contempt for some, sympathy for others, and a few times been concerned for her safety, like the recent incident at the jail, though such episodes were rare.

Rian tried hard not to get personally attached to her clients, recognizing that most were guilty of the crimes with which they were charged. Kids like Sean Rowan were the exception to the rule. These days, there were so many to deal with that their names were forgotten as soon as the case was over and the file was closed.

Rian read the article that accompanied the picture, noting that poor Christy's devastated family had offered a reward for information leading to the arrest of their daughter's killer. Rian looked again at the sweet face of Christy Price at a happier time, her smile beaming from what could have been her senior prom picture. Rian was older now and had experienced a lot more of life in the past six years, yet she noted that some of the insecurities she'd felt before she left Birmingham were beginning to return from that place where she'd locked them so long ago. She didn't like the feeling. It made her weak and vulnerable, and she didn't consider herself either. She wouldn't let fear control her life again.

Rian picked up the cordless phone and dialed her brother's number in Birmingham. She was a little surprised when a female voice answered.

"Uh, Amanda?" asked Rian.

"Yeah . . ."

"Hi, this is Rian Coulter, Brian's sister."

"Oh, hello. Wow, Bri's told me so much about you."

"Don't believe any of it," Rian joked. "Is he in?"

"No, we just got up actually. He ran out to get us breakfast."

We just got up? So now they're living together?

Rian felt guilty that it had been so long since she'd last spoken to her brother. Apparently, his relationship with Amanda had progressed quickly.

"Is there a message you want me to give him or can I have him call you back?" Amanda asked.

"Sure, that would be great." An awkward silence followed.

"So, Amanda, when are we going to get the chance to meet?" Rian asked.

"It's funny that you ask because Bri and me were just talking about that last night. We're planning to go to Tallahassee to see his, well, your folks, and we thought we'd swing over there on the same trip. If that's okay with you, of course."

Since Brian left for college, he'd never brought a girl home to meet the Coulters. This must be serious, Rian thought. Although her parents wouldn't be especially thrilled about Brian and

Amanda living together, they were open minded enough that it shouldn't be a problem.

"That would be great," Rian replied. "Either that, or I can drive over to Tallahassee. I'd love to meet you."

"Me, too. Sounds great. I'll have Bri call you."

Rian clicked off and thought about the conversation. With all that had been going on, she had temporarily lost touch with her only sibling. During that period, he'd become involved with someone whom Rian knew nothing about. She didn't even know Amanda's last name. This could be a serious, possibly even permanent relationship, and she was on the outside looking in. Guilt stabbed at her heart and Rian resolved to stay in closer contact with her brother and not let this happen again.

She needed to go for a run to clear her head. Mannix had plopped down on the counter next to her while she was on the phone, and Rian reached over to give him a scratch behind his ears. He responded by cleaning her hand with his sandpaper tongue.

Rian picked up the *Herald* and was about to toss it into the recycle bin when she looked again at the composite of the man on the front page.

HAVE YOU SEEN THIS MAN? the headline screamed again. His expressionless eyes stared at Rian and she studied his face intently.

Had she?

CHAPTER TWENTY-FIVE

"Shit," Palmer muttered under his breath as he looked at the report he was holding.

The crime scene technicians had taken scrapings from beneath Christy Price's fingernails for DNA testing in the hope that she had scratched her murderer and some of his skin was under her nails. The results were negative. They had taken skin scrapings from her neck, combed through her hair, vacuumed her clothes, and tested the belt used to strangle her, all without any positive results.

The medical examiner had determined that Christy had not been sexually assaulted, so there was no semen left behind and no need to take vaginal swabs for testing, although Palmer had requested it anyway.

Just like the other cases, they had little scientific evidence. Palmer was astounded that a killer this prolific was careful enough not to leave any DNA behind at any of the crime scenes so far.

There was a knock on the door and Sanchez stuck his head in.

"They're ready for you, L.T.," he said.

Palmer picked up his file and walked down the hall to a conference room. Several men in shirtsleeves were already there, drinking coffee and standing around a large oval-shaped conference table. The conversation ceased when Palmer entered the room.

"Good morning," Palmer said as he took a seat at one end of the table. The others nodded, muttered greetings, jockeyed for positions around the table, and settled into the faux leather reclining chairs.

The room was nice by county standards. A large color photograph of the Sheriff's Department dominated one wall. The opposite wall bore a portrait of the sheriff himself surrounded by the department hierarchy. On the far wall facing Palmer was a large, flat screen monitor which, at the moment, was dark. A star shaped conference phone speaker was in the center of the table.

To Palmer's left sat Dr. Crawford, the District Medical Examiner, Charles Ausley, the head of the Florida Department of Law Enforcement's Crime Scene Technical Unit, and Alan Banning, newly promoted to the position of "special prosecutions" within the State Attorney's Office.

On Palmer's right was Frank Shepherd, the Escambia County crime scene supervisor, Ellen Wright, the sheriff's public relations officer, Sanchez, and the three sergeants in charge of each watch patrol.

Each person had a yellow legal pad and pen on the table in front of them. Palmer made a mental note that the county people had lined up on one side of the table and the state people on the other as though this was some sort of face off. Not a good sign for a group who would need to cooperate with one another.

"I'll begin by having Dr. Crawford and Chuck bring everyone up to speed on where we are now. Sanchez, you have the notes." Sanchez nodded, grabbed the pen in front of him and began scribbling.

Dr. Crawford gave a summary of Christy Price's autopsy results and compared it with the reports of Marie Pettigrew and Monica Jessup. The cause of death in all three cases had been strangulation. In each case, the victims had been first disabled by a severe blow to the throat which crushed their larynxes and left them incapacitated and unable to resist.

Each victim had alcohol in her system, Monica Jessup the least and Christy Price the most. In Dr. Crawford's opinion, alcohol wasn't a contributing factor in the death of any of the victims, other than perhaps causing them to be less inhibited and therefore more vulnerable at the time of the attack.

Monica Jessup had been sodomized with a foreign object made of wood, possibly a broom or rake handle. Severe tissue damage in the vaginal area meant that Marie Pettigrew had also been sexually violated although Dr. Crawford was unable to tell what instrument had been used. Christy Price hadn't been penetrated, although there was bruising on both of her nipples indicating that someone had pinched them viciously.

Finally, Dr. Crawford mentioned that each victim had bruising about the neck and ruptured blood vessels in the eyes, indicating that death by strangulation had been relatively quick, but most definitely not painless for these women.

"Sick fuck," muttered one of the watch sergeants when Dr. Crawford finished. He then caught Ellen Wright's eye and apologized. She just smiled at him.

Chuck Ausley next summarized the crime scene evidence in each case, such as it was. Each victim had been bound in a similar manner, though the materials used in each case were different. Rope had been used in the Jessup case and an extension cord in the Pettigrew case. Both victims had been bound around the neck, then the feet with a slipknot between and the legs pulled forward toward the head. Any lowering of the legs would increase the pressure on the throat. Christy Price had been bound by a belt looped around her neck and feet. Ausley believed that there were enough similarities to convince him that she had been murdered by the same killer as Monica Jessup and Marie Pettigrew.

"Are you saying that these women strangled themselves?" interrupted Alan Banning.

Dr. Crawford fielded the question. "No," he said, "with a crushed larynx and the extensive bleeding in their throats, they would likely have suffocated even if nothing else had been done. There was evidence that each victim aspirated their own blood. The killer applied severe strangulation pressure to the neck that hastened the process and would have rendered them unconscious. The manner in which they were bound likely didn't cause their death but, depending upon when they were discovered, could have insured that any shred of life they were clinging to was extinguished."

Ausley pointed out that no bloody objects had been found at any scene, meaning the killer had taken whatever he had used with him and disposed of it elsewhere. Most disturbingly, no fingerprints or DNA evidence had been recovered at any of the scenes.

"That's very unusual," he said.

"Any link between the victims at all?" asked Banning.

"None that we've determined," said Palmer. "We think he stalked Marie Pettigrew and possibly Monica Jessup. We think Christy Price may have been a target of opportunity, but we don't yet know how he's selecting his victims."

There was a tap on the door and a secretary stuck her head in. "Call's coming in now, Lieutenant."

"Okay," he said, turning to the credenza behind him and grabbing a remote control, "put it through." He leaned forward and switched on the conference phone, then pointed the remote at the flat screen. It flickered to life, at first revealing only a color bar, then another office scene appeared. Two men in shirtsleeves and ties were sitting side by side.

"Good morning," said Palmer, and they returned the greeting. "Let me introduce Detectives Stephen Ennis and Tom Fanning from Birmingham. Detective Ennis is with the Jefferson County Sheriff's Office and Detective Fanning is with Shelby County." Palmer introduced everyone around the table and they mumbled their hellos.

Palmer began again. "Steve, can you let everyone in on what we discussed?"

"Sure," Ennis said. "Beginning eight years ago, we had a series of homicides here in metro Birmingham that we believe was the work of a single serial killer. There were a total of eight victims over two years, the last one in Shelby County."

Fanning took over at that point. "A woman named Connie Miller was killed in her home. She was divorced and lived with her two kids, both of whom were spending the night away, fortunately. The victim had been out for a night on the town with girlfriends and was killed later that night in her bed. The alarm system had been bypassed and the point of entry was the rear door."

A feeling of uneasiness was beginning to spread through the room. Palmer knew it was about to get worse.

"We never arrested a suspect and had little in the way of physical evidence at the scenes," Ennis continued. "Some of the victims had been sexually assaulted with an object of some sort, none of which we ever found."

"How did you conclude that the same killer was responsible?" asked Palmer, although he already knew the answer.

"Every one of the victims was hogtied. The rope was looped around their necks and ankles, then tied off in the center."

The tension in the room was palpable. No one spoke.

Ennis continued. "All of a sudden, after two years, the killings just stopped. We aren't sure why. There's been speculation that the killer died, went to jail on some other charge, or . . . moved to another area. But a few months ago, we had another homicide in Jefferson that made us rethink that. A realtor named Fran Manguson was killed inside a house she was supposed to be showing. Same signature as before. We're looking into whether it was a copycat, but after all this time, it seems unlikely."

"What leads were you able to develop?" asked Palmer.

"Very few from the first go round. No prints, no DNA. We think the killer has knowledge of security systems and may be some sort of laborer, but that was about it. No witnesses who had seen anything, although Connie Miller had new sensors put in her security system about a month before she was killed. We interviewed the owner of the security company, but didn't turn up anything. In the latest one, though, the Manguson case, someone saw a white work truck parked nearby, but no one got a tag or a description on the driver. It was a new subdivision, so a work truck wasn't out of the ordinary. We don't know whether it was related."

"How were the victims subdued?" Palmer asked and watched the faces around the room as the detectives answered.

"At first, blunt force to the head with a heavy object such as a pipe wrench or a hammer. Later, the victims were hit in the throat hard enough that their larynxes collapsed."

"Same here," injected Detective Fanning. "You can't put up much of a fight after that."

"Your cases have showed up in the media up here," said Ennis. "They're like a pack of wild dogs and may be headed your way. Maybe our guy has moved to Pensacola, I don't know. For your sake, I hope not. Any help we can give you, you can count on our cooperation."

"Thanks," said Palmer. "We'll be in touch." He clicked off the monitor and looked at the stunned faces around the table.

"You see what we're up against. This guy is experienced and, so far, he's been pretty damn careful. Our best angle is to figure out what went on to keep him silent for six years. If we can do that, we may catch a break."

Turning to the watch sergeants, Palmer told them to focus on any white work trucks in the area out of the ordinary places.

"No searches without contacting me," said Banning. "The last thing we want is to catch this bastard and have the case get kicked because of an illegal search." He gave everyone his cell phone number and told them to call him if needed at any time.

"One last thing," said Palmer. "Leaks will not be tolerated. No discussion about the investigation with anyone not a necessary participant. No, and I mean zero, comments to the media. All media requests go through me and Ellen. No exceptions." Everyone indicated their understanding.

The meeting broke up and people began to file out until only Sanchez and Palmer were left.

"Shit, L.T.," said Sanchez. "We don't really have anything to go on, do we?"

Palmer didn't respond, but he knew Sanchez was right.

"We will. He'll fuck up and make a mistake. We just need a break."

CHAPTER TWENTY-SIX

The witness fidgeted in her seat nervously as Rian continued to read the transcribed version of a statement that the woman had given to the police. Rian had subpoenaed Tonya Green for a deposition since Tonya had supposedly witnessed Rian's client, Charles Simpkins, fire the shots that killed Terence Gant. Simpkins was charged with first degree murder, and the State had announced its intention to seek the death penalty if Simpkins was convicted. Rian suspected that if she could poke enough holes in Tonya Green's testimony, she might convince them to offer Simpkins a plea to a lesser charge.

The deposition took place in a small, windowless conference room at the court reporter's office on the ninth floor of the building that adjoined the courthouse. Rian sat on one side of a rectangular-shaped conference table across from Tonya Green. Alan Banning sat next to the witness and, at the moment, seemed more interested in typing on his smartphone than in the deposition about to take place. To Rian's right, the court reporter sat at the end of the table, her fingers poised above her stenographic machine waiting for Rian to begin the questions.

Rian already knew quite a lot about Tonya Green. She had a history of several drug arrests and had been convicted twice for soliciting for prostitution. The circumstances of this case coincided with a drug deal that had gone bad. Simpkins and another man had shown up at the trailer where Tonya and Gant were living. The men argued, and Simpkins supposedly had shot Gant twice in the chest.

Rian slipped the witness statement back into her file and glanced over at Banning, who was still pecking away on his phone. She gave Tonya Green a big smile.

"Good afternoon, Ms. Green. I'm Rian Coulter and I represent Mr. Simpkins in this case." Tonya Green stared back at her. "I have a few questions for you but I'm not here to trick you or try to put words in your mouth. If I ask you a question that you don't understand, please tell me and I'll repeat it or ask it a different way. Okay?"

"Yes."

"I'm only interested in what you know, not what someone's told you, and I don't want you to guess. If you don't know the answer to one of my questions, just tell me. Is that okay?"

"I guess," Tonya replied with a shrug.

"Fine. Why don't you tell me what you and Mr. Gant were doing before Mr. Simpkins arrived."

"We wasn't doing nothing. I had been asleep 'cause I had to go to work that night. I don't know what Terence was doing."

"Had you or Mr. Gant smoked marijuana or taken any other drugs that afternoon?"

"No."

"Are you sure?" Rian asked with raised eyebrows. The police described an odor in the trailer similar to marijuana and that Ms. Green's eyes were "glassy" when she was interviewed at the scene.

"Yeah, I'm sure," Tonya responded defiantly. "I know I didn't smoke. Whether Terence did or not, I don't know. Like I said, I was asleep." She was defensive and evasive, both qualities that Rian knew wouldn't serve her well on the witness stand at trial.

"Tell me what happened when Mr. Simpkins arrived."

"Simp showed up with some other dude."

"Did you know who the other man was?"

"Never seen him before."

"Did Terence know him?"

"I don't know, but I don't think so. I think I heard Simp say his name was like 'Beemer' or something."

"Could it have been Beater?" Simpkins had told Rian that another man had gone with him to Gant's trailer to buy drugs. The man, Antonio Wilkins was called "Beater" because of his tendency to fight at a moment's notice.

"Yeah, it could have been."

"What happened when Mr. Simpkins and 'Beater' arrived?"

"I went back in the bedroom. Next thing I know, they're arguing and I hear somebody leave. Then the door opened again and I hear three shots, like 'pop, pop, pop.'"

"Where were you when that happened?"

"In the bedroom."

"Did you see who fired the shots?"

"No. I just saw Simp and the other dude jump in the car and leave. I ran out and saw Terence lying on the couch."

Rian knew that Tonya Green had told the police that she was in the living room of the trailer and had witnessed Charles Simpkins fire the shots that killed Terence Gant. She was now telling a different story and, although it was helpful to her client, Rian was suspicious.

"Are you saying under oath that you did *not* see Charles Simpkins fire a gun that day?"

"I didn't actually see him. Could've been him or the other dude. I don't know."

Rian glanced over at Banning who usually would be ready to pounce at this point. He sat there impassively, occasionally looking down at his phone.

"Ms. Green, I want to ask you this one more time. You told the police that Mr. Simpkins fired the gun and that you saw him do it. Today, you are saying, under oath, that you did not see him pull the trigger. Which is it?" Rian knew that however Tonya Green answered, she would have ample material to impeach her credibility at trial.

"I didn't see who fired the gun. I don't remember what I told the cops that day. I was too upset."

Rian narrowed her eyes at Tonya Green who held her gaze, convincing Rian that she would stick to this story at trial.

"I don't have any other questions," she said.

"No questions," said Banning, not looking up from his phone.

Tonya Green left and Rian gathered the file. She told the court reporter to hold off on transcribing the deposition for now and that she would let her know if she needed it. Hopefully, Rian could open the door to negotiate a deal for Charles Simpkins.

Banning was waiting at the elevator when Rian walked up. Before she could say anything, Banning spoke.

"Manslaughter, guidelines sentence," he said. Rian was stunned.

"What?" was all she could manage, wanting to confirm what she thought she'd heard. The elevator opened and they both stepped in.

"Simpkins can plead to manslaughter and I won't oppose a guidelines sentence." Rian quickly calculated in her head and determined that Simpkins would receive a sentence of five to seven years in prison and would likely be out in three. She thought she could convince Banning to offer second degree murder, but this was an offer she couldn't refuse.

"When did you get so generous?" she said, half jokingly.

Banning just shrugged. "One drug dealer kills another one. In reality, who really cares?" The elevator door opened and Banning stepped off. Rian followed him, assuming they would continue their negotiation in the hall. Instead, Banning just kept walking. He looked back over his shoulder and said, "Call me. We can do the plea at the end of the week." He left Rian standing in the middle of the hallway with an armload of files and a confused look on her face.

That was way too easy.

Abby wasn't at her desk when Rian returned, so she stacked the Simpkins file in Abby's chair. The washout of this case would free up a great deal of time on Rian's calendar, and she was already mentally filling in the blanks.

"Well, how'd it go?" Rian turned to see her secretary standing in the doorway. "Did you poke some holes?" she asked expectantly.

"Yeah," Rian said. "It was bizarre. The depo went well and I thought I had enough that I could talk Banning down to second degree. Before I said anything, though, he offers me manslaughter with a guidelines sentence. We go from a death case to manslaughter, just like that."

"I'm not surprised," Abby said.

"Why not?"

"My friend in the State Attorney's Office said that Banning has been moved to Special Prosecutions and, since then, he's been dumping his regular files left and right."

"Why?" Rian asked.

"Not sure. He supposedly said that he has to 'clear the decks' so he's been making offers to everyone that they can't refuse." Rian was a little disappointed that it hadn't been her brilliant questioning of Tonya Green that had convinced Banning to make such an irresistible offer.

"How are they going to assign cases now? Are they replacing him in Major Crimes?" Rian asked.

"I don't know, but I can find out," Abby said. "My friend said there's talk of moving Carla Richards up from misdemeanor."

"From the misdemeanor division to major crimes? She's just a rookie."

"I know. Weird, huh?" said Abby as she returned to her desk. Weird was an understatement.

What the hell is going on over there?

CHAPTER TWENTY-SEVEN

"They're pulling into the parking lot now," Rian said as she slipped her phone back into her purse. She looked across the table at Sam and gave him a weak, nervous smile. "I hope she likes me," she said without her usual confidence.

They were at Brendan's, a new fine dining restaurant on Pensacola Beach. It had opened three months before when the owner, Brendan Lewis, decided to sell his interest in his highly successful establishment in downtown Orlando and return home to realize his dream of an upscale seafood place on the beach. Brendan had attended one of the finest culinary schools in the country, and the restaurant was an immediate sensation with the local crowd.

As with most new places in the area, the wait for a table was long, but this wasn't a problem for Rian and Sam tonight. Naturally, Sam represented the owner and they now occupied a choice table overlooking the Gulf. If there was a new development within a fifty mile radius of Pensacola, Sam and his firm were usually right in the middle of it.

Brendan's occupied the premier spot on Pensacola Beach. The location had been a hub of activity since the 1940s and the most recent building there, a cheap sports bar, had been destroyed by a hurricane several years before. The restaurant was built on pilings with the main dining area thirty feet above the beach. Rich cherry furniture and expensive white tablecloths were surrounded by large glass windows that, in daytime, offered stunning views of the Gulf of Mexico. At night, the room was candlelit and dominated by a large saltwater aquarium in the center that was lit from above and stocked with a wide variety of colorful tropical fish.

Sam watched Rian across the dimly lit table. She wore a simple black dress with spaghetti straps. A diamond Rolex watch, a gift from her father, caught the light and was accented by the diamond circle necklace and earrings, both gifts from Sam. Her blue eyes sparkled in the light and, for a moment, Sam could do nothing more than just stare at her. Rian was always beautiful, but when she dressed up like this, she was simply stunning.

"What?" she said, meeting his gaze.

"I was just mesmerized by your beauty, my dear," he said with his typical half smile. She frowned at him and rolled her eyes.

They were meeting Rian's brother Brian and his girlfriend Amanda. After the brief telephone call a few weeks ago, Brian had called back to arrange dinner so that Rian and Amanda could finally meet. Brian thought that Amanda would be less intimidated by his older sibling in a public place.

Rian saw them approach and jumped up to embrace her brother in a bear hug, leaving Sam and Amanda looking at each other awkwardly.

"Hi, I'm Sam," he said, extending his hand. "You must be Amanda." At that Rian and Brian broke their embrace.

"Oh, shit, I'm sorry, babe," Brian said. "This is my sister Rian and her significant other, Sam McKinney. Guys, this is Amanda Baker." The girls hugged, the guys shook hands, and they all sat down. A waiter was there instantly to take drink orders. They all ordered cocktails, and Sam ordered a bottle of wine for the dinner.

"How was the trip down?" Sam asked when they were all situated.

"Great," Brian said. "We actually spent last night in Eufaula at Amanda's parents' place." He was more than a little nervous and Rian hadn't yet noticed the ring on Amanda's left hand. She was keeping that hand in her lap. The drinks arrived shortly.

"Uh, look, guys, I'd like to get this out of the way off the bat," Brian stammered. Sam glanced at Rian and, judging from the puzzled look on her face, she was still clueless.

Brian swallowed and continued. "Uh, Amanda's not my girlfriend. She's my fiancé. We're getting married."

The look of shock on Rian's face was one that Sam hadn't seen before. Her eyes opened wide and she looked immediately at Amanda who slowly brought her left hand from under the table and wiggled her fingers.

"Oh my God . . . Oh my *GOD*!" Rian said, her eyes filling with tears. She and Amanda both jumped up and wrapped their arms around each other. Both were now crying. Brian looked at Sam, relief in his face. Sam slapped him on the back and they shook hands.

"Well done," Sam said as Brian downed most of his cocktail in one gulp. The girls sat back down and dabbed at their eyes with napkins.

"Do Mom and Dad know?" Rian asked her brother.

"No, net yet. That's why we went to Eufaula, to tell Amanda's parents. We're heading to Tallahassee tomorrow to break the news to Craig and Bev. I wanted to tell you first." Rian's eyes began to water again.

"You're not mad?" he asked.

"Of course not. I'm incredibly happy for you both. I want to know everything; how you met, everything."

"Here it comes, babe." Brian said to Amanda. "I warned you that you'd be cross examined."

"Stop it," Rian said, winking at him and smiling.

Amanda went through her history, and Brian told the story of how they met when he was subpoenaed to give a deposition on behalf of the bank. A different waiter approached the table with a champagne bucket and a bottle of Dom Perignon that he handed to Sam, a gift from Brendan Lewis. Sam popped the cork, drawing the attention from nearby tables, and poured for everyone. The interrogation ceased while they looked over the menus and ordered dinner.

"Brian tells me that you're a paralegal," Rian resumed when the menus were placed. She passed her champagne glass to Sam without looking at him, intending that he refill it, which he did.

"I am, but I'm hoping to go to law school eventually."

"Where do you work?" Rian asked.

"A firm downtown, Ashton, Baker, Pennington, and Moore."

"You're kidding?"

"Nope, been there two years."

"Wait a minute. Amanda Baker; you're not related to Michael Baker, are you?" Rian asked, referring to one of the senior partners at Ashton, Baker.

"He's my uncle. My dad's older brother."

"Holy shit," Rian said, and the two then launched into a discussion of who Rian had worked with at the firm, who was still there, and who had gotten divorces. The two obviously hit it off well, much to the relief of Sam and Brian, who downed most of the wine and started on a second bottle.

While the girls were absorbed in conversation, Brian turned to Sam.

"How's she holding up?" Brian asked.

"What do you mean?" Sam asked, slightly puzzled.

"The murders. We've been reading all about them and about how similar the killings here are to the ones that happened in Birmingham several years ago." Sam just looked at Brian, but didn't respond. Brian glanced over at Rian, still deep in conversation with Amanda, then back at Sam. He seemed uncomfortable talking about this in her presence.

Sam reached over and touched Rian's arm gently to distract her. "I'm going to hit the head before the food gets here," he said. Rian smiled and resumed her conversation.

When Sam got up, Brian said, "I think I'll check out the Gulf view from the balcony. Be right back." The girls paid him no attention. He met Sam on the balcony. They stood in silence for a minute, taking in the waves crashing on the beach and the salty breeze that blew in from the water.

"Okay. What's up?" Sam said.

"About six or seven years ago, there was a series of murders in Birmingham and the surrounding area. A bunch of single women were killed, and the cops said it was a serial killer. It was going on while we were both living there. I was in college and drunk half of the time, so I didn't think much about it, but I think it freaked Rian out pretty bad. She was working at Ashton, Baker at the time, single, living alone, just like the women who were killed."

"Did anything happen to her?" Sam asked.

"No, but every young female in the entire area was spooked. She said a couple of the women at the firm claimed that they had been followed. Everyone was pretty hysterical, and Rian was really bothered by it. It's what drove her here eventually."

"Doesn't sound like her," Sam said.

"The thing is, all of a sudden, the killings just stopped. Nobody knew why. Now they're happening here and the media in Birmingham keeps saying what's going on here is connected to the killings in Birmingham. I figured it would be dragging up old memories for Ri and just thought you should know about it."

"I understand," said Sam. "Thanks."

They returned to the table and found Amanda and Rian seemingly unaware that they had left. The food arrived and they dined on grilled fresh fish, oysters, and a shrimp and grits dish that was one of Brendan Lewis's creations. The food and service were outstanding, and Rian was so preoccupied with Amanda that she paid little attention to the server who brought the entrees from the kitchen.

When the plates were cleared, they ordered coffee and the same server brought a silver coffee urn to the table. When he served Rian, she noticed him for the first time.

"Didn't you used to work at Mancini's?" she asked him as he poured her coffee, a slight slur to her voice when she pronounced the name of the restaurant that went unnoticed by everyone else. Rian held her liquor well and was never sloppy when she drank.

"No, ma'am," the man said, not looking at her.

"You've waited on us before somewhere," she said.

"No, ma'am, that's not possible. I just moved here," he said and moved away.

No one noticed that a different server brought their refills.

They finished dinner and got up to leave.

"You and Amanda come stay at my place. I have plenty of room," Rian said. She had spent most of the day cleaning her townhouse in anticipation of this invitation.

"We have a place at the Grand Marlin," Brian said. "We're planning to get an early start to head out. I want to show Amanda the place at St. Theresa tomorrow, too."

"Are you sure?"

Brian reached out and grabbed Amanda's hand. "I'm sure," he said. "Maybe next time." Rian got the hint.

Rian and Amanda hugged again, and Amanda promised to tell everyone at Aston, Baker hello for her when she returned.

Rian and Brian held each other for a long time. Sam could hear her sniffling.

"I love you so much. I'm so, so happy for you," she said.

"I love you, too, Ri. More than you know."

They left and Rian excused herself to go to the bathroom. Sam waited for her in the lobby area. She returned, and he slipped his arm around her. As he did, another local lawyer walked up with his wife.

"Congratulations, you two. I know you'll be very happy," he said. Sam shook his hand, as did Rian. They started to go, but stopped and looked at each other, then burst out laughing. They walked out arm in arm.

CHAPTER TWENTY-EIGHT

He watched them leave and cursed himself. The first time he'd encountered her she hadn't given the slightest hint of recognition. Though they hadn't spent much time together, she questioned nothing, and he was convinced that enough time and distance had faded the memory. Just to be sure, he'd deliberately brushed past her, not once but twice, that day in the square. She seemed not to notice him at all. That emboldened him and added to his strength and power, enabling him to perform deeds he'd never thought possible. He was truly invisible.

Now he wasn't so sure. Tonight was different. True, she'd had a lot to drink and her guard was down, but she had definitely remembered him, though he wasn't sure whether it was from before or not. His hair was dark now and his face was clean shaven. Contact lenses had changed the color of his eyes from pale blue to brown, which were hidden behind glasses, so he doubted that she matched him to the drawing in the paper. No one else had. He could walk among these stupid people and no one would give him a second look.

Except for her.

It was probably just the alcohol, and she wouldn't even remember the incident at all tomorrow. Still, he couldn't be certain and, for the first time, he was worried. The noises in his head returned and began to build again. The job at the restaurant had been stupid, and he cursed himself again. He would not return tomorrow, certain that he couldn't be traced.

His heart began to race, and the noise in his head grew louder still. He looked around, expecting that others nearby would hear them, too, but no one seemed to notice. They didn't understand. He knew the noise wouldn't stop. He needed to get out of here, fast.

He walked to the men's room and sat in one of the stalls for several minutes, trying to quiet the noise. When he was sure that he was alone, he took off his white uniform coat and stuffed it into the trash can. Slipping unnoticed through the front door, he made his way quickly to the parking area. The big white truck roared to life and he eased out of the parking lot and turned toward Pensacola, careful as always to observe the traffic laws.

He would change his plans now. He would keep a closer eye on her than before, and he contemplated making a visit to her house now, but dismissed the idea.

There was something else that he had to take care of first.

CHAPTER TWENTY-NINE

Brianna Larson stepped into the shot and sent the ball rocketing across the net, moving to her left as she did so. The return was to her backhand, and she tried to put enough topspin on it at such an angle that her opponent couldn't get there in time. The ball came back again and Brianna sent it across, this time charging the net. Her opponent saw this and lobbed the ball over her head, causing Brianna to turn and sprint toward the baseline after it. It dropped just inside the corner for a point.

"Great shot, Hannah," she said, out of breath and sweating. "You got me on that one."

"Well, I've been trying that all night and finally got one in," Hannah said. "You want to go again?"

Brianna thought about it for a second, then shook her head.

"Nah, I better not. I've got chem lab at eight and an econ paper I haven't even started on yet. Thanks, though. Give me a rematch next week."

"Okay. See ya," Hannah said and headed to her car.

Brianna was beat. Classes all morning, followed by work at the pharmacy, and then two sets of hard charging tennis had left her drained. She was a pre-pharmacy major in her junior year at West Florida, a mid-sized school located on 1,600 acres in northeast Pensacola. Home to about 12,000 students, the university was built in, and still surrounded by, a nature preserve that offered scores of hiking and biking trails and provided a beautiful but secluded campus where the buildings weren't close together and separated many times by dense woods. It wasn't particularly pedestrian friendly, and students had to drive to get to facilities like the tennis courts located at one end of the campus, particularly at night because the area wasn't well lit.

Brianna fished a water bottle out of her bag and took several deep drinks while she sat on the bench, trying to summon the energy to pack up her stuff and head back to her dorm. She heard Hannah's car pull out of the parking lot.

"Scuse me, ma'am?" a voice called out, but Brianna didn't react. "Ma'am?" the voice repeated a little louder and more urgently. It was the maintenance man calling her from across the court. He was standing next to the light pole by the fence.

"You 'bout done here?" he asked. Brianna glanced at her watch. It was 10:30. The courts were supposed to close at 10:00 on week nights.

"Oh, yeah. Sorry," she said. "I guess we lost track of the time." With that, the maintenance man pulled a lever and shut off the lights to the court, plunging her into darkness. It took a minute for Brianna's eyes to adjust to the change in light, and there was barely enough ambient light from the parking area for her to see to gather her racquet and bag and head to her car. She slung the bag over her shoulder and made her way through the gate in the chain link fence down the path to the parking lot. Her silver Honda was the only car in the lot, and the area was otherwise deserted. She reached into the bag for her car keys but couldn't find them. She fumbled around for several more seconds and came up empty.

"Shit," she mumbled under her breath, realizing that her keys must have fallen out back on the court or somewhere in between. She might never find them in the dark. As she made her way back up the trail to the court, she looked around for the maintenance man who had been there only a couple of minutes before. There was no sign of him, and she didn't see his truck anywhere.

"Hello?" she called out. "I can't find my keys. Could you turn the lights back on?" Only the crickets chirping in the nearby woods responded.

Brianna retraced her steps back to the court all the way to the bench where she'd been sitting earlier. She didn't see any keys. She got down on her hands and knees and ran her hand along the smooth court surface but found nothing. Her keys weren't there. She would have to call someone to come get her so that she could get the spare key from her dorm, then come all the way back here to get her car.

Frustrated, she let out a sigh and started back to her car to get her cell phone that she'd left in the bag. She made her way across the court again and stepped through the fence gate, thankful that the maintenance guy hadn't locked it behind her.

She never saw him. As she stepped through the gate, something struck her violently in the throat with enough force to send her stumbling backwards into the chain link fence. She bounced off the fence and stood there unsteadily as the pain in her neck began to intensify.

Her confusion turned to panic as she tasted something warm in her mouth and realized that she couldn't catch her breath. She tried to scream, but only managed to cough out some fluid and a word that was unintelligible. She tried to run, but her legs buckled and she dropped to her knees on the path. Her mouth filled with more fluid, and each time she gasped for air, it was sucked down into her lungs, making her cough and gasp even more. She felt like she was drowning. Her head began to spin, and she felt sick to her stomach.

Suddenly, someone from behind kicked her hard between her shoulders, sending her sprawling face first into the dirt. Whoever it was flipped her over, lifted her by the arms and began to drag her away. She tried to scream again, but the sound never left her throat. She was aware that she was being dragged over leaves, and the branches of small shrubs scratched her legs and face as they went deeper and deeper into the woods. The darkness seemed to engulf them, and the person dragging her eventually threw her roughly on the ground.

Brianna lay on her side for what seemed an eternity, but in reality was only a minute or two. She was on the edge of consciousness, aware only of the sound of her own gasping for air and the gurgling sound in her throat when she did so. Just as her panic began to subside, she heard the rustling of leaves and was suddenly kicked over onto her stomach. Within seconds, a crushing weight bore down on her back that forced what little air was left in her lungs out through her mouth and nose.

The last thing she knew was that something was being wrapped around her throat.

CHAPTER THIRTY

Rian slid her card into the slot and the mechanical arm slowly raised, allowing her access to the courthouse complex parking garage. She waved to Albert, the attendant who returned the gesture with a, "Mornin' Ms. Coulter," as he'd done every day for the six years that she'd worked in the Public Defender's Office. She rolled the window down and stopped to speak, as she had likewise done every day.

"Have a blessed day," he said as she pulled into the garage.

Rian negotiated the first left turn and was prepared to slip directly into her reserved parking place, but was surprised to see that another vehicle was already parked there. She sat there for a minute, contemplating whether she could block this trespasser in without impeding other traffic and without jeopardizing her car in the process. She'd done this once with her previous car and a different space, taking great pleasure in pissing off the private attorney who had parked his Mercedes in her space.

She determined that her car might be in danger if she parked behind this car, Rian thought about parking in the adjacent space. The problem was that all of these spaces were reserved and, if she took someone else's space, she would set off a chain reaction of complaints on this whole level of the garage. Just because some asshole decided to start her day off like this didn't justify her doing the same to everyone else.

Visibly annoyed, Rian hit the gas, causing her tires to squeal as she zoomed up two more levels to the public parking area. Slamming the door as she got out of her car, she stomped down two flights of stairs and approached the offending vehicle. She didn't recognize it and noted that it didn't have the required courthouse parking decal on the left front windshield. It did have a blue and green chambered nautilus, the symbol for the University of West Florida on the rear window with a number beneath it, which Rian correctly assumed was a UWF campus parking sticker.

The car had Florida license plates from Brevard County, indicating that its owner was from the Melbourne area. Rian peered into the driver's window and noticed an iPod, two Starbucks coffee cups, and assorted fast food wrappers on the floor.

Probably one of the interns in the clerk's office. Rian walked back down the incline and approached the guard booth. Albert stood as she approached.

"Somethin' wrong, Ms. Coulter?" he asked.

"Albert, do you know whose silver Honda that is that's parked in my place?"

"No, ma'am. It was here when I got here at six this mornin'. I thought you might be drivin' it; that is, 'till I saw you just pull in. You want me to call the tow truck?"

She thought about it for a moment. Had it been some private lawyer she would have it towed in a second. The space was clearly marked "Reserved Coulter" and she would not mind pissing off another arrogant dickhead. But this was just some college student. If he, or she, had gotten here that early, chances are his eyes weren't open enough to even read the sign.

"Nah, to hell with it," she said. "Do me a favor, though, will you Albert? When they leave, tell them that if they park there again, it'll cost them eighty dollars to get the car out of hock."

"Will do, Ms. Coulter."

Rian trudged back up the incline and entered the building. She tossed her briefcase onto the chair in her office and plopped down in her chair with a loud sigh. She swiveled to her right and logged in on her computer.

"Uh, good morning. Something wrong?" Abby called from the doorway.

"Some kid took my parking place this morning. Of all the many perks of this glamorous and highly sought after position, it's the one I hate to lose most," Rian said sarcastically.

"Maybe I should refer them over to Clyde Taylor," Abby said, laughing, referring to the lawyer who had last committed this offense. "I'll never forget how he had to walk around in the rain all day because you blocked him in and they wouldn't tow you away."

Rian smiled at the memory. "Well, we haven't had that problem with him again, have we?" she said.

"Nor with anyone else. Did you have it towed?

"No. It's just some college kid, I think. I told Albert to give them a bunch of crap when they leave to scare them from doing it again. I parked up on three."

Rian's morning proceeded uneventfully. She met with two witnesses who could allegedly provide an alibi for one of her clients accused in a robbery/homicide of a motel clerk. Experience had taught her to view alibi witnesses with suspicion, and Rian interviewed the two women separately. As she feared, their stories sounded contrived and too rehearsed to be believable at trial.

She reviewed and revised the pretrial legal memorandum in a case set for trial in two weeks and went through plea offers in cases with two of the other assistants in the office. If this was any indication, it would be a busy month in trial for the whole office.

Rian glanced at her watch and was surprised to see that it was already 11:45. The morning had flown by and she sent Sam a message.

"Lunch?" she texted. A minute later, her phone buzzed.

"Can't. Kenner closing @ 1 – problems. Call u," he responded.

Rian sighed and contemplated buzzing one of her assistants to go to lunch but decided instead to run by the bank and grab a quick sandwich someplace. She let Abby know and went out the back door, forgetting for the moment that she had parked on the third level. She remembered as soon as she emerged in the parking lot, noting that the car was still parked in her reserved space. She headed back into the office and stopped at Abby's desk.

"Please call the clerk's office and tell them that their intern is parked in the reserved section and ask them to come move their car. If it's still there when I get back from lunch, I'm going to have it towed."

"Yes, ma'am," Abby responded, snapping off a salute as though addressing a superior military officer.

Rian rolled her eyes. "Oh, stop it. You're such a smart ass," she said as she turned and headed for the elevator, leaving Abby laughing in her wake.

She cashed a small check at the bank drive through window and decided to pull into the deli next door for a quick lunch. This was a place that Rian frequented, but hadn't been to in a couple of weeks. One of the waitresses recognized her and hurried over when Rian sat down.

"Hi Ms. Coulter. Haven't seen you for a while. Whatchya drinking today, Diet Coke?" she asked.

"Hi, Lisa. Um, unsweet tea instead, I think." She perused the specials written on the white board behind the counter but opted for a cup of vegetable soup and half of a turkey sandwich on wheat toast. She smiled when the sandwich arrived, noting that Lisa had omitted the obligatory pickle slice next to the sandwich. Rian hated pickles.

I guess I'm getting pretty predictable.

Rian immersed herself in the free local weekly paper that she pulled from the stack by the door and nibbled quietly at her food until she became aware of activity around her. Looking up, she noticed that everyone's attention was directed to a small flat screen television mounted in the corner of the deli. She could tell that the station was tuned to CNN and that there was some "breaking news" being reported, but the screen was too small and too far away for her read the other writing. Rian went back to her lunch, but looked up again when she became aware that all activity in the restaurant had ceased and a strange quiet had settled over the room.

"Turn it up," one of the customers said. Lisa the waitress pointed a remote at the screen and the volume increased. Rian could see a map of the state of Florida on the screen with a highlight on Pensacola. Beneath the "Breaking News" logo, she could now read "Body Found."

"Again, if you're just joining us, a body has been found in a wooded area in Pensacola near the campus of a local university," the CNN reporter said. "As I said, we don't know much, and the police are not saying whether this incident is related to other recent homicides in the area. If it is, it would be the third such murder in the last six months, unusual for a town this size. CNN has a crew en route to Pensacola and we will continue to keep you posted on this story as it develops."

A distraught looking Lisa came over to refill Rian's tea glass.

"This stuff is just freakin' me out," she said. "I'm so damn scared I'm thinkin' of getting a gun."

Rian nodded in agreement.

"I know what you mean. Something just like this went on when I lived in Birmingham several years ago. The whole town was in a panic. This is a bad time of year for this to be happening here."

Rian's appetite had suddenly vanished, so she asked Lisa for her check and paid at the counter. She tuned the car radio to CNN on the drive back to the office, but there was nothing reported about any bodies in Pensacola. She pulled through the gate to the garage and Albert informed her that the car was still parked in her space. Fuming mad, she burst through the door to the office and marched down the hall, determined to call the towing company. When she reached her office, she found Abby at her computer with several other secretaries crowded around.

"Did you hear the news?" Abby asked.

"Yeah. Did you call the clerk and tell them to get their intern's car out of the parking lot?"

Abby stood and walked around the half wall that separated her from Rian. Another secretary immediately sat in her chair and started clicking the mouse to Abby's computer.

"I called. The clerk's office said that they don't have any interns right now."

"Then call the State Attorney's Office," Rian said.

"Already did," Abby replied. "They don't have any either. I tried Probation and Parole and even the Court Administrator. There are no interns working here today."

"Then call the towing company. Tell them I want the car gone today."

Rian turned and started into her office, but caught herself. Abby had returned to her seat and was studying her monitor intently.

"What are you all looking at?" Rian asked.

"The *Herald* website. They're streaming updates on the body that was found."

"I saw something on CNN at lunch. They didn't know much."

"The *Herald* has a guy at the scene who's updating everyone on Twitter, and they're streaming updates on their website."

Rian was impressed. "Not bad for a paper supposedly in financial trouble. What are they saying?"

"Victim is a white female, no identification yet. She was found in the woods near the tennis courts about an hour ago."

Rian knew exactly where Abby was referring. She had used those same tennis courts many times. A chill ran down her spine, and she headed back to her office.

"Her car is missing," Abby called to her. "Cops are looking for a silver Honda Accord with Brevard County plates."

Rian froze.

"What did you say?" she asked Abby.

"The *Herald* says that the victim was last seen last night around 10:30. Her car is missing and they are looking for a silver Honda with Brevard County plates."

Rian forced herself to remain calm and modulate her voice.

"Abby, can I see you in my office for a second?"

"Now?" Abby asked, clearly not wanting to leave her computer again.

"Yes, now please," Rian said, forcing a smile.

Abby followed her into the office.

"Close the door," Rian said.

"Uh-oh," was Abby's response. She started to explain why everyone was crowded around her desk, but Rian held up her hand and cut her off.

"I don't give a shit about that, Abby. Who's in charge of the investigation out at UWF?"

"I don't know. Why?"

"Find out, but do so quietly. Tell the other staff people crowded around that I just chewed you a new one and that they'd better hightail it back to their work stations. Then, quickly and quietly, find out who's in charge out there and how to get in touch with them. Do it now."

Abby started to ask another question, but stopped when she saw the look on Rian's face. She had an easy relationship with her boss on most days, but no one would say something flippant when Rian had that look. She simply nodded and opened the door.

"Close that behind you," Rian commanded.

Unsure of what to do, Rian just sat there, drumming her fingers on the desk for a minute. She turned to her computer and pulled up the *Herald*'s website. The newspaper had already uploaded some photographs from the scene, but they showed little more than the tennis courts and the adjacent woods blocked off by yellow crime scene tape. The site had a button at the top that would refresh the page automatically every thirty seconds, and Rian clicked on that feature.

Scrolling down, she read where the police hadn't released the name of the female victim, but reported that an all points bulletin had been issued for her silver Honda Accord. The page went blank for a second, then refreshed with a phone number for the Escambia County Sheriff's Office to contact with any information. Rian was about to call that number when there was a tap at her door. Abby opened it and closed it behind her.

"The S.O. desk wasn't particularly forthcoming but I was able to get through to investigations. The guy heading it up is a Lieutenant Glenn Palmer, but he's at the scene now. There's no way to reach him."

"Call them back. Palmer will have at least one other investigator working the scene with him. Tell them to have either him or one of his assistants call me on my private line as soon as possible."

"What's this about?" Abby asked. Her nerves were beginning to show.

"Abby, please. Just make the call."

"Rian . . ." Abby pleaded. Tears were starting to well in her eyes.

"I need you to hold it together, Abby. Come on, you can do this, just please make the call."

Abby gathered herself and recovered.

"Then tell me what this is all about."

Rian met her gaze and they looked at each other for a long moment. Rian sighed, then spoke in a flat voice.

"There's a silver Honda Accord with Brevard County plates that's been parked in my space since last night."

CHAPTER THIRTY-ONE

Deep in the woods on the University of West Florida campus, out of range from the gathering media crowd, Glenn Palmer and Sheriff Vince Milam stood together and surveyed the scene before them. The shallow grave that had held Brianna Larson's body was empty, except for the crime scene techs who came in and out looking for evidence. Brianna's body was on its way to the morgue where Dr. Crawford would perform an autopsy later today, even though Palmer already knew the cause of death. He would have a detective in attendance to take possession of any physical evidence that might be recovered.

As he looked around, Palmer considered it fortunate that Brianna had been found so quickly. Although the woods on the campus were intertwined with jogging and nature trails, this location was out of the way of any of these. If not for two biology students combing the woods early this morning looking for fungi, Brianna may not have been discovered for weeks, long after the trail leading to her murderer had gone cold.

The fact that they already knew her identity was also unusual. Her roommate had called this morning to report that Brianna didn't return home last night and gave police a description of Brianna and her vehicle. Ordinarily, a college student staying out all night would be no cause for alarm for either her roommate or the police, but everyone had been on high alert since the murder of Christy Price only three months ago. Brianna's roommate was able to tell the police exactly what Brianna was wearing, and the body that had been found this morning fit that description exactly.

Palmer's cell phone buzzed, and he pulled it out of his pocket and looked at the number. It was Sanchez.

"Go," he said.

"L.T., I talked to the roommate who said that Brianna left to play tennis around 8:00 last night. She plays with several different people, but most often with a girl named Hannah Padgett. She lives in one of the sorority houses and we went by, but she isn't there now. Campus police pulled her class schedule and we're headed over there now to talk to her."

"I take it she doesn't know what's happened?" said Palmer.

"Don't think so. I wanted to check with you to be sure it was okay to tell her since we haven't released the girl's name yet."

Palmer considered this for a moment. It was Sheriff's Department policy not to disclose the name of a homicide victim until the victim's family had been notified of the death. Usually this wasn't a problem, but in the hypersensitive environment surrounding this case, word would spread like wildfire. No one wanted Brianna Larson's family to learn that she'd died through the media that would surely descend on them like locusts.

"What's your ETA?" Palmer asked.

"About five minutes." Not much time, Palmer thought.

"Stand by," he said and hung up. He punched in the number for Sandy Evans, the department secretary who had been detailed exclusively to the task force.

"Sandy, what's the status of notification of the family?" he asked when she answered.

"Brevard was sending officers to the house to inform the mother. I haven't had confirmation yet."

"Okay. See if you can confirm and let me know asap. Thanks." He called Sanchez back and told him to go ahead and let Hannah Padgett know what had happened, trusting that by the time this all hit the fan, Brianna's family would already have been notified of her death. Fresh leads would have to take priority now anyway.

Palmer hung up the phone and realized that he'd wandered away from Sheriff Milam while he was talking. He walked back and stood next to the sheriff, who was still silently looking at the scene.

"We've located the person that the victim was playing tennis with last night," he informed his boss. "Maybe we'll catch a break."

Milam nodded slowly, then looked at Palmer.

"You know, we might have to consider the fact that this is bigger than we are." When Palmer didn't respond, he added, "We might need some help."

"You mean the Feds," Palmer said. The FBI was often called in on serial killer cases, although less frequently in the years since 9/11. They had a tendency to run roughshod over local law enforcement when asked for assistance, and Palmer didn't need the inevitable turf war that would develop despite his best efforts to avoid it.

"Vince, don't do that yet. We have our best people on this. I can't see what the Feds could do that we aren't doing. If we get any physical evidence that we can't deal with, maybe. But not yet."

Milam pursed his lips and turned back to the crime scene. "It's not my idea, but the time may come when it's not our call." As an elected official, the Sheriff had to deal with political implications of which Palmer was blissfully ignorant. Palmer recognized it as a warning shot across the bow.

Palmer's cell phone buzzed again. Sandy Evans was calling back, probably to confirm that the Larson family had been officially notified.

"Palmer," he said.

"Lieutenant, I got a call from a woman in the Public Defender's Office wanting to know who was in charge of the investigation of the scene at UWF."

"How would they know anything about it?" he asked.

"That was my question. She said the *Herald* has reporters on scene streaming updates on Twitter and the *Herald*'s website every few minutes." Palmer looked back in the direction of the parking area where the media was concentrated. There was no way that they could see what was going on here.

"Anyway," Sandy continued, "I tried to blow her off, but she called back and was persistent. I told her that you were in charge of the task force. Then I got a call from one of the Assistant Public Defenders, a woman named Rian Coulter. She wanted your cell phone number, which I obviously didn't give her, but she wanted you to contact her immediately on her private line. Says she has information bearing directly on this investigation."

"What sort of information?" asked Palmer. He recognized the name of Rian Coulter as the Chief Assistant Public Defender who was usually involved in defending high profile cases. He'd met her a few times and had a generally favorable impression of her, although he distrusted most defense lawyers instinctively and suspected an ulterior motive here.

"She wouldn't tell me," Sandy said. "She said she would only talk to you or your assistant at the scene."

Palmer cursed silently, irritated at the interruption and the tendency of lawyers to try to control everything.

"Give me her number."

"I'll text it to you now," Sandy said.

* * *

Rian sat at her desk staring blankly at the work before her. She still had the *Herald*'s website up, and it continued to update every thirty seconds, but no new information had been added for a while now. Jack Brown sat across the desk from her. Rian had informed him of the situation immediately, and they had both decided that this was the best course of action. They had discussed the implications of the vehicle possibly belonging to a serial killer's victim being parked in Rian's parking place and whether the act was intentional or not. Now, they simply waited silently.

Rian's desk phone rang, and she looked at the caller ID window that indicated that the call came from a private, unpublished number.

"This is it," she said to Jack as she picked up the phone.

"Rian Coulter," she said into the receiver.

"Ms. Coulter, this is Lieutenant Glenn Palmer with the Escambia County Sheriff's Office. I received a message to contact you at this number reference possible information concerning an investigation at UWF."

"Yes, Lieutenant. Thank you for calling me back."

"What's this all about?" Palmer asked impatiently.

"I understand that you're looking for a silver Honda Accord with Brevard County plates, is that correct?"

Palmer was amazed at how information traveled these days. It was both a blessing and a curse.

"Yes, that's correct," he said. "Do you have any information?"

"A silver Honda Accord with Brevard County plates was parked in my reserved parking spot in the courthouse parking garage when I arrived this morning. The lot attendant told me that it was already there when he got to work at six o'clock this morning."

"Where's the vehicle now?"

"It's still there. Courthouse security has been guarding it since I learned that it was possibly linked to a homicide at UWF. It has a university parking decal."

"Where is your parking space?" Palmer asked.

"Take the Claggett Street entrance. It's on the first level next to the building."

"I'll have officers in route. Where is your office located?"

"Same building. We're on the first floor."

"Stand by, please. We'll want to talk with you also."

"I anticipated that. I'll be waiting."

Palmer hung up and dialed Sanchez's number.

"Are you still with the witness?" Palmer asked when Sanchez answered.

"Yeah. We're just finishing up."

"Meet me at the downtown courthouse parking garage asap. The victim's car has been located there. Courthouse security is standing by, but contact city and ask that they send officers to secure it until we get there."

"Okay, L.T. On my way."

"Sanchez," Palmer continued, "Code Three," meaning that Sanchez was to travel without emergency lights or siren.

"Yes, sir. Got it," he said.

Palmer clicked off and looked at Sheriff Milam who simply nodded. He then took off and sprinted through the woods back to his car.

CHAPTER THIRTY-TWO

Rian continued to glance at her computer monitor which was still displaying the *Herald's* website. Every few minutes, it refreshed the page and soon after she spoke to Palmer, the words "Update 1:52 p.m." appeared in bold, red letters at the top of the page, followed by a short notation:

> "Lt. Glenn Palmer, head of the Homicide Task Force and the lead investigator in the case, was seen sprinting to his vehicle and hurriedly left the scene. Updates will be posted as events dictate."

"How long before they show up here, do you think?" Rian asked.

"They've probably only got one guy at the scene," Jack Brown responded. "He'll have to decide whether to stay put or follow Palmer. My bet, if he's any good, is that he realizes there's no more news there and follows him here."

"Terrific," said Rian, sarcastically.

While they waited, Rian and Jack discussed what connection, if any, this victim or the killer would have to the office or to Rian personally. Every so often, a disgruntled client would make a veiled threat to one of the lawyers, promising to do this or that when they got out of prison. These were part of the job, and Rian had her share of them as well, although none recently, and none that she'd taken seriously. As the elected Public Defender, Jack Brown's duties were more administrative. He hadn't stepped into a courtroom in years and didn't personally represent clients. Even so, Jack had a few threats thrown his way, too. Neither could think of a link between their duties and whatever was going on at the university.

"I'm going to let Commissioner Simpson know what's going on. Let me know if you need me to step in when they get here," Jack said and went back to his office.

Rian stared down at the work on her desk and knew that she wouldn't get to it today. She wasn't afraid as much as puzzled.

What does this have to do with me?

She grabbed her iPhone and tapped out a quick text message to Sam. Things had moved so quickly that she hadn't even had a chance to let him know what was going on.

A few minutes later, Abby tapped on the door and stepped in.

"Lt. Palmer and Detective Sanchez are here to see you. I put them in the large conference room."

"Thanks, Abby," Rian said and got up from her desk.

"Do you need anything?" Abby asked.

"Nope. I'm good," Rian said as nonchalantly as she could.

She strode confidently down the hall and opened the door to the conference room. Palmer and Sanchez were seated at the table. Both rose as she entered the room.

"I'm Rian Coulter," she said, extending her hand and giving Palmer a firm handshake. His six foot, two inch frame towered over her, but Rian wasn't the least bit intimidated by him.

"Glenn Palmer," he said. "This is Detective Sanchez." Rian shook his hand and they all sat at the table. Sanchez pulled out a small digital recording device and placed it on the table. Rian started to protest, but changed her mind. She didn't want to start the meeting off on the wrong foot.

"How can I help you?" she said.

Palmer began by thanking her for calling him.

"When did you discover the vehicle?" he asked.

"I pulled into the garage at about 6:45 this morning," she began. "The car was already here, parked in my reserved space."

"Does the space have your name on it or is it just marked reserved?" Palmer asked.

"There's a bumper that's painted yellow. The words 'Reserved Coulter' are stenciled on it in black."

"Do all of the attorneys here have reserved spaces?"

"Yes, but not all of them are marked by name. Most of them just say 'Reserved.' Jack Brown and I are the only two who have our names on the bumpers. One of the many perks that we have with our positions."

Palmer smiled at the joke. Sanchez was busy taking notes and missed it.

"Please continue," he said.

"I was irritated and considered blocking it in, but parked on another level instead. I checked with the attendant at the gate and he said the car was here when he arrived for work."

"Who's the attendant?" Sanchez asked.

"His name is Albert. He's been here for years."

"What happened next?" Palmer asked.

"I did look at the car and noticed that it had a UWF parking sticker. I looked through the windows and decided that it must be a student intern working in the courthouse, so I didn't give it any more thought. I asked my assistant to have the clerk's office move the car while I was at lunch. I was about to have it towed when we learned of what was going on at UWF."

"How did you learn of what was going on?"

"When I came back from lunch, my assistant and several staff members were following the story online. The *Herald* was tracking the story online and updating it every minute. From that I learned that you were looking for a car that fit that description, so I called you immediately."

Palmer was thankful that she'd called him instead of the *Herald* and made a mental note to discuss this with Mike Donovan.

"Is there a back way to the garage?" he asked.

"Sure. I'll show you the way. My space is right by the door."

Rian led them out the back door to the parking garage. The silver Honda was still parked in her space, guarded by two deputies. Rian could see a marked sheriff's cruiser blocking the Claggett Street entrance to the garage.

"Where can we find Albert the attendant?" Palmer asked.

Rian pointed to the entrance. "He's in that booth there."

Sanchez took the hint. "I'm on it," he said and left to interview Albert.

Palmer walked silently around Brianna's car, peering in through the windows as he did. He looked up at a security camera attached to the wall just above the door to the courthouse.

"Does that work?" he asked.

"I assume so, but I'm not positive," Rian answered. "Security has a monitoring station on the fourth floor. I know they monitor all of the courtrooms and the judge's chambers. I'm not sure about the parking areas."

"How do you gain access to the parking garage?"

"You can enter from either the Claggett Street side or from Bayfront. Both entrances have an electronic card slot that raises the arm to let you in."

"How would someone without a card get in there at night?"

"They leave the barricades up at night. Somebody complained to the County Commission about not being able to park in a county owned garage during the festivals that they have down here at night."

"So any Joe Blow could park in here after hours without having to swipe a card to get in?"

"Correct," said Rian.

Palmer made a note to check with the company that maintained the electronic barricades to see if they had a record of whose card was last used to enter the garage last evening. Sanchez rejoined them.

"Can we step back inside?" he asked Rian.

"Sure," she said and punched in the code for the electronic lock on the courthouse door. It clicked and they stepped into the building. As they passed through the door, Palmer pointed out the security camera to Sanchez and dispatched him to the fourth floor monitoring room to see if there was a recording of who parked the car here the night before. Rian and Palmer went back to the conference room. Abby brought them both Diet Cokes.

"Ms. Coulter," Palmer began when Abby left the room, "have you received any threats of any kind recently?"

Rian briefly recalled the ugly incident with Anthony Stallworth at the jail. He had reacted badly to her suggestion that he enter a plea in his case, but hadn't actually threatened her.

"No, not really. Like everyone here, I've had my share of comments made over the years, but nothing that I've ever considered an actual threat."

"Do you know a UWF student named Brianna Larson?" he asked.

Rian shook her head. "That name isn't familiar to me. I don't know anyone in Brevard County at all."

"Do you have any connection to any of the other victims in this case that you can think of?"

Rian gave him a puzzled look. She hadn't considered that angle before.

"Lieutenant, I assumed that whoever parked that car here did so randomly. Are you telling me that there's some connection between me and this serial killer?"

"Ms. Coulter, I didn't say that and I never used the term 'serial killer.' The car was parked in a space marked specifically with *your* name. Not Jack Brown's. Not someone else's. Yours. That tells me that it was meant to be a message either to you or about you, specifically. I'm trying to find out what connection you may have to these events."

Rian thought for several moments, then pursed her lips and shook her head.

"No, I can't think of a thing. I don't know the girl you just mentioned. I didn't know the girl out at the Border Line either. I've represented people who've been arrested out there before but I don't see how that could be related. To my knowledge, I never met the woman who was killed back at Christmas in Cantonment. I can't see what this has to do with me at all."

Palmer looked at her intently and she held his eyes with hers.

"Didn't you used to work in Birmingham?" he asked.

CHAPTER THIRTY-THREE

Sanchez was waiting on the courthouse steps when Palmer emerged.

"What did you find out?" he asked as Sanchez fell in stride beside him.

"Get this, L.T. No video of the parking area. They got cameras everywhere in that building. Every courtroom, every judge's office, every hallway. Even the friggin' snack bar's got a camera. I bet you can't take a crap in the building without somebody knowing it. They're all monitored in a room on the fourth floor staffed by our people."

"Do they tape what's going on?" Palmer asked hopefully.

"Yeah, a continuous loop. It only stores twenty-four hours before it re-records over itself and erases what's there. But here's the deal, most of the cameras on the exterior don't work. They don't monitor them and don't maintain them, so most of them have gone down due to lack of maintenance."

Palmer stopped and looked at him.

"Are you kidding me?" he said.

"I shit you not," Sanchez said. "Budget cuts," he said, holding his hands up and mimicking quotation marks with his fingers as he spoke. "They say their job is to maintain security *inside* the building, not outside."

"So what happens if there's an incident outside?" Palmer asked.

Sanchez smiled at him. "Then they call the city 'cause it's their 'jurisdiction,'" he said, using air quotes again.

Palmer just looked at him, then shook his head and resumed walking.

"God damn petty political bullshit," he said. "God forbid that they'd do something outside of their jurisdiction. Meanwhile, we miss a golden opportunity to get our boy on tape."

"You don't think this guy knew about all that, do you, L.T.?"

"No, I just think he's a lucky son of a bitch," Palmer said.

They walked in silence together until they reached Palmer's car.

"So how'd it go with the lady PD? Did she know anything?" Sanchez asked.

"I don't think so," Palmer replied. "She said that she didn't know any of the victims and claims that she hasn't received any threats and couldn't think of anyone who would target her like that."

"You think she'd tell you if she could?" Sanchez asked skeptically.

Palmer shrugged. "I don't know. Lawyers are lawyers no matter where they work. I felt like she was being straight with me, though. I didn't get the impression that she was holding out on us." He paused and stared back at the building for several seconds.

"There's a connection here, though. I can feel it. I just can't put my finger on what it is."

He looked back at Sanchez and gestured toward the parking garage. "Where's the car now?" he asked.

"Crime scene guys are towing it as we speak," said Sanchez. "I expect it'll be at our garage in an hour or so."

"Tell them that it gets top priority over everything else they've got going. Maybe the asshole left a print and we'll get lucky."

Palmer got into his car and drove back to the West Florida campus, taking the most direct route there from downtown. Along the way, he noted several secluded spots where the killer could have easily disposed of evidence if this was the route that he'd taken the previous night.

It was at least twelve miles from the site of the murders to the courthouse parking garage, and Palmer noted that it had taken him a little over twenty minutes to make the trip in daytime traffic. The killer might have made better time at night. He was bothered by the fact that the guy was so bold as to drive the car right into the parking garage like that, not knowing or apparently caring that he might be caught on tape.

If his vehicle was at West Florida, how did he get back out there after dumping Brianna's car? If he walked back, it would've taken hours. He pulled out his cell phone and dialed Sanchez.

"What time did the witness who played tennis with Brianna say that they finished?" he asked when Sanchez answered. While asking the question, Palmer heard a beep on his phone indicating that someone else was calling him.

"She said it was after 10:00, maybe closer to 11:00 when they finished," Sanchez said.

"Have our people search every trash can on Bayfront east of the courthouse, and along East Bay Boulevard, particularly the secluded spots. Our guy may have stashed something along there on his way back here."

"Okay," Sanchez said. "Anything else?"

"While they're at it, have them check to see if anyone saw somebody walking north on East Bay between midnight and 5:00 this morning," he said.

"Wow, L.T. That could take a while," Sanchez said.

"It's all we've got at the moment," Palmer said and clicked off.

He checked his messages, but had no new voicemails on his phone. He checked his text messages and saw that there was one new message from "mdonovo65." Mike Donovan. Palmer opened the message.

"Meet?" was the only message. Palmer texted back.

"1 hr, usual spot. Confirm," he texted.

"Done," was the reply a few seconds later. Palmer deleted the messages, both incoming and outgoing, from his phone.

* * *

Donovan was already sitting at the bar when Palmer walked into O'Steen's. Palmer pretended not to notice him and walked directly to the Powerbroker's Club in the back. It was just after

3:00 in the afternoon, and Palmer assumed that the club would likely be empty since the lunch crowd would be gone. It was still too early for the after work drinkers.

He walked in and made a quick sweep of the room. A man and woman neither of whom Palmer recognized occupied only one booth. They looked like they were just finishing and about to leave and didn't appear to notice him. The waitress approached, and Palmer asked her to set him up in the corner booth while he excused himself to go to the men's room.

Donovan was washing his hands when he entered, and Palmer gave him a silent nod and headed back to the private room. Donovan was pretty good at the cloak and dagger stuff, Palmer thought, as he settled into the booth. A minute later, Donovan joined him. The waitress appeared and already had a glass of sweet tea for Palmer. Donovan ordered bottled water.

"I take it that was you tweeting from the scene," he said to Donovan after she left. "What's next, a Facebook page?"

"Since when does an old guy like you know about Facebook?" said Donovan.

"You'd be surprised what some people will post. It's becoming an investigational tool," Palmer replied. "Like Twitter." He'd already read all of Donovan's updates on the *Herald* website and didn't think that Donovan realized that he was one of his followers on Twitter.

"News is instantaneous now and comes in all forms. We've had three times the number of hits on the website today than we normally do," said Donovan.

"Congratulations. Maybe it'll win you a Pulitzer."

"So it was the victim's car in the parking garage?" Donovan asked.

"Yeah," Palmer answered. "It was parked in one of the Public Defender's parking spots. Her name's Rian Coulter. Do you know her?"

"Yeah, kind of."

"How well do you know her?" Palmer asked.

"I've talked with her a few times on some of her cases. She's the number two person in the office just beneath Jack Brown himself. She handles all of the high profile cases in the PD's office."

"How forthcoming is she?"

"What do you mean?"

"Does she talk to the media or is she one of those who avoids you guys like the plague?"

"She's pretty savvy if you ask me. She's not adverse to talking to us, but usually plays her cards pretty close to the vest. Why? Is she involved in all of this?

"Not directly, no. But parking the victim's car in her spot as opposed to anywhere else in the entire vacant parking garage means something. It may mean that there's a connection to her somehow. I need you to help see if you can find out what it is."

Donovan looked surprised that Palmer had asked for such assistance. "What kind of help?" he asked cautiously, and Palmer assumed he was wary of becoming part of the investigation himself and compromising his independence as a reporter.

"Just to see what you can dig up," Palmer said. "My resources are spread pretty thin. I interviewed her earlier today for the first time. I felt she was a pretty straight shooter, but still guarded in what she told me. Lawyers like to be the ones asking questions though, not being on the receiving end."

"What can you tell me about this one?" Donovan asked.

"The victim was a student at UWF. She was attacked after playing tennis last night, we think around 11:00."

"Hogtied like the others?"

"Yeah, bound with rope. This time, he buried her in a shallow grave in the woods."

"Who found her?"

Palmer gave him the names so that Donovan could contact them before any of the other media outlets. Giving him primacy on information such as this helped to solidify Donovan's cooperation without compromising the investigation in any way. For his part, Donovan could get information in some cases quicker than Palmer that he could pass on without compromising the integrity of his story. It was an unusual, symbiotic relationship.

Palmer also gave Donovan the name of the victim and what little background he had on her at the moment. Donovan started to slide out of the booth, then stopped and looked at Palmer again.

"Is this escalating?" he asked.

"Meaning?" Palmer replied, even though he knew exactly what Donovan meant.

"Meaning four murders in twelve months, beginning with Jessup, but three in the last six months. Are we going to see more sooner rather than later? Is he escalating?"

This guy is no dummy, Palmer thought.

"Off the record, maybe. It's something we're looking at." A non-answer.

Donovan slid out of the booth.

"Thanks," he said. "I'll let you know if I get anything on Rian Coulter."

"Okay," Palmer said. "And we didn't have this conversation."

* * *

Rian stared out of her window at the channel 4 news van setting up at the entrance to the parking garage for the evening news broadcast. There was also one from the Mobile, AL station, and Rian suspected that most of the others were set up to broadcast from the university campus. She was contemplating how she would get her car out of the garage without having to deal with the media.

"Madame, your Knight has arrived and your chariot awaits," Sam's voice called. Rian wheeled around and saw him standing in the doorway, leaning on the door frame with one leg crossed over the other and his arms folded across his chest. He was wearing a suit, but had loosened his tie. As usual, Sam had a half-smirk, half-smile that exuded self-confidence. Rian welcomed it because she was feeling a little off her game at the moment.

"Get in here," she said. He walked toward her, kicking the door shut as he did. She met him halfway, and he wrapped his arms around her and held her. She looked up and he kissed her lightly and brushed her hair away from her eyes.

"You okay?" he asked. Rian nodded.

"I saw the news vans and thought I could kidnap you instead," he said.

"Thanks," Rian said. "You read my mind. I was just sitting here wondering how I was going to get my car out of the lot."

"I didn't go in the garage, but I suspect they're camped out there, too. We can take the exit on the south side and slip past them. Can you leave now?

"Yeah, I have nothing else today. Let me tell Abby." She punched some numbers on the phone and Abby tapped on the door a few seconds later, then opened it.

"I hope I'm interrupting," she joked as she entered. "Hey, handsome," she said to Sam, her usual greeting.

"Hey, gorgeous," he said, giving the usual reply with a wink.

"Break it up, you guys," Rian said. "Abby, Sam and I are going to slip out early through a different exit and avoid the news in the garage." Abby had fielded calls throughout the day from all of the local television and radio stations, as well as several from nearby towns and as far away as Birmingham. Rian hadn't talked with any of them.

"Okay. Someone from CNN called a few minutes ago. I told them you were in court. I don't think they believed me," Abby said.

"They're probably trolling all over the courthouse right now," Rian said. "You may run into them too. Make sure you just say 'No comment.'"

"Okay. You guys be careful," Abby said.

Rian sat on the corner of her desk and took Abby's hands in hers. Abby was a top notch legal secretary and fiercely protective of Rian, but her tender, sweet nature would be no match for an aggressive reporter if they ambushed her out of the office.

"This will all blow over in a couple of days," Rian told her. "Biden or Sarah Palin or somebody will say something stupid and my fifteen minutes of fame will be over. We just need to ride it out. Have security walk you to your car, okay?"

"Okay, no problem. I'm fine. Now, go!" Abby said.

Sam and Rian left through the front entrance and took the stairs up a couple of flights. They crossed the atrium in the courthouse without incident but, instead of taking the public elevators, Sam walked around to the other side, motioning with his head for Rian to follow. He pulled out a set of keys and inserted one into a lock beside the private elevator reserved for the judges. It opened instantly.

"How in the hell . . .?" Rian started to ask, but Sam put his finger over his lips and gently guided her in with his hand. They took the elevator to the ground floor and followed a narrow hallway to an exit door, emerging in the reserved judicial parking lot.

"Don't tell me you parked in here," Rian said as they stepped out. Sam just smiled and made a sweeping gesture with his left arm extended. His Mercedes was parked three spaces from the door.

Rian shook her head. "I swear, McKinney. You never cease to amaze me."

"It helps when your partner's former law partner is the Chief Judge," he said, laughing. "But I'll still take the credit, if there's something in it for me."

They got in and slowly nosed the car to the edge of the parking area protected by a large wall. The security door opened automatically and they eased out into the street. Rian looked to her right and saw the phalanx of reporters, apparently lying in wait for her to leave through the garage where her car was parked. They hesitated for a second, then turned the other way and left.

CHAPTER THIRTY-FOUR

Sam drove a zigzag route away from the courthouse complex to make sure that they weren't followed, then turned west along the bay. Rian gazed out the window at the water shimmering in the setting sun. Sam always drove with his right hand on top of the gear shift, and Rian's left hand rested on top of his as she absent-mindedly stroked his hand with her thumb. Neither spoke, and Rian became aware of an increasing fatigue gnawing at the edge of her consciousness. After a while, she turned and looked at Sam, who kept his eyes on the road.

"Thanks," she said simply. Sam cut his eyes at her and smiled his half smile.

"Where are we going?" she asked, not that she really cared much. She was content just to be with Sam and away from that scene at the courthouse.

"Alton's condo. I figured the press would be camped out at your place and you'd be easily spotted anywhere else in town. We'll have peace and quiet over there until this all blows over in a day or two." Alton Ashburn was the senior partner of Sam's firm. He was a trial lawyer turned developer, had made a fortune in both, and owned the penthouse condominium in the largest and most exclusive high rise just across the Alabama line in Gulf Shores. Corporate executives from all over the country had units there, as did sports and entertainment stars and other big shots, most of whom were friends of Alton's. Security was paramount there. Rian had never seen the place, but had heard that it was fabulous.

Rian continued to daydream out the window as they crossed over the intercoastal waterway bridge, emerging onto Perdido Key. She could feel the tension beginning to ease until she noticed a weathered looking structure ahead with a parking lot overflowing with cars.

The Border Line Lounge.

Sam saw it too and felt her hand tense on his. He drove in silence for another minute, then gripped Rian's hand.

"What's this got to do with you, Rian?" he said. "Is there something that you're not telling me?"

Rian said nothing at first, then slowly shook her head. "I honestly don't know. At first I thought the car being parked in my spot was just a coincidence. You know, some intern or something, somebody who didn't know any better. But Lieutenant Palmer was adamant that it means something particular about me."

"Why?" Sam asked.

"Because it was *my* spot with *my* name on it. Of all the named spots in an empty garage, he picked *mine*."

"I don't know," Sam said, unconvinced. "Maybe. That seems like a stretch to me."

"Well, it did to me, too, at first," Rian said. "I've been turning it over in my head all afternoon and for the life of me can't think of why me." Sam just looked at her until she got it and they both laughed. "I know, bad choice of words," she said. "Gallows humor, I guess."

The sun was dipping below the horizon when they pulled into the guardhouse at Intimity, Alton Ashburn's condominium complex, appropriately named after the Italian word for privacy. The guardhouse shielded the car from the roadway and the parking garage was shielded from view as well. A visibly armed guard approached the car and Sam rolled down the window.

"Good evening, Mr. McKinney," he said to their surprise. "Please follow the road to your right. Your space is number 180 on the top floor." Sam thanked him and eased forward toward the parking garage.

"Have you been here before?" Rian asked.

"Nope. Haven't been invited. Alton must've called ahead."

They pulled into the parking garage, took the ramp to the top floor, and found the parking space located just below the heliport. The penthouse had its own private elevator that Sam operated with the key that Alton had given him. It was outfitted with rich mahogany walls and a floor of Italian marble and took them up eighteen stories, opening directly into the condominium with matching marble floors.

A Waterford crystal chandelier graced the foyer, and Rian could see straight through to the south wall made entirely of glass, offering a breathtaking view of the sun settling over the Gulf of Mexico to the west. A terrazzo tiled balcony extended the length of the south wall and wrapped around the east and west sides in a "U" shape.

Rian and Sam initially ignored the luxurious interior and headed straight for the balcony to catch the last bit of sunset. As they did, the interior lights came on automatically as did accent lights on the balcony.

"Jesus," Sam said under his breath as they stepped onto the balcony and leaned on the rail.

They stared out at the water and enjoyed the soft sea breeze and the sound of the waves crashing on the shore far below. Sam stepped back inside and reappeared a few minutes later with two crystal goblets of red wine, handing one to Rian. Fresh fruit and cheese had been laid out for them on a wooden cheese tray covered by a dome of glass. They helped themselves and moved back inside to sit on a large leather sofa. Rian stared intently into her wine glass and twirled it back and forth in her fingers.

"What else did Palmer say?" Sam asked eventually.

Rian didn't look up. "They checked to see if maybe the parking lot camera got a glimpse of the suspect," she said. "He wanted to know if I'd received any threats, which I haven't, at least not lately."

More silence, then Rian looked up at Sam. "He asked if I used to work in Birmingham."

"What did you say?"

"I told him that I'd been an associate at a law firm there right after I graduated, but he already knew that."

"So, what's the point?" Sam asked.

"He didn't say. I got the definite impression that he was holding something back. I told you I had a feeling that this was somehow related to that shit in Birmingham," she said.

Rian was getting agitated, so Sam proceeded cautiously.

"Look, it's their job to explore every possibility. I'll admit there are some similarities to what went on up there, and I know they never arrested anyone. But that was years ago. Besides, you had nothing to do with all of that then, other than living in Birmingham. You didn't know any of the victims, did you?"

"No. One of the secretaries in the office knew one, but I'd never met her."

Sam moved closer to her, took her wine glass, and sat it on the coffee table. "I know you're a little freaked and I don't blame you," he said, putting his arm around her and pulling her to him. "The whole town's flipping out but this has nothing to do with you. Do you hear me? *Nothing*."

"I hear you. I just don't get it," she said half- heartedly.

Sam changed the subject. "I'm starving," he said. "Let's walk over and get some dinner. We can stay here and just get drunk tonight and forget all of this." Rian had to laugh at the expectant look on Sam's face.

"I don't even have a change of clothes," she said.

"Clothes? We don't need any stinking clothes," Sam said in a Hispanic accent, paraphrasing a line from *Blazing Saddles*. That broke the tension, and they both dissolved in laughter.

"Okay, McKinney. You win. Just let me call my folks, though, and let them know where I am. If they see this on the news there and can't reach me, they'll be worried sick."

Rian called her parents and her brother to let them know what was going on. Brian hadn't heard about the latest episode, but Rian's father was up to speed and expressed his concern. He wanted Rian to come stay with them in Tallahassee and only relented when Rian promised to keep Sam close by and to come if things got any worse.

They walked down the beach to a small seafood place that had the most delicious crab cakes in remoulade sauce that Rian had ever tasted. She and Sam split a bottle of chardonnay and after dinner ducked into a little beach bar for a few Bushwackers, a local frozen concoction made of rum, Kalhua, and a lot of other things. They strolled barefoot on the beach, and by the time they reached the condo, it was after midnight. Rian felt relaxed and a little silly about how she'd reacted to the events earlier that day. Sam made one more round of drinks and they climbed between twelve hundred thread count Egyptian cotton sheets in the master bedroom and fell fast asleep.

CHAPTER THIRTY-FIVE

Rian checked her watch as she stuffed files back into her briefcase. It was almost noon, and she might have just enough time to grab a quick lunch before cattle call at 1:00. Two of the other assistant public defenders were in trial, so, once again, Rian had to pitch in to help, this time handling felony first appearances.

Under Florida law, every person arrested was entitled to reasonable bail, the purpose of which was to ensure that the defendant would show up in court when required. The initial bail was set either by the arresting law enforcement agency or by the judge who had issued the warrant for the defendant's arrest.

The person arrested could then either post the amount of the bail in cash or, as was more often the case, hire a bail bondsman and pay the bondsman ten percent of the total amount. The bondsman would then stand good for the remainder. If the defendant failed to show up, the court collected the remaining ninety percent and would refund the now highly motivated bondsman once he produced the wayward defendant in court.

Law enforcement agencies frequently set a ridiculously high bail for most offenses, and those unable to post bail were taken before a judge within forty-eight hours to review the circumstances of the arrest. These first appearances were mainly opportunities to appoint the public defenders office to represent the defendant and to argue over what amount of bail was appropriate.

Rian had been arguing these matters since 9:00, leaving her annoyed with little time to prepare for the motions she was arguing after lunch. These were matters usually handled by the junior attorneys in the office.

Most judges set aside a block of two hours every other week for all pending motions to be heard. All defense counsel, private attorneys, and public defenders alike, showed up at one time and waited until the clerk called their particular case in whatever order the particular judge wanted to hear them. Dozens of attorneys milled about in the waiting area outside the courtroom, checking emails, reviewing files, and signing documents that had been couriered over from their offices, hence the term "cattle call."

Knowing that judges tended to call the cases of the private attorneys first, Rian figured that she had enough time to grab lunch first. She pulled out her iPhone and dialed Abby's direct number. It went straight to voicemail, which meant that Abby was either on the other line or had stepped away from her desk.

"Hey, Abby, it's me," Rian said when prompted to leave a message. "I'm just now getting out of first appearances, so could you call Sally's and have them deliver a sandwich to the office so that I can go over the Velasquez file for this afternoon?" Just then her phone beeped and she looked at the screen. It was Abby calling her back.

Rian clicked over to the call. "Hey, I was just leaving you a message. I'm on the way down now."

"Don't come through the front," Abby said with obvious tension in her voice. When Rian was in a hurry, she often came through the front lobby because it was a shorter route to her office.

"Why?" Rian said.

"Lieutenant Palmer is waiting for you in the lobby."

Rian stopped where she was. "What does he want?" she asked.

"He wouldn't tell me," Abby said. "He just showed up unannounced. I told him you were in court and I didn't know when you'd be back. He's been waiting about twenty minutes."

"Okay, thanks. I'll see you in a minute," Rian replied and clicked off. As far as she knew, Palmer was working full time on the serial killer case. She hadn't spoken to him since the day that Brianna Larson's car was found in Rian's parking place at the courthouse several weeks before. With all that he had on his plate, for Palmer to cool his heels just waiting for her in the lobby was strange, she thought. She could sneak in the back door and avoid him.

What the hell does he want?

Rian took the stairs down and entered the lobby of the Public Defender's Office. Palmer saw her walk in and stood, but before he could say anything, Rian strode confidently across the lobby and approached him directly, switching her briefcase to her left hand and offering her right hand to Palmer.

"Good afternoon, Lieutenant. Nice to see you again," she said, shaking his hand, aware that there were clients waiting and nervously watching. "I understand that you wanted to speak with me?" she said.

At first, Palmer didn't respond, but just looked at Rian with a slight smile. He was significantly taller and larger than she was, but she held his gaze with no sign of intimidation as he looked down at her.

"If you have a few minutes," he said. "I just have a few questions."

"I'm actually between court appearances so I don't have a lot of time," Rian said. She turned to the receptionist nearby. "Jennifer, please take Lieutenant Palmer to Conference Room A." She turned back to Palmer. "I'll drop this stuff in my office and join you in a minute."

Rian punched in the security code and let herself into the main office while Jennifer escorted Palmer to the conference room in the other direction. She tossed her briefcase into a side chair in her office as Abby walked in.

"You came in through the front?" Abby asked.

"Yeah," Rian said. "I put him in A and will meet him in there. Can you pull the Velasquez file and have it ready to go?"

"Already done," said Abby.

"Thanks. And bring my lunch in if it gets here," she said over her shoulder as she walked down the hall toward the conference room.

Palmer was seated when she entered and declined her offer of something to drink. He seemed relaxed with his legs crossed, and Rian noticed a thin manila file folder on the table next to him.

"So, what's this about?" she asked.

Palmer wasted no time. "You worked for a firm called Ashton, Baker, Pennington & Moring in Birmingham." It was more of a statement than a question. Rian waited for more, but Palmer remained silent.

"Yes, I did," she answered cautiously. "So?"

"What sort of firm was it?" Palmer asked.

Where is he going with this?

"The firm handled mostly civil litigation and property matters," she said, confident that Palmer already knew that.

"What sort of matters did *you* handle?"

"I was just out of law school. I did a lot of different things to gain experience."

"Did you work with any of the attorneys in particular?"

Rian paused for a second to consider the question, but could see no harm in answering. "I worked with and for most of the partners while I was there," she said, being intentionally vague.

"Any one in particular, more than the others?" Palmer persisted.

"Each associate was assigned a partner as a mentor. Mr. Baker was mine, so I guess I worked with him more than anyone else. Why is this important?"

Palmer ignored her question. "Did you or the firm do any criminal defense work while you were there?"

Rian's radar sensed danger. She wasn't sure how far she was willing to let this go. "Look, Lieutenant," she said, "I have a full day today as I'm sure you do. Ashton, Baker has a website that I'm sure you've already seen that indicates the types of cases that the firm handles. I don't see what this has to do with --"

"Did you or any of the partners you worked with handle criminal cases?" he interrupted, somewhat aggressively.

"Why do you want to know? That was years ago," Rian responded.

Palmer fought for self-control. He smiled and calmly asked, "Did you or the firm handle criminal cases, Ms. Coulter?"

Now Rian was mad, so much that she couldn't remember any of the criminal matters anyone at Ashton, Baker had worked on. She vaguely recalled a tax fraud case that Allan Pennington handled, but there certainly were more than that. As she thought, Palmer reached over and tapped the manila folder on the table impatiently.

"I'm sure there were some, for family or friends or whatever. It wasn't the firm's main focus."

"I'll need the names," Palmer said matter-of-factly.

"What do you mean, you'll need the names? What names?" she asked.

"The names of the criminal clients and who worked on their cases," said Palmer. As he spoke, he produced a small notebook out of his jacket pocket and pulled his pen from his shirt pocket.

Rian was incredulous. "Are you kidding me?" she asked. Palmer just looked at her, pen poised above his notepad.

Rian pushed her chair back and stood. "Lieutenant, I fail to see what this has to do with me or any investigation that you may be working."

"Are you refusing to cooperate, Ms. Coulter?" he asked.

Rian started to react, but noticed the glint in Palmer's eyes, convincing her that he knew that he'd just pushed her button. She swallowed her response and calmed herself. She'd been antagonized by prosecutors and chewed out by frustrated judges and wasn't about to let Palmer get under her skin any more than he already had.

"Lieutenant," she said softly, smiling. "Nothing could be further from the truth. If you recall, I was the one who called you to report Ms. Larson's car when I knew you were looking for it. I believe I've been most cooperative."

"Yet, I still don't have any names," Palmer said.

"I simply can't recall any. And even if I did, I couldn't tell you. That is confidential and privileged information," Rian responded.

They stared at each other for a long moment, then Palmer put his notepad away and stood.

"I can have a subpoena issued," he said.

Rian chuckled and said, "Have a nice day, Lieutenant."

Palmer started to leave, but stopped at the door and turned back to Rian.

"You know, Ms. Coulter, despite what you may think, I'm not the enemy here. We should be on the same side. If you had contact with this asshole in some way in Birmingham and he's now here, have you stopped to think that he just might remember you?" Rian just stared at him. "Just a thought. You have a nice day too, Ms. Coulter," Palmer said and walked out.

Rian was still standing there when Abby walked in with the Velasquez file and handed it to her. "Your lunch is on your desk," she said.

"Never mind," said Rian. "I'm not hungry anymore."

* * *

Outside the courthouse, Palmer sat behind the wheel of his unmarked car contemplating his next move. Rian Coulter was no wallflower, that was for sure. Although he was suspicious that she'd been singled out by the killer and that there was some connection between the killer and Coulter, he was certain that she hadn't made that connection yet, if she ever would. She'd been neither threatened nor attacked, and his next move could put her in jeopardy; or spook the killer. He phoned Sanchez.

"Hey, L.T. How'd it go?" Sanchez asked.

"Pretty much as I thought. Polite, but gave me nothing to go on," Palmer said.

"You think she knows and just ain't sayin?" said Sanchez. "You think we should subpoena her?"

"Not yet," said Palmer. "I want surveillance on her for a little while. Light surveillance. More for her sake than for ours. Put Corcoran and Dyson on it and tell them to keep their distance. I don't want her to know."

"On it, L.T." said Sanchez.

Palmer hung up, then pulled another phone from his pocket. It was a TracFone, a throwaway cellular phone that he'd paid cash for at Walgreen's. He bought air time with a prepaid Visa card that he'd also paid for with cash. He'd had to register the phone online and he did so with a false name and gave 1060 West Addison Street in Chicago as his home address. Wrigley Field. Palmer pulled down a menu and punched in a preloaded phone number. When the person answered, Palmer said, "It's me. Run it," and hung up. He turned the phone off and put it back into his pocket.

On the other end, Mike Donovan hung up and turned back to his computer monitor. He pulled up the story, proofread it again, and clicked "Send."

CHAPTER THIRTY-SIX

Rian pulled the BMW into her driveway and checked the time on the dashboard clock. Nestled beneath the canopy of live oaks that lined her street, her house was still dimly lit even though the sun was beginning to rise. The glowing orange lights on the clock told her that it was 5:39 a.m. She switched off the car and grabbed her gym bag from the back seat. As she circled the rear of the car, she was startled by the image of a man standing on her front porch. She froze as the man stepped forward, and it took her a few seconds to realize it was Sam.

"Jesus, McKinney," she said as the adrenaline began to subside. "You scared the shit out of me. What the hell are you doing here?"

Sam stepped forward, his expression blank. "Where were you?" he asked. "I called, but you didn't answer."

"My knee was acting up again, so I went over to the club to work out on the elliptical," Rian said. Several local businessmen had gotten together and purchased an old warehouse and turned it into a private fitness club. Rian had bought a membership several months ago and had a key so she could use the facility at any time.

"Where's your phone?" Sam asked.

"I left it. I didn't count on anyone calling at this hour," Rian said as she walked toward him. As she did, she noticed he was holding the newspaper in his hand. She looked back at him and stopped walking.

"What's going on?" she asked.

"I think you should come in and read this," Sam said as he held the folded paper up. Rian shrugged and brushed past him, wondering why he was waiting on the porch for her when he had a key to the house. He followed her inside and watched as she tossed the gym bag onto the table and headed over to make coffee.

"Rian," he said sternly. She turned and looked at him, the annoyance obvious on her face. He opened the paper, turned it to face her, and slid it across the counter. Rian could see the headline from across the room. POLICE EXPLORE LINK BETWEEN BIRMINGHAM AND AREA MURDERS, it read.

Rian's expression turned from annoyance to quizzical.

"So?" she said. "That's not a surprise."

"Read the article. Particularly the paragraph in the middle."

Rian sat on a bar stool and scanned the opening paragraphs of the article which recounted the local homicides and the fact that the police were comparing these murders to a series of unsolved murders in Birmingham several years earlier. Midway through the article, Rian saw the part that Sam had referred to.

"Investigators are exploring any common connections, and sources close to the investigation have revealed a possible link to Chief Assistant Public Defender Rian Coulter. A vehicle belonging to Brianna Larson was found parked in Ms. Coulter's private parking space at the Justice Center after the murder. Ms. Coulter was a private attorney in Birmingham during the time of the previous crimes and investigators are interested in learning whether Ms. Coulter has information relevant to the investigation. Ms. Coulter has refused to comment. The sources spoke with the *Herald* on condition of anonymity."

"God DAMN it," Rian shouted, slamming her hand down on the counter. "That son-of-a-bitch Palmer did this."

"Did what?" Sam asked.

Rian was pacing around the kitchen, gesturing with her hands. "He showed up in the office yesterday unannounced wanting to see me. 'Just a few questions' he says."

"What did he want?"

"To bullshit me mostly. He wanted to know if I worked in Birmingham, but he already knew I did. He wanted to know which partners at the firm I worked with and whether they did any criminal work, but I'm sure he knew that, too. Then he wanted the names of any clients we'd handled criminal cases for."

"What did you tell him?"

"I told him I couldn't remember, which is true, but even if I did I couldn't disclose them because it's confidential."

"Okay, so how'd you leave it with him?"

"Told him to have a nice day and showed him the door, that's how. He gave me some crap about whether I had considered that if it's the same guy that he might remember me, trying to scare me."

"That's not unreasonable," Sam said.

"Oh, no, not you, too," Rian said. "He's trying to play me, can't you see that?"

"Do you know anything?" asked Sam.

"No, Sam, I don't. I don't know a damn thing. I left Ashton, Baker because the whole deal freaked me and everyone else in Birmingham out."

"I don't like it," he said.

Before Rian could respond, her phone buzzed on the counter. She picked it up, looked at it, and rolled her eyes. "Oh *great*," she said, sarcastically. She turned the phone toward Sam so he could read the identity of the caller. It was Jack Brown, Rian's boss. She let it go to voicemail without answering.

"Jack'll be pissed," said Sam, suppressing a smile.

"Let him. Maybe he'll do me a favor and fire me," she said as she headed upstairs to the shower. Sam watched her go, then reread the article as Rian's phone buzzed again with a call from Jack Brown. Sam let himself out, wishing that he could be a fly on the wall of the meeting between Rian and Jack.

* * *

Rian stopped for coffee on the way to work and pulled into her parking space right at 8:00. She wasn't late, but had deliberately not come in early, knowing that the first order of business was likely a tense confrontation with Jack about the office "image." She let herself in through the back door and went straight to her office. As expected, Abby appeared in the doorway, and Rian looked up when she heard Abby sniff.

"Abby, are you crying? Are you okay?" she asked. Abby burst into tears and wobbled into the office. Rian got up and put her arms around her.

"It's just so awful," Abby blurted out between sobs.

"It's okay, Abby," Rian said. "It'll blow over in a couple of days." Abby snapped her head up off Rian's shoulder and stepped back.

"What an awful thing to say," she said and started crying again. "How could you be so insensitive?"

Insensitive?

"Abby," she said, "they have their information wrong. Palmer will realize it and that will be the end of it."

Abby stared at her and her eyes suddenly grew wide.

"You don't know, do you?" she asked. "Oh, God. You don't know."

"Know what?" Rian asked, a feeling of dread beginning to creep into her consciousness.

"Barry Sellers was killed this morning."

"What?" Rian gasped. "When, how? What happened?"

"Someone ran him over this morning on Broward Avenue. A hit and run. Jack's been trying to reach you all morning."

Guilt washed over Rian like a wave. So Jack was trying to reach her to tell her about Barry, not to bitch at her for tarnishing the image of the Public Defender.

"Oh my God," she said, collapsing into her chair and putting her face in her hands. She thought of Barry's wife Angela and their little girl, Gracie. They had been through a scare earlier in the year when it was thought that Gracie had a tumor behind her eye. Fortunately, it hadn't been true and Rian knew that Angela was trying to get pregnant again. Her phone buzzed and she pulled it from her purse. This time, she took Jack's call.

"Where the hell have you been?" Jack said when she answered.

"I just walked in. I'll be right there," Rian said, sheepishly.

Rian hugged Abby again and stepped into the hallway. Jack's office was next to hers, but she paused to look at Barry Sellers's office across the hall. She could hear other staff members sniffling and crying nearby. She turned and stepped to Jack's office, knocking rapidly twice, then entered without waiting for a response.

Jack was sitting behind his desk with his elbows on the desk and his fingers steepled before him. He wore a crisp white dress shirt and, as always, his red suspenders. His red and grey striped tie was pulled down and his collar was unbuttoned. His steel grey hair was unkempt, which was unusual for him. Jack glanced at Rian when she entered, but said nothing as she walked in and sat on the other side of the desk. She could see the morning edition of the *Herald* on the corner of his desk.

After a long silence, Jack lowered his hands and looked at Rian.

"You heard about Barry?" he asked.

Rian nodded. "Abby just told me," she said. "Do we know anything?"

"Not a lot. I just hung up with Sheriff Milam. Seems Barry took his morning jog early this morning and got hit on Broward not far from his house. No one saw it, but apparently someone in a house nearby called 911 and said they saw a light colored pickup truck. No license plate."

"Not much to go on," Rian commented.

Jack looked away and was silent for a long moment. He looked back at Rian and said, "Milam thinks it might have been intentional."

"Intentional?" Rian said incredulously. "Why in the hell would anybody want to kill Barry Sellers?"

"I don't know. Disgruntled client, maybe?"

Rian started to respond, then got Jack's double entendre. Her eyes flashed.

"Look, Jack . . ." she started, but he held up his hand and cut her off.

"Rian, I know how the other side works. I know Palmer was here yesterday and obviously didn't get what he wanted from you. Now he's trying to ratchet up the pressure on you. I get it."

Rian relaxed and eased back in her chair. He was on her side after all. "I just wish you'd brought it to me yesterday. We could've done something proactive and headed things off. We'll be under siege today and this thing with Barry on top of it."

Guilt washed over Rian again. She looked at Jack and her smile thanked him for standing with her. "What do you need me to do?" she asked.

"Give the press a 'no comment,'" he said. "With any luck the bozos in Tallahassee will do something to take us off the front page," he said.

"What about Barry?" Rian asked.

"I'm going by to see Angie this morning. I'll buzz you when I'm leaving if you want to come. Take a look at his caseload and make sure we have the immediate stuff covered for the next few days, then reassign everything else."

Rian got up to leave and paused at the door. Jack was back with his fingers steepled, staring down at his desk. "Jack?" she said. He cocked his head up at her. "Thanks," she said.

Jack smiled tiredly. "I'm getting too old for this shit," he said.

* * *

Rian and Abby spent the rest of the morning checking Barry Sellers's calendar and arranging for someone to cover any hearings that he had on his calendar for the next week. Barry had no trials scheduled in the next three weeks, so those cases could be reassigned to other attorneys in the office. He did have several important motion hearings on his book, and Rian made calls to the opposing attorneys asking for their consent to continue those hearings. She then contacted the assigned judges and requested continuances of the hearings until the cases could be reassigned.

In the afternoon, Rian and Jack met with the entire office staff to discuss the division of Barry's caseload as well as the news story that had come out that day. Everyone was instructed not to talk to any reporters and warned of the possibility that they could be contacted at home or elsewhere away from the office.

It was after 6:00 when Rian stepped across the hall and into Barry Sellers's office. For a long while she stood there, looking at the pictures of his daughter, his diplomas and certificates on the wall. The files and papers on his desk looked as though he'd just gone home for the day and would be back tomorrow, ready to pick up right where he'd left off. His clients wouldn't care; he was appointed to represent indigent defendants, and someone else would be assigned to their cases shortly. The judicial process would grind on and Barry Sellers would soon be forgotten by everyone but his family.

Rian put the file boxes that she'd brought with her on the corner of Barry's desk and began to pack up the pictures, paperweights, and mementos on his desk. She heard a sound and looked up to see Abby in the doorway wearing jeans and a Florida Gators sweatshirt holding two more file boxes.

"I figured you'd be here and that you needed some help," she said.

Rian smiled at her. "I didn't want Angela to have to come and do this," she said. "Thanks, Abby." Together they packed the few personal items that Barry had in his office and carried them out to Rian's car. Rian made one last sweep of the office and was about to leave when she noticed the closet in the corner. She opened it and noted that it was empty except for some legal pads and an old, battered green canvas duffel bag on the bottom. She grabbed it and threw it into her trunk along with the other boxes.

After making sure Abby got to her car safely, Rian walked back to her own car and climbed in. She unlocked the brackets in the ceiling and hit the button that activated the roof that folded itself neatly into the compartment behind the back seat. It was a nice night to drive with the top down, and she looked forward to feeling the wind in her hair and the smell of the salt air from the Gulf on the drive home.

Her phone buzzed and she looked at the caller ID screen that said "Private." She'd had two other calls from "Private" earlier in the day that she'd let go to voicemail. She hit the ignore button and started the car, turning up the satellite radio and gunning the engine as she left the garage and headed up Claggett Avenue.

As Rian left, a white pickup truck pulled away from the curb and drove down Claggett Avenue, three cars behind.

CHAPTER THIRTY-SEVEN

J.T. Spencer squeezed himself into the crowded elevator and stared blankly at his reflection in the polished chrome door as it closed. It was hot and, when combined with his nervousness and the hustling from building to building for meetings, he was sweating profusely. He dabbed at the sweat on his forehead with his handkerchief as the elevator deposited him in the basement of the Senate Office Building. He exited and ducked into the men's room quickly to splash water onto his face. Composed, he strode as confidently as he could into the room and the meeting of the Senate Republican Caucus.

The Florida Senate had forty members and, this session, twenty-seven of them were Republicans, including Spencer. With a solid majority in the House of Representatives as well as the Governor's Mansion, the Republican Party now dominated every facet of the Florida political landscape. Republicans held all of the committee chairs in the legislature, special interest funds flowed unceasingly into the incumbents' reelection accounts, and the party leadership was poised to embark upon an ambitious legislative agenda that would undoubtedly leave its mark on the state for decades.

As a freshman senator, Spencer was unaccustomed to the intense pressure from lobbyists and special interest groups that began long before the session even started. He'd attended the freshman orientation shortly after the election, or "rookie school," as Governor Chambers referred to it, and been assigned his office in the Senate Office Building. He'd had only a few weeks to hire his staff, set up his district office back in Pensacola, and scrounge around Tallahassee for a place to live during the two-month session set to begin the next week.

Almost immediately, Spencer had been bombarded with proposed legislation drafted by nearly every conceivable special interest group, and his calendar was rapidly filling with appointments with lobbyists wanting his commitment to vote in favor various proposals. It was a lot to digest, and Spencer felt overwhelmed, though he desperately tried not to show it.

As he entered the room, Spencer recognized many of his Republican colleagues, but there were an equal number of men he didn't know. They appeared to know him, however, and quickly moved to shake his hand. There were representatives of several insurance companies, chambers of commerce, political action committees, and even the National Rifle Association, all of whom warmly congratulated him and said how much they were looking forward to working with him. The energy doubled when the governor himself appeared, and Spencer silently laughed as he was nearly mauled by the crowd in the crush to see and touch Arden Chambers. Soon, the lobbyists cleared the room, and Chambers walked over and put his arm around Spencer's shoulder.

"Well, Senator, are you all settled in? Ready to get your feet wet?" he said, much to the delight of the others.

"Governor, only one of us can walk on water, and it's certainly not me," he responded. Chambers and the other senators howled with laughter. Chambers hugged his shoulder and patted him briskly on the back.

"See there, fellas? I told you he was special. Old J.T. here is cut from the same cloth as I am. He's gonna do us all proud." After several more minutes of mingling and small talk, Chambers pulled Spencer aside for a private conversation.

"I want you to be the point man for 1930," he said, referring to the number of the Senate Bill that would remove oversight of the legal profession from the Florida Bar and place it with the legislature. Chambers himself had introduced the bill before the election.

"Me?" Spencer said, stunned. "Why me? Governor, I have no clout at all."

"You're better off than you think, J.T.," said Chambers. "You just do like I tell you and manage this thing through, and you'll have all the clout that you can handle. Okay?" All J.T. could do was nod in meek compliance. Chambers smiled, clapped him on the back again, and was off, glad-handing and waving as he left the room. The doors were closed and locked, and Senator Victor Fernandez, the Senate President and Chair of the caucus, called the meeting to order.

"Ladies and gentlemen, let's get started," he said. "We have a lot to cover today." As the senators and the caucus staff members took their seats, Fernandez continued. "Let's start with Senate Bill 119," he said and looked directly at Spencer. "Senator Spencer, I understand that you'll be taking over as sponsor of the bill."

All eyes turned to J.T. He swallowed hard and responded in a surprisingly confident tone, "Yes, Senator, that is correct."

"All right then," Fernandez continued. "Senators, we all know what a priority this bill is for the Governor. We can expect significant opposition from all of the legal groups, so we all have to stand firmly behind Senator Spencer on this. We clearly have the numbers, so there's no need to negotiate whatsoever. I've spoken with the Speaker and he's assured me that the House will do the same." Fernandez scanned the room, searching out each senator. "We hold the line on this. No amendments, no mercy. Understood?" Everyone nodded and murmured their agreement, then quickly moved to the next item on the agenda.

CHAPTER THIRTY-EIGHT

Rian stared at the files on her desk, but couldn't focus on them. She absently twirled a pencil between her index and middle fingers so that it made a tapping sound on the desk, but she wasn't even aware of it. All morning she had tried to work, but the meeting with Palmer and the subsequent news story had competed for dominance of her attention. She had plenty of work to keep herself busy, but each time she tried to engage, her mind drifted back to the question of whether there was any connection between her and the murders in Birmingham and here in Pensacola. Despite her efforts, she had come up empty, but the sense of unease inside her was growing.

Rian picked up the phone and dialed a number. Almost immediately, a bright, perky female voice answered. "Good morning, Ashton, Baker, Pennington and Moring. How may I direct your call?"

"Amanda Baker, please," Rian said.

"Who may I say is calling?" bright and perky asked.

Rian had forgotten this part and she struggled for a name. "Uh, Penelope Martin," she said, plucking a name out of thin air.

"May I ask what the call is in regard to?" was the response, a little less cheerful. This always irritated Rian and she was tempted to say no, but didn't want this call to be memorable.

"I'm a friend of hers from college," she said as cheerfully as she could. "I'm in town for a few days." Rian heard a few clicks, two rings, then got Amanda's voicemail.

"Hey, Amanda, it's Rian Coulter. Can you give me a call on my cell when you get a chance?" she said without any urgency in her voice. She left her cell number and hung up. She sat thoughtfully for another minute, then retrieved Barry Sellers's home number from her iPhone. More than a week had passed since Barry's funeral and she still dreaded making this call. A small, weak voice answered.

"Angela? Hi, it's Rian Coulter," she said.

"Oh, hello," Angela said in a barely audible voice. Rian could feel the pain of her husband's death through the phone line.

"I'm sorry to bother you. Is this a bad time? I can call back later."

"No, no. It's okay," Angela responded, a little more composed.

"I just wanted to let you know that I have Barry's personal things from his office. I can drop them by whenever it's convenient. I also have the life insurance and pension fund information you requested."

"Um, okay. Thank you," Angela said, her voice breaking. "If it's okay, can I call you, uh, a little later?"

"Absolutely," said Rian. "Angela, you call me anytime, day or night, if there's anything you need, okay? There's no rush on this."

"Okay. Thank you, Rian. Thank you for calling." Angela was starting to cry and could barely get the words out. Rian hung up and tried to imagine the pain that Angela Sellers must be feeling. She turned to her computer and busied herself for thirty minutes with an outline for the deposition she was to take the next day when her phone rang. Rian glanced at the screen and saw an unfamiliar number, but the area code indicated the call was from Birmingham so she answered.

"Hey, Rian. Sorry I missed your call. I was in a meeting," Amanda Baker said.

"No problem. I was wondering if I could ask you to do me a favor," Rian said.

"Sure, anything."

"Does the firm still use LegalPro?" Rian asked. LegalPro was the case management software that allowed the law firm to categorize all cases and store information about each case. Information concerning the names of the parties, the attorneys responsible for the case, and the type of case was entered into the system when the file was created. All other documents were either generated by the system or scanned into it so that a complete, virtual file was maintained that could be accessed remotely from anywhere. Users logged in through a secure Internet portal and could access the files from home or while traveling. When Rian worked there, a hard copy of the file was also kept as a backup.

"Yeah, unfortunately," Amanda said. "We went through a huge upgrade last year and it was a nightmare. Why?"

"Could you pull up a list of my cases? Not just the ones that were assigned to me, but the ones that I worked on?" Rian asked.

"I'm not sure. They archived a bunch of older stuff to make room on the server, but I can check. What's going on?"

"I'm applying for board certification and they need an incredible amount of detail about the types of work that I've done," Rian lied.

"Oh, okay. No problem. How soon do you need it?"

"No big rush, but I'd appreciate anything you can do. Also, you'd better not mention this to anyone else either, unless they've relaxed the rules up there on doing unbillable work," Rian said, and they both laughed. Amanda promised to let Rian know what she could find as soon as possible and they hung up.

Rian often grabbed a quick lunch over at Sally's, a small deli a short walk from the office. Although the place was a hangout for the local legal establishment, she could usually sit at a small table in the back and quietly work on a file or check emails on her phone in relative peace.

Upon entering, she soon realized that this wasn't going to be one of those days as lawyers, some of whom she barely even knew, immediately approached her to comment on her newfound notoriety. One of them actually handed her a business card, in the event she "needed assistance." As Rian looked around, she saw secretaries, clerk's office personnel, and other courthouse workers glancing at her as though they, too, wanted her to know they'd read the article about her. She knew they were mostly just curious, but the unwanted attention bothered her. She ordered her grilled chicken and artichoke wrap to go.

Abby was at lunch when Rian returned, but had left a message taped to Rian's computer monitor that Angela Sellers had called back and apologized for not being able to talk earlier. Rian could bring Barry's stuff by any time.

It was past five but Rian was still at the office when Amanda Baker called back.

"It took some digging, but because you were in the old system, I could pull your information up from the archive," she said. "I ran a name search for every file that your name was associated with, whether or not you were the primary attorney on the case."

"Fantastic," Rian said. "Can you send me the list?"

"I'm emailing it to you now. Let me know if it's not what you need or if I can help further."

"Thanks, Amanda. See you soon. Give Bri a kiss for me," Rian said and clicked off. A few seconds later her computer chimed, indicating she had a new email. She opened the email message and the attached document and sent the attachment to Abby's printer. She could hear the document start to print at Abby's desk and, when it was finished, Rian deleted the email and the attachment from the system.

Grabbing a Diet Coke from the small refrigerator in her office, Rian sat down to review the list of matters she had worked on in Birmingham, focusing initially on criminal matters only. There was the tax fraud case that she'd remembered and mentioned to Palmer as well as a few other assorted criminal matters, but nothing proved to be a revelation to Rian at first.

She scanned the list again, but nothing stood out, so she put the list into her briefcase and left the office.

A few minutes later, she pulled into the driveway of a house in Silver Cove, a community of mostly starter homes that had been built before the real estate market had crashed in the recession. Most of the homes were small and built on zero lot lines with little yard to speak of. Rian sat in her car for a moment, contemplating the scene around her. A child's walker was on the sidewalk and several toys were strewn about the yard. Barry Sellers's silver Toyota Camry was parked in the driveway. Rian shook her head slightly, still not quite believing what had happened the week before. With a sigh, she got out and grabbed the two file boxes from the back seat and headed to the door.

Angela Sellers looked as though she'd aged ten years. She asked Rian to set the boxes on a table in the adjoining room, and they sat and talked for a few minutes while Rian explained the life insurance forms and the options that Angela had for the funds Barry had accumulated in his pension account. It wasn't much, and Rian knew that, without Barry's salary, Angela, Aiden, and Gracie would have a hard time.

"I'm thinking of moving back to Mom and Dad's in Ocala," Angela said. Rian didn't know what to say, so she simply gave Angela a long and heartfelt hug. She thanked Rian for coming and walked her to the door.

Rian started down the walkway, then turned back. "Hang on a second, Angela," she said. "There's one more thing in the car that I forgot." She popped the trunk and removed the old canvas duffel bag that she'd found in the closet in Barry's office and brought it to Angela, who was still waiting at the door.

"What's that?" Angela asked.

"What do you mean?" said Rian.

"What's that bag for?"

Rian was confused and she frowned. "I, um, found this in the closet in Barry's office," she said, wishing she had bothered to look inside before this awkward moment. "Isn't it his?"

Angela shook her head. "I've never seen it before. I'm sure it's not Barry's. What's in it?"

Rian felt increasingly uncomfortable and just wanted to get out of there. "You know what?" she said. "This probably belongs to the office. I must've just grabbed it by mistake." She turned and quickly headed back to the car. "I'll call and check on you and Gracie in a few . . ." she said over her shoulder, but stopped when she noticed that Angela had already closed the door.

Rian tossed the duffel back into the car and headed straight home. She brought it inside and set it on the coffee table while she attended to Mannix, who was loudly complaining for his dinner. Grabbing a beer from the refrigerator, Rian sat on the couch and stared at the bag in front of her. It was olive green and made of canvas with handles and a strap of the same type material. Although it looked as though it could have been an old military bag, no name or other identifying information was stenciled on the outside. It was dirty and had what looked like small, old oil stains in several places. She debated whether to open it or not, then leaned forward, unzipped it, and looked inside.

Rian reached for her phone instantly and called Sam.

"I have a major problem," she said when he answered. Sam could hear the tension in her voice.

"I'll be there in five minutes," he said.

CHAPTER THIRTY-NINE

Rian and Sam looked down at the inventory of the duffel bag that was laid out on Rian's coffee table. She had covered the table with a plastic tablecloth that she had bought for the tables on the deck and she and Sam had on latex gloves that Rian just happened to have on hand. They had removed the items in the duffel bag and laid them out side by side on the table; several rolls of green nylon rope, three rolls of duct tape, a large buck knife, a pair of sandals, two clear plastic cups from the Border Line Lounge and, most disturbing of all, a round wooden stick that appeared to be a sawed off broom handle. One end of it was stained.

Rian sat on the couch and put her head in her hands, then ran her fingers through her hair. "Okay," she said, clapping her hands together, "we have to find out why the hell this was in Barry's office and who put it there."

"No," Sam said sternly. "*We* don't have to do anything. *You* need to call the Sheriff's Office right now and turn this stuff over to them."

"Not until I find out who this came from. What if this stuff belongs to a client of the PD's office? What if *he's* a client of the PD's office?"

"Who cares? This is likely evidence of a crime, or multiple crimes, and you have a duty to stop this asshole from killing someone else if you can."

"My *duty* is to protect the confidences and secrets of my clients," she shot back.

"He's not *your* client."

"Don't bullshit me, Sam. If he's a client of Barry's or someone else's in the office, it's the same thing as being my client. Whatever knowledge Barry had is imputed to everyone else that works there. You of all people should know that."

"Rian . . ." Sam started, but she cut him off.

"I think I should call Arlene tonight and see if she knows anything about this stuff," she said. Arlene was Barry Sellers's secretary. She had taken a week off after Barry's death, but was back at work helping to parcel his files out to other lawyers before she was reassigned to another position. Rian reached for her iPhone, but Sam snatched it out of her hand.

"Wait just a minute," he said. "That's an extraordinarily bad idea."

"Why?" she asked, her eyes flashing.

"Because you need to think this through first and sort out the ethical considerations, not to mention the possible crimes that you may be committing here. If this gets out, and it will, all sorts of hell will rain down on you."

Rian had to acknowledge that Sam had a point, even if she was pissed at him at the moment. She got up, snapped off the gloves, and walked to the kitchen, then back to the couch. She stood with her arms crossed in front of her.

"So, what do I do?" she asked.

Sam didn't hesitate. "My first suggestion is that you turn this crap over to Palmer immediately. Since you're apparently unwilling to follow that advice, I think you should try to find out as quietly as possible which of Barry's cases this stuff fits." Rian nodded slowly in adoption of his plan.

"Who else knows you have this duffel bag?" Sam asked.

"Abby knows because she was there when I found it. Arlene knows that we cleared out Barry's office so if she knew it was in the closet, then she knows I have it. I doubt she knows anything about what's in it. Neither does Abby. I just opened it myself for the first time tonight."

Rian put the gloves back on and they carefully placed the items back into the duffel and zipped it shut. She took it to the coat closet by the front door, put it on the floor inside, and walked back to where Sam was standing.

"Thanks," she said. "Sorry if I was bitchy. Serial killers bring out the worst in me, I guess." She wrapped her arms around his waist and buried her face in his shoulder. He folded his arms around her, and they held each other for a long moment.

"I do have one other suggestion," he said. Rian leaned her head back and looked at him.

"What?"

"Hire a lawyer," he said.

CHAPTER FORTY

"You wanted to see me, Ms. Coulter?" Arlene Daigle asked apprehensively. Rian looked up from her desk at the thin woman in her mid-fifties standing nervously in her doorway. She smiled to put Arlene at ease, then got up and walked over to meet her.

"I did, yes. Please come in, Arlene," she said, motioning to a chair in front of her desk with one hand and closing the office door behind them with the other. Rian enjoyed a good relationship with the staff in the Public Defender's Office. She had gone to bat for them for salary increases and fought for them when budget cuts threatened to eliminate clerical positions. Other than the investigators and one paralegal, the entire staff was female, and they connected with and admired Rian for what she had achieved. Jack Brown was more the aloof boss whom they hardly knew.

Rian normally conducted such meetings from behind her desk, keeping the barrier between herself and the staff member unmistakable. This time, she took the seat next to Arlene with only a small table separating them. Rian sensed her unease and smiled again.

"How are you holding up, Arlene?" she asked with sincere concern. Arlene had been with the Public Defender's Office for over fifteen years and had worked for Barry Sellers for the past four. Her performance evaluations had been good, and she was a mother hen to many of the twenty somethings on the staff.

"Okay, I guess," Arlene responded. "I've finished all of the file memoranda for Mr. Sellers's cases and Mr. Owens asked if I would help with scheduling some depositions in a few of the files he has taken on."

While Rian was genuinely interested in how the case reassignments were going and how Arlene was adapting, that wasn't the purpose of this meeting. They chatted for a few more minutes about mundane matters before Rian switched the subject.

"Is there anything that you feel I should know about any of the clients that isn't in the file materials?" she began. Arlene looked puzzled and didn't answer. Rian pressed on. "I'm thinking in terms of the reassignments and whether we've paired the clients with the right attorney. I wouldn't want to put an aggressive career criminal with Amy Johansson, for example," she said, referring to one of the new Assistant Public Defenders who had just been promoted from the Misdemeanor Division. Rian already knew the exact history of each defendant that she had reassigned and had given careful consideration to those factors. She was trying to find a way to ease into the topic she really wanted to discuss with Arlene without raising any alarms. Arlene seemed to be considering her question and was silently shaking her head in response.

"Does anyone in particular stand out in your mind? Anyone unusually aggressive or odd?" Rian asked.

"No. Not more than usual," Arlene said.

This is going nowhere, Rian thought.

"Had Barry received any threats in the last several months?" she asked as matter-of-factly as she could, forcing any anxiety out of her voice as she did. Arlene seemed taken aback by the question.

"Threats? No, not that I know of. Why?" she asked.

"No reason," Rian said, deadpanned. "We're just making sure that we know everything. Are all of Barry's notes in the files?"

"Except for those that he kept on his laptop, they should be," she said. Rian hadn't considered this. Barry Sellers had one of the few laptop computers in the office. Fortunately, it was still in his office and hadn't yet been issued to another attorney.

"Would you mind bringing it to me?" Rian asked and Arlene left, returning a few moments later with a Dell notebook computer.

"I think the password is Aiden32207," she said, referring to Barry's son and his birth date. She handed the laptop to Rian and turned to leave quickly, seemingly eager to escape the office before other subjects could come up. Rian had planned to let Arlene know that they no longer had a position for her, but decided to let it wait for a couple more days. At her age, Rian knew it would be difficult for Arlene to find another job in the legal community and she wanted one more chance to argue with Jack about keeping her.

"Oh, Arlene, one more thing," she said as Arlene reached the doorway. "There was an old green duffel bag in Barry's closet. I figured it was his, but Angela Sellers said that it wasn't. Do you know where it came from? Did some client bring it in?"

"No, but I'll check the inventory log," she said. Rian thanked her and she left.

It was a violation of office policy for the attorneys to keep items that might be evidence in an ongoing case and Rian couldn't imagine that Barry Sellers would have willingly done so. Since the Public Defender's Office was inside the courthouse, all clients had to go through security screening at the entrance. Rian knew that the buck knife in the duffel would have been seized immediately.

She plugged in the laptop and booted it up. In a minute, the ubiquitous Microsoft Windows theme played and Rian entered the password Arlene had given her. She was soon greeted with a photograph of Barry and Angela Sellers at the beach. Taken before Gracie was born, their son Aiden was riding on his daddy's shoulders and they were all smiling broadly; a blissfully happy picture that would never be repeated.

Rian clicked on an icon on the desktop entitled "Case Files." This opened a list of folders arranged alphabetically that Rian immediately recognized as Barry Sellers's active client list. She knew that Barry had seventy-three active cases at the time of his death, but there were only fifty-nine files listed.

She clicked on a few random names and saw that Barry had sub folders in each file entitled "Case Notes." Most had notes of some sort, and it would take a while to go through them all. She surmised that these were Barry's personal notes that he jotted down when thinking about his cases at home or elsewhere away from the office. She read through a few of them, which seemed pretty ordinary, so she logged out and turned off the computer.

Rian's computer chimed, indicating an incoming email message. She clicked on the envelope on the screen and saw that it was an interoffice message from Arlene Daigle: "No property listed on inventory sheet, but I do remember Barry griping about something a client left here. He tried to call the guy, but couldn't reach him." Rian didn't want any sort of paper trail left, electronic or otherwise, so she picked up her phone and buzzed Arlene's desk.

"I got your message," she said when Arlene answered. "Do you know who the client was or when this happened?"

"I don't remember the guy but it was a couple of months ago. It was before that time you had to cover his plea day because Angela went into labor with Grace." Rian considered this for a moment. She could get a list of the defendants who appeared for pleas that day from the clerk's office, but it would be faster for Arlene to retrieve it. She opted for the latter.

"Can you print me a list of Barry's docket for that day I covered for him?" Arlene said she would and ten minutes later, it was on Rian's desk.

Three days later, Arlene Daigle was laid off from the Public Defender's Office due to budget constraints.

CHAPTER FORTY-ONE

Sanchez knocked on the doorframe and entered the office as Palmer looked up from his desk. He handed a manila folder to Palmer as he sat in the side chair opposite the desk.

"We went through Sellers's caseload for the past year," he said as Palmer opened the file and began to flip through the pages. "Looks pretty typical for a PD handling felonies. Burglaries, agg assaults, sexual batteries. Any one of these dirtbags could've had an ax to grind with him, L.T."

"Any of them file a 3.850 motion?" Palmer asked, referring to the criminal procedure rule that allowed a convicted defendant to seek a new trial by claiming that his lawyer had been ineffective at trial. It was a frequent tactic for convicted felons to continue to protest their innocence and blame their "incompetent" lawyer for losing the case.

"Yeah, but we checked and they're all still locked up," Sanchez said. Palmer closed the file and stared at it on the desk.

"Maybe it isn't related, L.T. If you still think Coulter is the key, then this could just be a coincidence. Maybe we should just let Persons keep it," Sanchez said, referring to the Crimes Against Persons unit in the Sheriff's Department that usually handled such matters.

Sanchez had a point, Palmer acknowledged to himself. It could be a rabbit trail they were chasing that risked wasting valuable task force resources, but his instincts told him that Barry Sellers's death had something to do with his investigation of the serial murders.

Other than the fact that Barry Sellers and Rian Coulter both worked in the same office and she was his superior, there seemed to be no connection between them. They could spend weeks running down all of the dirtbags whom Barry Sellers had come into contact with and still end up right back where they were now. He didn't have the manpower for that, and he was starting to feel pressure from his superiors to break something in this case.

On the other hand, he thought, had he been wrong about Rian Coulter being targeted by the killer? Palmer had to now question that, but parking a victim's car in Coulter's parking place in an otherwise empty garage seemed far too specific to be just a coincidence.

Palmer was at a crossroads and he knew it. He threw his pen across the desk in frustration and sat back in his chair.

"Shit," he muttered, handing the file back to Sanchez. "Pull all of Coulter's cases over the same time period and see if there's anything in common. If nothing jumps out, give it back to Persons.

* * *

Rian walked into the break room and poured herself another cup of coffee. As she did, she picked up on a conversation that three other Assistant Public Defenders were having nearby.

"He's lucky he wasn't killed," one of the young lawyers was saying. "I just hope I don't get the case if they catch the fucker." He turned and saw Rian and looked embarrassed when he noticed that she'd overheard him. "Sorry," he said.

"What are you guys talking about?" she asked.

"Somebody took a shot at a deputy sheriff this morning," the young lawyer said. Rian hadn't heard about it. "Abandoned car out on County Road 79, and when the deputy got out to investigate, somebody shot at him from the woods," he continued. "The bullet just grazed his temple. Turned out the car was stolen," he said.

"Wow. Glad he's a bad shot. A cop killer case would probably land on my desk," she said. "Who was the deputy?" she asked as she turned to leave.

"It was that guy who used to work court security here. Vince," said one of the other lawyers.

Rian stopped. "Vince Peters?" she asked, and the others nodded. Rian walked away feeling badly for Vince, whom she liked immensely. She hadn't seen Vince since . . .

Suddenly, it hit her.

The shock of it was as though someone had poured ice down her back and she stopped dead in her tracks in the hallway to catch her breath. Abby saw the look on her face and asked what was wrong, but Rian didn't even hear the question. She almost ran back to her office and locked the door behind her.

She hadn't even made it to her desk before Abby buzzed her. "Rian, are you okay? Is everything all right?" she asked when Rian picked up the phone.

"I'm fine, Abby, really. I just remembered something that I needed to research quickly. Can you hold all of my calls?" she asked and hung up. She grabbed her briefcase and pulled out the list of the cases that she'd handled for Barry Sellers months ago when he was out because his child had been born. She ran down the list and found the name she was looking for; Henry Lee Duncan. She remembered the guy. He was charged with burglary and had been late for court. She'd only had a few moments with him and remembered that there was an odd demeanor about him when he showed up. Rian wracked her brain trying to remember the details of their conversation.

She picked up her phone and buzzed Abby. "I need you to pull a closed file for me," she said when Abby answered. "The client's name is Henry Lee Duncan. It's one of those cases I covered for Barry when he was out the day Gracie was born."

"Okay," Abby said, "but it may be in archives. They moved all of Barry's physical case files. I can call over there . . ."

"No!" Rian said, cutting her off, wincing because she knew she'd been too abrupt. "I want you to go get it yourself. Quickly and quietly. Tell no one else, Abby, do you understand?"

The tone in Rian's voice quelled any response from Abby other than a simple "Okay."

While she waited, Rian pulled out Barry Sellers's laptop and booted it up. She clicked on the case files folder and pulled up Barry's active client folder list. There was no folder named Duncan. Puzzled, she went back to the main list to see if there was a folder for closed files, but there was none.

Come on, Barry. Help me out here. Where did you put the file notes when you were finished?

She clicked through several files to see if one could have been misnamed by chance, but came up empty. As a last resort, she went to the trash bin icon and clicked on it. There was the closed files folder.

Barry didn't take out the trash.

Rian clicked on the file and found a long list of folders arranged alphabetically. She scrolled down until she found one named *Duncan* and clicked on it. She quickly found Barry's initial notes in his own shorthand about his client Henry Lee Duncan:

> "Clt clms no pvs record – "misunderstanding" during divorce in Bham yrs ago – no conv. Working temp as landscaper for past 3 mos. Not B&E – door unlocked and trying to locate "vic" to discuss landscaping. Clt evasive when answering – psych?" Depo of vic?"

Holy shit.

Rian noted that Barry had attempted to contact the prosecuting attorney to discuss the case and had even made a note to call Duncan's ex-wife. Abby's distinctive knock on the door interrupted her and, remembering that she'd locked the door, Rian got up and opened it.

Abby started to enter and Rian stopped her.

"Is that the Duncan file?" she asked, pointing to the file in Abby's hand. A bit taken aback, Abby simply nodded, handed the file to Rian, and went back to her desk. Rian realized that Abby's feelings were hurt, but she didn't have time to deal with that at the moment.

She opened the file and noted the sparse details inside. There was no criminal history on Duncan, and her own personal notes about the plea bargain that she'd worked out for him were inside. She pulled out the arrest report which also contained few details, but Rian didn't care. What she was looking for was there. Duncan's physical description showed him to be 5'10" tall, weighing 205 pounds with blond hair and blue eyes. He had a scar on the right side of his chest.

That fits, she thought. But she had to be certain.

She went back to her briefcase and pulled out the list of cases that Amanda had sent her from Ashton Baker. She found the one she was looking for on page five. Donny Ray Cooper. He was the son of one of the firm's largest construction clients, a spoiled, privileged brat who'd partied his way through school and was working for his father as a landscaper. He was going through a divorce and had come home drunk one night and threatened to kill his wife. Rian had represented him and, after several calls to the right people by Donny Ray's father and Hammond Baker, the charges had been dismissed and his record expunged from the court files. She'd only met with Donny Ray a couple of times but, if Rian was right, Donny Ray Cooper and Henry Lee Duncan were one and the same.

She picked up her iPhone and started to make a call, then hesitated. Cell phones were notoriously unsecure and she didn't want to take any chance that someone could intercept her calls. She grabbed her land line and placed a call to Ashton, Baker, taking several deep breaths to calm herself while she waited for Amanda to answer. Fortunately, she was in.

"Hey, Amanda, it's Rian," she said as cheerfully as she could when Amanda came on the line. They chatted for a few minutes even though Rian's heart was trying its best to jump through her chest. Finally, she couldn't stand it any longer and interrupted Amanda in mid-sentence.

"Amanda," she said a little too abruptly, but Amanda stopped talking. Rian softened her voice. "Sorry, I'm just a little short of time. I didn't mean to be rude. I was calling to see if you could do me one more favor."

"Sure," Amanda said without any hurt in her voice. "Anything, you know that."

"I've been over the list and was hoping that I could get you to pull one of those old files for me."

"Which one?" Amanda asked.

"The client was named Cooper, Donald Raymond Cooper," Rian said, holding her breath in fear that Amanda would recognize the name even though the case arose years before Amanda went to work there.

"Sure, no problem," Amanda said without hesitation. "I can bring it with me next week."

"Next week?" Rian asked, confused.

"Yeah, when Bri and I come down for the shower. You will be able to come, won't you?"

Shit, Rian thought. Friends of her parents were throwing Brian and Amanda a wedding shower in Tallahassee next week. Rian had forgotten all about it.

"I wouldn't miss it," she said. "I can't wait to see you and Bri. Just bring the file with you then, that would be great. Thanks," she said even though she couldn't bear the thought of waiting until then to look for the information that she needed from the file.

After she hung up, Rian went back to Barry's laptop and read the addendum that he'd written in his personal file which, according to the date, was about ten days after their initial conference:

> "Clt approached me in pkg lot – wanted me to keep alleged BT. Told him PD does not hold evid but he said BT not seized @ arrest. Green duffel – looked in but didn't inventory. Clt insisted so put in office closet."

Barry Sellers was the only one who knew about the green duffel bag and he was now dead. Rian was convinced he was murdered, although there had been no public announcement of Barry's death as a possible homicide. Vince Peters had been the court security officer when Henry Lee Duncan appeared in court, and someone had tried to kill him earlier in the day. Rian would confirm the details about Donny Ray Cooper's case when she could, but she already knew the dilemma she was facing.

As she contemplated what to do, her computer chimed and she checked her email. She had a new message from Amanda Baker. "Hard copies shredded, but scanned version in archive was small enough to send. See attached," it read. Rian clicked on the paper clip icon at the bottom which opened the attached file. Donny Ray Cooper's arrest report was the third page and it described him as 5'10" tall and weighing 195 pounds with a skull and crossbones tattoo on the right side of his chest. Rian remembered that the firm's policy had been to have photographs of each client in the file and she scrolled through until she found Donny Ray's. He'd had dark hair then and was younger, but the resemblance was unmistakable. It was Henry Lee Duncan.

There was one more thing that Rian needed to do. She opened her web browser and pulled up the *Escambia Herald* website. She searched the name Christy Price and found the series of articles that detailed the girl's murder at the Border Line Lounge the previous spring. Rian clicked through the articles until she found the one containing the composite drawing of the suspect beneath the headline "Have You Seen This Man?" She stared at the face of the man with pale eyes looking back at her from her computer monitor.

Oh my God.

CHAPTER FORTY-TWO

Mike Donovan was putting the finishing touches on an article about possible corruption in the county building inspection department. His deadline was 3:00, and he glanced at the clock on the opposite wall. It was 2:47. He would just make it. His phone buzzed and he paused, annoyed with himself that he'd neglected to hit the Do Not Disturb button to forward calls to his voicemail. He started to ignore it, then reached over and hit the intercom button without missing a beat on his keyboard. "Yeah?" he said and continued typing.

"Mike, call for you on 27," the receptionist said. "Some guy from Birmingham."

"Tell him I'll call him back," Donovan said, still typing. A few seconds passed and she buzzed him back.

"Mike, he says he works the crime desk at the *Birmingham Examiner* and that you definitely will want to talk to him." Donovan snatched up the phone receiver so that anything further that she had to say wouldn't be overheard. He tucked the receiver between his shoulder and jaw. "He says he has some information for you on the murders," the receptionist continued.

"Okay, thanks, Annie," Donovan said and reached over to punch the blinking line. "Donovan," he said with the phone still tucked in his neck.

"Mr. Donovan, this is Jason Thompson. I'm with the *Birmingham Examiner.* I'm following up on a series of unsolved murders up here and have some information I thought would be of interest to you."

"Okay," Donovan said, glancing at the wall clock again and continuing to type.

"I just spoke with a detective with the Birmingham PD. They believe there's a definite connection between the killings up here and the ones y'all have going on there. They think it may be the same guy and have contacted the feds."

"What's the connection between here and Birmingham?" Donovan asked, scanning his monitor for typographical errors and scrolling through his story.

"They were very interested in your article about the defense lawyer down there who used to work here. They think the guy may have been a client of hers or something. What's her name, Colton?"

"Coulter. Rian Coulter," Donovan corrected him.

"Yeah, Coulter. Do you know her or can you put me in touch with her?"

Donovan chuckled to himself. "She's the Chief Assistant Public Defender here," he said. "I doubt seriously if she'll talk to you."

"Well, things may be heating up for her," Thompson said. "They're looking into her, and it wouldn't surprise me if she hears from them herself. The guy told me off the record that the M.O. of the killings there are almost identical to the ones up here."

"What's the detective's name?" Donovan asked.

"Fanning. I don't know what role the feds will have and I'm trying to run that down now."

"Thanks, Jason. I appreciate the call," Donovan said and hung up. He uploaded the county commission story just in time, then pondered the new information he'd just been given. He grabbed his keys and cell phone from the desk and headed for the door.

He grabbed a coffee at the Starbucks drive through a few blocks away, then parked at the plaza overlooking the bay. A few fishermen gave him a passing glance, but paid no further attention to him.

Donovan reached into his pocket and pulled out his prepaid phone, clicked on the only name in the menu and sent a text message: "Need 2 talk." Five minutes passed before the phone buzzed and Donovan flipped it open.

"Got a call from the crime desk guy in Birmingham," he said without any preceding pleasantries. "A detective named Fanning called him and said they're pursuing a connection between their homicides and ours with your girl Coulter as the missing link. Says the details of the killings are the same."

"You can't run with this yet," said Palmer on the other end. "Nothing's confirmed, and leaking it will either scare him off or put her in danger."

"So you already knew about this then," Donovan said. It wasn't really a question.

"Fanning and another guy named Ennis have worked the Birmingham cases," said Palmer. "We've had some video conferences to compare notes, nothing more."

"Look, Palmer, I have a damn job to do, too," Donovan said, his anger rising. "This little 'partnership' of ours seems to be only a one way street in your direction. You're supposed to clue me in."

"I have and I will," said Palmer, his voice tensing.

"They're calling in the feds," said Donovan.

"*What*?" Palmer nearly shouted.

"Didn't know *that*, huh?" Donovan replied sarcastically. "The *News* is on it, and I'll bet you're about to be elbowed out of the way."

"Listen to me, Donovan. The feds are not taking over. Don't run with this until I tell you. Give me the name of the reporter in Birmingham."

"Bullshit," Donovan said. "No, I tell you what; I'm going to do my job. Thanks for nothing."

"I'm telling you, don't leak this," Palmer virtually yelled into the phone.

"Tell you what, Palmer," Donovan said. "How 'bout you kiss my ass?" He flipped the phone shut and threw it into the glove box.

CHAPTER FORTY-THREE

The Rules of Professional Conduct govern the professional actions of all lawyers in Florida. These rules were enacted by The Florida Bar, an organization to which all 90,000 lawyers in the state must be members. Violations of the these rules have led to charges being brought by the Bar against a lawyer and to discipline such as public reprimands or even disbarment by the Supreme Court if the transgression was serious enough.

Lawyers are officers of the court, charged by the rules with a responsibility for the administration of justice. They are also required by the rules to be zealous advocates of their clients' interests and rights. These competing roles frequently conflict with each other, yet the rules of professional responsibility offer little guidance on how to resolve those conflicts. Lawyers and judges are supposed to police themselves and report any violations of the rules by their colleagues to the Bar.

One of these rules, Rule 4.1, clearly states that a fundamental principle in the client-lawyer relationship is that, without a client's consent, a lawyer is prohibited from revealing information related to the representation. The rule of confidentiality applies not only to statements made by the client in confidence but also to "all information relating to the representation, whatever its source."

Rian re-read the rule again, secretly hoping that it would somehow read differently this time. As her resolve settled in, she looked up at Sam, who was staring down at the table in his kitchen that was littered with copies of statutes, cases, and research that he and Rian had compiled over the last several hours. Sam pursed his lips, then began to slowly shake his head. He looked up at Rian and his head shaking increased.

"I don't think it applies," he said.

Rian looked at him incredulously. "What do you mean, you don't think it applies?" she said. "How could it *not* apply?"

Sam leaned back, threw his left arm over the back of the chair and gestured with his right.

"Look, this guy, whoever he is, is not your client. He was Barry Sellers's client, so any information obtained during the representation was obtained by Barry, not by you."

Rian hadn't told Sam that Donny Ray was the killer, only that she was pretty sure that she knew it was a former client of hers. She wasn't sure why she hadn't told him, except that she wanted to sort it all out in her own mind first before dragging Sam into the middle of it.

Rian started to speak, but Sam held his hand up to stop her.

"Let me finish," he said. "You have no reason to protect the confidences of Barry's client. That obligation died with Barry."

"That's bullshit and you know it," Rian said angrily. "The guy was a client of the Public Defender. Any obligation that Barry had to a client of the office extends to me as well. I also filled in for Barry when he was out so, in essence, he was my client, too." She stood and began to pace.

"Yeah, well, if you want to split hairs like that, fine," Sam shot back.

They both remained silent for several minutes before Sam spoke again.

"You know, you could tell me who he is and I could leak it." Rian turned and looked at him, but said nothing. "I have no professional obligation here. I could casually mention it and make sure that the name gets to the right people," he continued.

Rian just stared at him. "How is telling *you* any different from picking up the phone and calling Palmer?" she said. "The rule doesn't say you can't disclose a client's confidence to anyone except your boyfriend."

"So you're willing to risk your whole career to protect some scumbag serial killer? For what? So you and your ACLU buddies can sit around and congratulate each other on how you preserved justice?"

"Spare me the sarcasm," Rian said, her anger rising. "I don't need it. There are higher principles at stake here."

"You're damn right there are," replied Sam, now on his feet, his voice rising as well. "Like protecting the public. You could be putting yourself in danger, too. Have you even bothered to consider that?"

"That's a risk I'll just have to take," she said.

"Oh, yeah, I forgot. You're Superwoman," he said sarcastically.

Rian's vision went white and her temper boiled over. She reached out to slap him, but he anticipated this and grabbed her by the wrist before her hand could reach his face. She tried the other hand, but he grabbed that one also. Resistance was futile so Rian just stood there with her arms in the air and stared coldly at Sam.

"So, what would you do if you were me?" she asked, struggling to keep her voice even.

"I'd give him up in a heartbeat and save my own ass."

"Convenient," Rian said, taking advantage of the distraction brought on by her question to snatch her arms free of Sam's grasp. She walked back to the table and began to gather her purse and briefcase.

"Where the hell are you going?" Sam asked. Rian ignored him and continued to gather her things.

"Just tell me who he is. No one will know where the information came from. He could kill some other unsuspecting woman while you're mulling all this over."

Rian stopped and just looked at him. The smug look on his face made her want to slap him all over again. Instead, she shook her head wordlessly and turned for the door. In an instant, he was behind her and grabbed her left arm with his right, turning her back to face him.

"You do this and the whole world will come down on you. The cops, the Bar, everybody."

"Let go of me," Rian said, almost in a growl. She tried to free her arm, but Sam tightened his grip.

"You're making a huge mistake," he said. Rian tried to free her arm but it wouldn't budge.

"Take your fucking hand off me," she said, but he held her even tighter.

"Look, Rian," he said, restoring the calm in his expression and voice. "You also have a professional obligation to the administration of justice. You're an officer of the court, goddammit."

Rian summoned all of her strength and jerked her arm free of Sam's grasp. She said nothing and turned and reached for the door.

"I'm still your attorney," Sam said, "and I'm advising you to disclose what you know."

Rian had her hand on the door handle, but turned back to give Sam an evil smile.

"You know what? You're fired," she said. Rian snatched the door open, hearing glass break as it hit the opposite wall, and disappeared into the night. The tears didn't start until she reached her car.

CHAPTER FORTY-FOUR

Rian reached for a towel as she stepped out of the shower. Nothing cleared her head like running, and she'd been out this morning before sunrise, altering her usual route in favor of a more intense workout through the hills north of downtown. She had pushed hard to rid herself of the tension that had been building inside and had felt it ease as she emerged from North Hill and cruised at a good pace back down to her townhouse. There was little traffic at this time of the morning, and she saw no one along the way. She felt much more relaxed after a long shower and was actually looking forward to what lay ahead for her later in the day.

Rian had left her cell phone charging on the nightstand and, as she toweled off, she heard it ring. The theme from Star Wars meant that it was Abby calling from her cell phone. Puzzled, Rian wrapped herself in the towel and stepped into the bedroom, knowing that the call would go to voicemail before she could answer it. She glanced at the clock on the opposite nightstand and noted that it was 8:07, which meant that Abby should be at the office.

Rian unplugged the phone and noticed that this was the fourth missed call she'd had from Abby in the last three minutes. There was also a missed call and a voicemail from Amanda and two calls with voicemails from numbers she didn't recognize. One of those originated from area code 205, which meant the call was from northern Alabama. The other was a local call.

Worried that something had happened to Abby, Rian ignored the other calls and started to punch in Abby's cell number. Before she could finish, the phone sprang to life again blaring the Star Wars theme and with Abby's picture on the screen.

"Abby, wh—-" Rian began to say, but Abby interrupted her.

"Where are you?" Abby asked, almost in a whisper.

"What?" Rian asked.

"Rian, where are you? Are you on your way to the office?" Abby asked, still whispering, but the urgency in her voice was unmistakable.

"No, I'm at home," Rian said. "I went for a run this morning. Abby, what's wrong?"

"You need to leave," Abby said, her voice starting to break.

Rian took a deep breath. "Abby, calm down and tell me what's going on."

"The FBI is here looking for you," Abby told her.

"What? What does the FBI want with me?" Rian asked.

"I don't know. They showed up just before 8:00. They started asking a bunch of questions about you, about Barry, where your files were stored and who had access to them."

This can't be good, Rian thought.

"Why are you whispering?" she asked.

"I'm in the bathroom. I didn't know what else to do but to come in here and call you. Rian, are you in trouble? Are they going to arrest you?"

"Of course not. I haven't done anything wrong. Abby, go back out and tell them I'm on my way in and should be there in about thirty minutes. Put them in the conference room across from my office. And tell Jack."

"He already knows. He was talking to them when I left to come in here," Abby said.

"Okay. I'll be there as quickly as I can," Rian said and hung up. She dressed quickly, dumped some food into the bowl for Mannix, and went out the side door to her BMW. She started the car and glanced in the rear view mirror as she started to back out. As she did, she noticed two men get out of a nondescript car parked on the curb across the street. Rian shifted her gaze to the driver's side mirror and saw them approaching, both wearing dark suits, crisp white shirts, and muted ties, the trademark uniform of the FBI. One was about 6'2" and built like a linebacker with short, dark hair.

Ex-military, Rian thought.

The other was much shorter and thinner. He wore dark sunglasses, and Rian instantly took him to be the junior agent. He carried a thin, black padfolio that appeared to be made of leather.

As Rian got out to meet them in the driveway, both had their credentials extended at arm's length.

"Rian Coulter?" the tall one asked as she approached. Rian nodded.

"I'm Agent Morris, this is Agent McDavid. We'd like to speak with you," he said. It was more of a command than a greeting.

Rian flashed her best smile. "Of course, gentlemen. How can I help you?"

Agent Morris looked around, then nodded toward Rian's house. "Can we speak inside?" he said.

Rian had encountered FBI agents before, but she had not met these two. Even so, she wasn't easily intimidated. At this point, she was more annoyed than intimidated, but a sort of unease was starting to build inside her. She didn't particularly want these two agents in her house, but she neither wanted to appear uncooperative nor have this conversation out here within earshot of her neighbors.

"I was just heading to my office. It's not far from here," she offered, knowing that they'd already been there looking for her. "Can you meet me there?"

Morris remained expressionless. "We'd rather talk here, ma'am," he said, then allowing a sarcastic smile to cross his face, "if you don't mind."

Seeing no other option, Rian walked to the door and stepped back into the house. Morris and McDavid followed her inside, and she gestured for them to take a seat on the sofa, which they did. As she did, the smartphone in her pocket chimed with Amanda's ringtone. Rian quickly reached inside and muted the call without removing her phone. It kept buzzing, and went to voicemail.

"Can I get you gentlemen anything to drink? Water, coffee?" Rian asked.

"No. Thank you," Morris answered for them both. McDavid just shook his head. Rian sat in the chair opposite them, the coffee table between them. She noted that McDavid glanced around the room, but Morris never took his eyes off her. She met his eyes and waited for him to speak.

"Ma'am, I'll get right to the point," he began. As he spoke, McDavid pulled a sheet of paper from his padfolio and handed it to Morris. He studied it briefly, then turned it upside-down and slid it across the coffee table toward Rian along with a cheap pen. "I'm sure you know your rights, but I'm obligated to advise you of them anyway," he said.

Rian glanced at the paper, but she already knew it was a form containing her Miranda rights. Before a statement could be used against a criminal suspect in court, the person must be advised of the constitutional right to remain silent, to not answer questions, and the right to speak with an attorney before answering. Any incriminating statements made without first giving these rights wasn't admissible later in court. The paper Morris had presented to Rian was a pre-printed form with those rights and a place for Rian to sign, waiving her rights. She'd seen thousands of these same forms used by law enforcement officers. Rian made no move to pick up the form or to sign it.

"You mind telling me what this is all about, since you're getting right to the point?" she asked. She was aware that McDavid was pulling out other documents, but she kept her eyes on Morris. He smirked as if he knew she wouldn't sign the form.

"Ma'am, you made a total of nine telephone calls in a one week period to an Amanda Baker both at her office and to her cell phone, all from your cell phone," McDavid said. Stunned, Rian looked at him, then down at the table where McDavid had laid out her cell phone records from Verizon. He pointed to each call she'd made to Amanda which he'd highlighted in yellow.

"You subpoenaed my telephone records?" she said, recovering and mustering all the indignation she could despite the nauseating sensation growing in her stomach.

"Ms. Coulter, do you know Amanda Baker?" Morris asked. Rian looked at him but didn't respond. "Ma'am?" he asked again.

Rian was off balance and she knew it. She secretly kicked herself for letting them into her house and for allowing them to gain the upper hand. She desperately wanted to call Sam, but they hadn't spoken since she stormed out of his condo. The phone in her jacket pocket buzzed again, but she ignored it.

"You should know that Ms. Baker is cooperating with us," Morris said.

"Look, Agent Morris. Amanda Baker is going to be my sister-in-law. She's engaged to marry my brother. Of course I know her and of course I've called her. So what?" she said.

"What did the two of you discuss?" he asked. Rian knew then that he hadn't talked with Amanda or he would already know what they had discussed. She also knew that his statement about Amanda's cooperation was therefore a lie. Morris seemed to recognize that he'd made a mistake.

"Am I under investigation?" she asked, trying to seize the initiative. Her phone began to buzz again, and again she reached inside her jacket to mute the call. Morris took note of it and motioned toward her pocket.

"You need to get that? Someone really must want to talk to you," he said with a smirk.

"You didn't answer my question," Rian said. "Am I under investigation?"

Morris sighed and glanced momentarily at McDavid before looking back at Rian. "Ma'am, we have reason to believe that you may know the identity of the individual who committed several homicides in Birmingham six years ago and that you're withholding that information," he said.

"What's that got to do with Amanda Baker?" Rian asked.

He ignored her question and continued. "We also have reason to believe that the same suspect is committing homicides in this area and that you may be withholding that information as well," he said.

"So you subpoenaed my telephone records, found a Birmingham connection in Amanda, and drove all the way down here to shake me down? That about it, Agent Morris?" Rian said angrily. She stood and glared down at the two agents.

"Ma'am . . ." Morris started to say, but Rian cut him off.

"Do you have a warrant for my arrest?" she demanded. Morris sat back on the sofa and sighed.

"No," he said.

"Do you have a warrant to search my house?"

"No."

"Then I'm going to have to ask you to leave," Rian said, stepping to the side and gesturing to the front door.

"Look, Ms. Coulter. Maybe we got off on the wrong foot," Morris said. The accusatory tone was gone from his voice, yet he made no effort to leave.

"Agent Morris," Rian said. "I'm sure that you know that remaining on premises after the owner has advised you to leave is considered trespassing. That's a misdemeanor in this jurisdiction. Do I need to make a call?" she asked, pulling her cell phone from her jacket and waving it in the air.

Morris set his jaw and stood, while McDavid grabbed the phone records and stuffed them back into his pad.

"That won't be necessary," he said and started for the door. Rian held it open for him, but he stopped before leaving. "We'll be back," he said.

"Better bring that warrant," Rian said and closed the door behind them.

She looked at her phone and noted that she had three more calls from Abby, three from Amanda, one from her brother Brian, one more from a local number that she didn't recognize in addition to the others that had been there before she left the house. Several had left voicemails.

There were no calls from Sam.

Rian clicked on Amanda's number and started to hit redial, but stopped herself, remembering Agent McDavid's highlighted copies of cell phone records. She went to her voicemail instead and saw that Amanda had left a message as had the Birmingham number and the two local numbers that she didn't recognize. She clicked on Amanda's number to hear the message:

> "Rian, it's Amanda. It's Wednesday morning at about 8:00. The FBI showed up here this morning wanting to talk to me and asking questions about you. Uncle Mike took them into the conference room, then they left. I don't know what they wanted but it seemed serious. Uncle Mike has been huddled with the partners ever since, then he asked me for your cell number. Are you in trouble? I'm worried about you. Call me."

She bypassed the messages from Abby and went to the call that originated from area code 205. As she suspected, it was from Michael Baker, her supervising partner from Ashton, Baker in Birmingham. He was calling to advise her that the FBI had informed him that an investigational subpoena was being issued to the firm to turn over all files that Rian had worked on while she was employed at Ashton, Baker. The firm was opposing it, he said, but he asked that she have no contact with the firm, or Amanda, except through the firm's legal counsel. He provided the name and contact information for the firm's attorney.

Great, Rian thought.

Rian scrolled to the local numbers and listened to the first voicemail:

> "Ms. Coulter, this is Lt. Glenn Palmer with the Escambia County Sheriff's Department. I think we need to talk. Call me at your earliest opportunity."

Rian clicked on the other local number:

> "Ms. Coulter, this is Michael Donovan with the *Escambia Herald*. We've met before, though it's been a while. I'm calling to let you know that we're running with a story in tomorrow's *Herald* that links the murders here with the murders in Birmingham six years ago and including the fact that the authorities believe that you have information critical to the investigation that you are withholding. I wanted to give you a chance to comment. If so, you can reach me at 823-9990 before 3:00."

Shit.

Rian looked outside to see if the agents were still there. The car was gone, so she got into the BMW and, taking care to make sure she wasn't being followed, she drove to her bank and withdrew $400 from the drive through ATM, then headed to the Walgreens five blocks away. She bought a Tracfone and a reloadable minutes card with 1,000 minutes, paying cash for both.

Rian returned to the townhouse, walked upstairs, and retrieved her Macbook from its neoprene case. She plugged her phone into it and backed up all the data onto the laptop's hard drive. Next she registered the Tracfone on its website under the name of Samantha McCafferty, her high school Latin teacher. When the registration form asked for an address, she listed 1700 West Mallory Street, the Escambia County Sheriff's Office. She replaced the computer into the case, went to her closet, and removed an old steamer trunk in which she stored sweaters and other winter clothes she rarely got the chance to wear in Florida. She put the laptop inside among the clothes and returned the trunk to the closet.

She returned to the car but, instead of driving to the office, she drove east across the bay bridge into the adjoining county, stopping at one of the scenic overlooks that dotted East Escambia Bay. Rian got out of her car, walked to the rail, and gazed out at the tranquil bay 300 feet below. Jet skiers chased one another across the water and she could see a parasailer in the distance. She contemplated how her life could have taken such a dramatic turn so quickly.

Rian took out her beloved iPhone and stared at it. She longed to call Sam. Neither had called the other since that night, and Rian wasn't sure whether this was out of sheer pride on both of their parts or if their relationship had actually sustained a fatal blow. She'd never felt more alone, and she was angry with Sam for not being here when she needed him most.

The visit from the feds that morning, coupled with the calls from Donovan and Palmer, convinced Rian that she not only knew for sure who the killer was, but that the police knew that she knew his identity. Part of her wanted to just tell them and let this all be over with. She was withholding information, but the voice inside her screamed that ethically she had to keep the information confidential. How ironic, she thought, that she had to protect the identity of a serial killer to remain ethical. Would they really disbar her if she revealed him?

She was under investigation and could be disciplined or even prosecuted. Her reputation would surely suffer, and she suspected that she'd be fired when she returned to the office. More importantly, her community was in danger and other women could be hurt or killed because of the information she was withholding. Rian was sure she would never be able to forgive herself if that happened.

Rian put her hands on her head and squeezed as if to keep her head from exploding. Her cell phone records had been subpoenaed, and now her privacy was compromised. If Palmer and Donovan had her cell number, who else had access to it? Were her calls being traced and recorded? Were her whereabouts being tracked through her cell phone?

There was no other way, she decided. She would stick to her guns, regardless of the consequences. She was in this alone, but she wouldn't go quietly.

"Bring it," she said, and launched her iPhone into the bay.

CHAPTER FORTY-FIVE

Palmer was furious. He picked up his cell phone and tried Donovan's number again, but he didn't answer and the call went to voicemail. Palmer laid the newspaper out on the kitchen table and read the article again. Quoting "sources close to the investigation," the article was a full front page bomb that compared the similarities between the murders in Birmingham with those along the Gulf Coast in detail.

Each victim was pictured, as was Barry Sellers. Donovan had spoken with Angela Sellers and had speculated whether Barry's death wasn't accidental and was somehow related to the murders. He included a photo of Angela holding little Gracie. The article went on to mention that FBI agents from Birmingham had "joined the investigation," confirming for Palmer that they were the "sources" quoted in the article.

Palmer's picture was there, too, an old stock picture that the *Herald* had on file. The article mentioned that the head of the Gulf Coast Strangler, as they had now named the killer, task force couldn't be reached for comment. Palmer snorted at this, knowing that Donovan never even made an attempt to call him.

He flipped back to the front page. There were two large photographs, one of Rian Coulter and one of the composite drawing of the suspect created after Christy Price was killed. Between the photos was a large sub-headline: "Does she hold the key?" The article mentioned that Rian had refused to comment and was under investigation for possible criminal offenses. In frustration, Palmer wadded the paper into a ball and threw it toward the trash can, missing badly.

His phone chirped and he saw that it was Sanchez.

"I swear to God, Sanchez," he said when he answered, "if anyone on our side has leaked information to this piece of shit, I'll see to it personally that they go to jail. I'll arrest Donovan's sorry ass, too, if I can."

"So, you've seen the article," Sanchez said carefully.

"Yes, I've seen the goddammed article," Palmer yelled. "I'm just trying to decide who I'm going to shoot first."

"Captain's pissed," Sanchez said. "He wants to see you right away. He got a call from the mayor, who had a call from the mayor of Birmingham. It's a real shitstorm."

"Tell him I'll be there when I can. You go see Donovan and tell him that if he wants to publish any further confidential information, he'll be doing it from Leonard Street," Palmer said, referring to the location of the county jail.

"I thought you'd want the pleasure of that visit," Sanchez said, surprised.

"Nah. I've got another visit to make. Where's Coulter?" Palmer had been tracking Rian's movements through her phone for over a week.

"Don't know, L.T. Signal's dead. It went down yesterday," Sanchez reported.

Palmer didn't like that information. He knew that, like most people these days, Rian was addicted to her phone, checking it for messages every few minutes.

"She's gonna get herself killed," he said.

Palmer placed a call to the local FBI office and received assurance from the Special Agent in Charge that they hadn't contributed to the *Herald* story. Agents Morris and McDavid hadn't bothered to check in with the local field office when they arrived as was customary when agents crossed jurisdictional boundaries.

"We didn't even know they were here," he said.

Palmer left in his unmarked cruiser and drove to Galvez Lane, the street where Rian lived. He drove slowly past her townhouse, noting that her car wasn't there and that there didn't appear to be anyone surveilling her house at the moment. He drove to the courthouse and found her BMW parked in its usual parking space in the garage. Palmer parked in a nearby space and waited.

* * *

Rian was in Jack Brown's office, pacing the floor as she did when she was excited or upset.

"I'm not suspending you," Jack was saying. "It's a leave of absence, with pay. Just a few days off until this blows over a little."

"You can call it what you want," Rian said. "It's still chickenshit, Jack. You of all people should be backing me up on this."

Jack Brown was in a difficult position. As the Public Defender, he knew he should be supporting Rian's effort to preserve the confidences and secrets of a client whom the law required his office to represent. On the other hand, he was also an elected official and not immune to the growing chorus of people screaming for someone's head on a platter in connection with the murder investigation. At the moment, the most likely person to donate that head appeared to be Rian.

Jack got up from his desk, walked over, and put his arm around Rian's shoulders. He'd been her mentor, and she'd been like a daughter to him since she first came to work for him. He truly loved her.

"I am supporting you," he said softly. "Not just because you work for me but because you're right. I'm putting out a statement later today."

Rian leaned her head back and looked at him. He was a good and decent man who had always done right by her. He was just a few years from retirement and didn't deserve to have his career end with the firestorm of criticism surely headed his way. Once again, the thought crossed her mind that she was alone.

"Maybe you're right, Jack. I could sure use a few days off," she said. He smiled at her and rubbed her arm. She pulled away and started toward the door. "Can I use Abby if I need anything?" she asked.

Jack's smile broadened. "Of course. You're still the Chief PD. This'll all be over within a week or two, tops," he said.

"Thanks," Rian said. "I'll see ya." She left Jack's office and headed back to hers, followed silently by every other eye in the office. She wondered which ones supported her and who thought she was harboring a murderer. She glanced back at Barry Sellers's empty office and felt a wave of guilt wash over her.

* * *

Palmer was leaning against the side of her car when Rian entered the parking lot. Rian saw him and marched up to him with purpose.

"I suppose you're here to tell me that my visit from the M and M boys was *not* your idea and to blow some other smoke up my skirt," she said.

Palmer held his hands up in mock surrender. Despite the fact that he believed that she was the key to his entire investigation, he actually liked Rian Coulter.

"You know how these things go," he said. "They didn't even let their pals in the local office know they were here, so they sure wouldn't check in with little ole me. Birmingham politics; what can I say?"

Rian smiled at that and seemed to relax a little. She walked up to her car and rested her back against it, turning to look at Palmer.

"So, have they elbowed you out of the way?" she asked.

"Not exactly. Just a flexing of muscles and a few leaks to the paper to get your attention."

Rian stood straight and turned to face him. "Look, Lieutenant, I haven't done anything wrong. In fact, I haven't done *anything* but my job for which my life has been turned into a pile of shit." As she spoke, she looked over Palmer's shoulder at a man approaching them from the other end of the parking garage. As he drew closer, she recognized Gerald Brooks, the chief investigator for the State Attorney's Office. She'd never seen him down here before. Palmer saw Rian's puzzled expression and turned to look at Brooks, whom he knew as well.

"Oh, hello, Lieutenant," Brooks said as he approached. "Didn't expect to see you here. Sorry to interrupt." Palmer nodded at him in response. Brooks turned to look at Rian, reaching inside his coat pocket as he did to remove a folded piece of white paper.

Rian had always had a good working relationship with Jerry Brooks and considered him an honest, straight up investigator. Now, she looked at him warily, the hair on the back of her neck bristling.

"Uh, Rian, uh, I'm sorry to be the one to bring you this but . . ." he stammered, holding out the piece of paper to her. Rian took it and unfolded it. It was an official subpoena for Rian to appear before the grand jury at 1:00 the next day.

Rian was stunned. "Are you kidding me?" she asked.

"What is it?" Palmer interjected. Rian looked at him coldly.

"It's a fucking subpoena to appear before the grand jury tomorrow. I suppose now you're going to tell me you didn't know about *this* either?" she said angrily.

"Ms. Coulter. I assure you, this is not my doing," he said, casting an unfriendly look at Brooks, who shrugged and backed away.

Rian was nearly blind with anger. She snatched open her car door, slammed it shut, and started the engine. Palmer had to jump out of the way to keep Rian from backing over him, and he watched her race out of the parking lot, squealing her tires as she turned onto Claggett Street.

Walking back to his car, Palmer pulled out his cell phone and dialed Sanchez.

"She just left. You got her?" he asked.

"Just a sec, L.T. Signal's coming up now," Sanchez said. After a brief pause, he continued. "Yep. There she is, turning onto Bayfront from Claggett. Going a little fast, too."

"I want this monitored 24/7," Palmer said. "No exceptions."

"Yes sir. It'll give us a tone when she moves from a stationary position," Sanchez said.

Palmer nodded and got into his car, pleased that the GPS tracking device he'd placed under Rian's bumper was working properly.

CHAPTER FORTY-SIX

Waterville Estates was one of Tallahassee's oldest and most exclusive gated communities. Occupying hundreds of acres northeast of the city, it was home to Supreme Court justices, physicians, lawyers, retired politicians, and the upper crust of Tallahassee society. Many of the stately mansions bordered the large lake in the center while others lined the private golf course that meandered through the subdivision.

Access to Waterville was controlled by a round-the-clock guard at the main gate and a secure iron gate at the rear that could only be opened electronically by a computerized passkey.

The guard checked Rian's name off a list that he kept on a clipboard, handed her driver's license back, and motioned her through the gate. She could feel the tension in her shoulders start to ease as she drove through the gate and down the entrance road lined with hundred-year-old oaks dripping with Spanish Moss.

The events of the past week were still on her mind. After being subpoenaed to appear before the grand jury, she had contacted an attorney friend who agreed to help and who was able to convince prosecutors to withdraw the subpoena.

He was able to confirm that Rian was the target of a criminal investigation and, therefore, would exercise her Fifth Amendment right to remain silent if called to testify.

Since Florida law prohibited the prosecution from calling a witness merely to force the person to constitutionally refuse to testify before the jury, Rian's appearance before the grand jury would have been meaningless, if not unlawful. Reluctantly, the prosecutor, Allan Banning, agreed and recalled the subpoena. The grand jury investigation would go on anyway but, for now at least, Rian was in the clear.

She was glad to leave Pensacola and all of that behind, if only for a day.

She made a quick right turn and slowly drove past her childhood home, pausing briefly in front to remember humid summer afternoons in the front yard on the Slip 'N Slide with her brother Brian and their friends. Her parents sold the home and moved to a high rise condo when she graduated from law school, and Rian wondered if the new owners had children who would find the notes that she and Brian had left each other in the nooks and crannies of the house. She smiled to herself and pulled away, driving a short distance and stopping at a house down the street behind a long line of cars parked at the curb.

As she entered the home, she was greeted by its owners, Carter and Patty Mann. The Manns, both physicians, were old friends of her family and had known Rian since she was a baby. They were also her godparents. She hugged them warmly.

"Where's Sam?" Patty wanted to know, looking over Rian's shoulder.

"He's not with me. We're, um, sort of on a little break," Rian said awkwardly. She hugged them again, then entered the family room where her parents were waiting with Brian and Amanda. Hugs were exchanged and everyone talked about the details of the upcoming wedding. No one mentioned Rian's predicament, which had received widespread attention, including some comments by Nancy Grace herself who criticized Rian for "harboring a serial killer." Soon, Rian's father disappeared, returning momentarily with a glass of red wine for her.

"No thanks, Dad. I have to drive back tonight," she said when he offered her the glass.

"Nonsense," he replied matter-of-factly. "Your mother and I won't hear of it. You'll stay with us," he said in a tone that usually meant the discussion was over.

"I have to, Dad, really," Rian said, but took the glass of wine anyway, rationalizing that she wouldn't be driving for several hours and that one glass wouldn't be harmful.

For the next two hours, Rian was immersed in the pleasure of being surrounded by her supportive family and the happiness of her brother and his fiancé. She greeted old friends, enjoyed excellent food, and gave no thought to the difficulties awaiting her back in Pensacola.

* * *

Across the room, Skip Sullivan watched it all closely. He had kept abreast of Rian's situation and soon slipped outside to make a call to his boss, Governor Arden Chambers. He also forwarded a photograph he'd secretly taken with his phone of Rian laughing it up with her family, holding a glass of wine.

"Perfect!" the Governor roared when he looked at the picture. "Not a care in the world," he said, laughing.

"The timing couldn't be any better, sir," Sullivan said.

"I agree, Skip. Good work. She's the poster child for what we're trying to do. Fucking lawyers," he said. "Give it to that stooge Spencer. She's from his district. Be sure to remind him of that," Chambers said. Sullivan soon placed the next call.

* * *

After the gifts were opened, and with the party winding down, Craig Coulter appeared at his daughter's side. Putting his hand on her arm, he wordlessly guided her into a nearby bedroom. He sat on the bed and patted the mattress, as though directing her to sit beside him.

"What's up, Dad?" Rian said, sitting beside him and knowing full well why he had pulled her in there.

"How are you holding up?" he asked.

Rian dropped her defensive posture along with her shoulders. "I'm okay, Dad, but it's been pretty rough. They seem to want to make me the killer instead of the real one."

"I don't know all the ins and outs of why you're taking the position you are, Peanut," he said, "but we all support you and will do whatever we can to help you."

Rian's eyes filled. Her father had always believed in her and, at that moment, he seemed to be the only person in the world on her side. She leaned over and wrapped her arms around him, hugging him tightly for a long time.

"Thank you, Daddy," she whispered in his ear.

As they stood, her father pressed something into her hand. When she opened it, she saw that it was a key.

"What's this?" she asked, puzzled.

"It's to the cabin," he said, referring to their getaway house in St. Teresa. "I thought you might need to get away for some peace and quiet. I've stocked the pantry and the fridge for you. Just go when you need to."

Rian smiled and hugged him again, holding him for a long time.

She said goodbye to her family and godparents and climbed back into her BMW for the three-hour drive back to Pensacola. Glancing at her watch, she noted it was 11:45, Tallahassee time. She would be home before 2:00.

* * *

The truck engine was already idling when he saw her come through the front gate. He put it in gear, falling in several cars behind her. He was in no hurry. He knew where she was going and that the cars between them would fall away when she turned onto the Interstate. He was patient and would wait for the right opportunity.

* * *

Rian set her satellite radio to a New York station that played continuous classic rock, avoiding any news talk stations that might be carrying stories about her. She settled back for the long, boring drive to Pensacola along Interstate 10, past the many small towns that dot the Florida panhandle.

There wasn't a lot of traffic this time of the night, which meant that the state troopers probably wouldn't be out in force either. She set the cruise control to 85 mph, hoping to get home a little earlier than anticipated. She glanced over at her purse in the passenger seat and considered calling Sam to let him know where she was. Sam didn't know that her iPhone was at the bottom of the bay and didn't have the number to her burn phone. He couldn't reach her even if he'd tried.

She felt a little uneasy that no one in Pensacola knew where she was, but she reconsidered and left the phone in her purse, directing her attention back to the Led Zeppelin song on the radio.

Just east of Bonifay, Rian was suddenly jolted out of her seat by something slamming hard into the rear of her car.

She was usually aware of traffic around her and had seen nothing behind her the last time she checked. Instinctively, she glanced at her rear view mirror. All she could see was the dark windshield of what appeared to be a large pickup truck directly behind her. Its headlights were off.

The darkness of the night coupled with the tinted windows of both vehicles made it impossible to see the driver's features.

She couldn't tell whether it was a man or a woman or whether others were in the truck, much less recognize them. Rian quickly looked at her side mirror, but the truck was too close to her to see any details.

What the *fuck* are you doing? she thought.

Just when she thought this might be some sort of a prank, the truck increased speed dramatically, its weight and mass forcing her smaller car forward and to the shoulder of the road to her right.

"NO!" she screamed, struggling to keep the car under control.

Rian tried to change lanes, but the truck was so much larger and heavier that she couldn't escape it. Looking ahead, she saw no other traffic. There was no one to help or to witness this attack.

She gripped the wheel and sped up, trying to outrun the truck and get back onto the road. In doing so, she overcorrected, and the car began to fishtail. The truck slammed into her again, causing her to spin and lose control, heading down into a ditch to her right. Rian fought to keep the car upright, but couldn't keep it from overturning. The airbag deployed, slamming her in the face and burning her left wrist. As the car flipped multiple times, the left side of Rian's head slammed into the driver's window, eventually shattering it. She landed upside-down in the ditch.

Rian's last conscious memory before all went dark was the water pouring in through the shattered driver's window.

CHAPTER FORTY-SEVEN

It took several rings before Palmer realized that his cell phone was actually ringing. Lying face down in the bed, he reached out with his left hand and grabbed it.

"This better be life-threatening," he said sleepily.

"Uh, sir, this is Stinson in dispatch," said a male voice on the other end. "Sorry to bother you at this hour, but we've lost contact with your subject, Ms. Coulter." Palmer shook the cobwebs from his head and sat up in the bed.

"What do you mean we lost her?" he said. Glancing at the clock on the nightstand, he noted that it was 2:42 a.m.

"Signal went dark at 11:38 p.m.," Stinson reported. Palmer did the math and his blood pressure spiked.

"That was three hours ago. Why the *fuck* am I just hearing about this now?" he yelled.

"She's been at a residence in Tallahassee all evening, sir," Stinson stammered, and Palmer could hear the tension in his voice. "I, uh, guess they thought she was staying put for the night. They, um, just checked back and saw that the signal was lost," he said.

Palmer was furious, but tried to calm down. "Where was she when the signal went out?" he asked.

"Just east of Bonifay, sir. On I-10," said Stinson.

"Notify Sanchez and have him meet me at investigations in thirty," Palmer ordered and hung up.

When he arrived at the Sheriff's Department, Sanchez was already there. Together they confirmed that the GPS system was working properly and that the problem was with the device that Palmer had secretly attached to the inside bumper of Rian's BMW.

"Maybe it came loose on the interstate," Sanchez said hopefully, but Palmer shook his head.

"No, it was secure," he said.

"There's nothing out there, L.T. Nothing to make her go off grid," Sanchez said as they both looked at the map of the Florida Panhandle. Just then, an officer stuck his head in the door and told Sanchez that he had a call. He walked to a nearby desk and took the call, returning a few moments later.

"Holmes County Sheriff reports that a BMW with Escambia plates was found upside-down in a ditch east of Bonifay. Sounds like our girl," he said.

"What about the driver?" Palmer asked.

"Unconscious at the scene, but stable. She's at Doctor's Memorial in Bonifay," said Sanchez.

Palmer breathed a sigh of relief. Although the little hospital in Bonifay handled trauma patients, he knew that if Rian's injuries had been truly life-threatening, she would likely have been airlifted to the much larger hospital in Tallahassee. He grabbed his coat off the back of a chair and slipped it on.

"Let's go," he said to Sanchez.

"Think it was just an accident?" Sanchez asked as the headed down the hallway.

"Guess we'll find out soon enough," Palmer replied, though he was already convinced that it wasn't.

CHAPTER FORTY-EIGHT

Rian tried to open her eyes, but shut them quickly because of the searing pain in her head.

As her head began to clear a little, she was aware that she was lying on her back in a darkened room. There was a soft beeping sound coming from her right, but when she turned her head toward it, she found that a stiff collar wrapped around her neck restricted movement. She also found that she could only open her right eye. The left side of her face was extremely painful and her left eye was swollen shut.

Where in the hell am I?

She couldn't raise her head off the pillow because of the collar, so she raised her right arm enough to see an IV taped to her hand and the blood pressure cuff around her upper arm. Her lower back hurt, and she tried to shift her position in the bed a little, letting out an involuntary grunt as she did.

"Rian?" she heard her mother's voice say. "Craig, she's awake." Instantly, the faces of her parents came into view.

"Wha . . ." Rian started to say, but her throat was so dry that her tongue stuck to the roof of her mouth. Her mother held a

Styrofoam cup and a straw to her lips, and she took a few sips of water. This made her cough, and she thought that her head would explode.

"Rian," her father said softly. He was holding her left hand and stroking it softly. "You've been in a car accident. You're in a hospital in Bonifay. You have a concussion and bad neck sprain, but you're going to be okay," he said.

"Thank God," her mother said softly, wiping tears away.

"I don't remember anything," Rian said. Her parents just smiled at her, but the look of relief on their faces was evident.

"Honey, Sam's here. He's been here all night," Beverly said. Rian glanced around the room with her one eye, but didn't see him.

"He's outside," her mother said. "He wasn't sure that you wanted to see him. Is it okay?" she asked. Rian nodded slightly, setting off another round of bombs inside her head.

A minute later the door opened and Sam walked in. He took Rian's left hand in both of his, pressed it to his lips and held it to his cheek as he leaned over the bed and kissed her forehead.

"You look like shit," Rian said.

Sam laughed. "Me? You want me to get a mirror?" he asked.

"What happened?" she asked.

"You ran off the road and flipped a couple of times," he said. "Ended up upside-down in a ditch filled with water. Cops say you must've fallen asleep at the wheel, given the hour." Rian didn't respond.

"You know, you're lucky to be here," he said, his voice cracking.

Rian smiled at him, and they sat together holding hands in silence. She drifted off to sleep and, when she woke again, Sam was calling her name and shaking her shoulder slightly. Rian opened her eye and could see that two other people were in the room, standing in the shadows just inside the door.

"Lieutenant Palmer and Detective Sanchez are here," Sam said. "You feel up to talking with them?"

Though they were the last people she wanted to talk to, she said okay, curious why they would drive all the way from Pensacola. Palmer and Sanchez stepped forward to the bed.

"You stay, okay?" she said to Sam, gripping his hand for emphasis. He took a seat in the chair to her left.

"Ms. Coulter," Palmer began. Sanchez nodded toward her in greeting. "I'm sorry about your accident, but I understand that you're going to be fine. I'm glad to hear that," he continued.

"Thanks," Rian said, matter-of-factly.

"Can you tell us what happened?" Palmer asked.

Rian suddenly wondered how they knew she was here and why two homicide detectives would be investigating a traffic accident.

"What time is it?" she asked.

"Three-thirty in the afternoon," Sam answered from her left.

Rian looked back at Palmer. "How'd you know I was here?" she asked. Palmer didn't flinch, but Sanchez glanced at him, then back at Rian. Both Rian and Sam noticed.

Palmer smiled. "Troopers contacted us when they discovered Escambia plates on your car," he lied. "They thought it would be faster for us to notify your family since your burn phone didn't have any numbers in it and your iPhone was nowhere to be found."

Rian knew Palmer's answer was a lie, but a damn good one, she thought, especially on the spot. She smiled back at him.

"Nice of them," she said.

"What happened, Ms. Coulter?" Palmer asked. He was no longer smiling. Neither was Rian.

"I can't remember. The last thing I recall was being at my brother's wedding shower in Tallahassee," she said. Palmer stepped closer to the bed and lowered his voice.

"The yokels are writing it up as though you fell asleep at the wheel. Your blood alcohol was almost zero, so there aren't any charges. There are, however, scuff marks on the interstate east of the crash scene," Palmer said.

Rian stared at him long enough for them both to be uncomfortable, then shook her head. Palmer leaned over the bed and spoke in a near whisper.

"I can't help you if you won't let me," he said.

"I just don't remember anything, Lieutenant," Rian said. "I'm sure they told you that I have a concussion. Maybe I'll remember in a few days. If so, I'll call you."

Palmer straightened and stepped back, cutting his eyes over to Sam, then back to Rian.

"You do that, ma'am. You do that," he said, his voice a mixture of frustration and sarcasm. He turned to Sanchez, jerked his head toward the door, and they left.

Sam stood and approached the bed.

"Something you're not telling me, dear?" he asked.

"Someone tried to kill me Sam," Rian said.

* * *

Rian spent another day in the hospital in Bonifay and was then discharged home with instructions to take things easy for a couple of weeks. She thought that was laughable. Her face was still bruised, but the swelling had gone down enough that she could see out of her left eye. She still had a headache, but the Lortab she'd been prescribed took the edge off enough for her to function.

She kissed her parents goodbye, and she and Sam headed west toward Pensacola, but not before driving through the accident scene a couple of times. The scuff marks Palmer referred to were still visible, though they were already starting to fade. Other than that, there was no visible evidence that there had been another vehicle involved.

"I still can't believe that no one saw anything," Rian said as they started for home.

"He picked the most deserted spot possible," Sam said. "Either he's lucky or damned smart."

They said little during the two-hour drive except disagreeing over whether Rian would stay at her place or at Sam's. Given all the attention, they finally decided that Rian would stay with Sam, but she wanted to go by her place and get some clothes and pick up Mannix, who Sam had reluctantly agreed could stay as well. As Sam's Mercedes approached Rian's townhouse, they both noted a dark colored sedan and a city police vehicle parked across the street. Sam turned into the driveway, and as he and Rian got out of the car, they saw the doors to the cars across the street open and several people get out.

"Uh-oh," Sam said under his breath as they approached. Rian saw two uniformed officers, several people she didn't know, and one she did; Allan Banning. As they approached, Banning spoke.

"Rian Coulter," he called to her. "I have a warrant for your arrest," Banning said smugly.

"Very theatrical, Allan," Rian said as they all squared off in the street. "I guess my line is, 'On what charge?'"

"Oh, you know the charge," Banning said sarcastically. "Obstruction of justice." He motioned with his head and a uniformed officer moved behind Rian and told her to place her hands behind her back.

"Is this really necessary?" she asked as the officer started to cuff her.

"I get no pleasure out of this, but if you resist, there could be more charges," Banning said, clearly relishing the moment. The cuffs went on. Rian was led to the marked patrol car and placed in the back seat. Sam was already on his phone making arrangements to bail Rian out.

As they pulled away for the ride to the jail, Rian noticed a solitary figure standing at the corner. As they drove past, Mike Donovan raised his camera and captured a perfect picture of Rian's bruised and battered face sitting in the back of the police car.

CHAPTER FORTY-NINE

Although he tried not to, Lincoln Phillips was enjoying the moment. As chairman of the powerful Florida Senate Judiciary Committee, he controlled all legislation that dealt with criminal laws and the judicial branch of government.

In recent years, the economic downturn had resulted in drastic cuts in funding for all aspects of the judiciary, including research assistants and the salaries for judges at all levels from the county courts to the Supreme Court. Judges now found themselves in the awkward position of having to beg the legislature for more money each year, which Phillips and Governor Chambers thought the perfect opportunity to keep "activist" judges in line and ensure that any rulings from the bench were in keeping with their philosophy.

Normally, even though Phillips occupied a significant position in the Senate, little attention was paid to the day-to-day activities of his committee. Senate Bill 119, the bill designed to transfer oversight of the legal profession from the Florida Bar to the legislature, had been assigned to Phillips's committee directly, bypassing the usual route through several subcommittees where it could be amended or defeated. Phillips and Chambers expected a fight from the Democrats and the Bar, but little interest elsewhere.

Rian Coulter had changed all of that.

Now Phillips looked out at a packed committee room, bristling with news media cameras from across the state as well as CNN and Fox News. The question of the regulation of lawyers had been transformed from a mundane matter to a national showdown between two equal branches of government, with Rian caught squarely in the middle.

Public sentiment was divided. Many people around the country expressed admiration for her and considered her position courageous. Others, particularly in the South, viewed her as a symbol of a profession that willfully flaunted the law and needed to be reigned in. Fox News had accused Rian of "coddling murderers," and Nancy Grace had gleefully reported on Rian's arrest.

Maryanne Patterson, the Florida Bar president, was before the committee to testify about the bill and had just completed her prepared remarks. Patterson, a corporate lawyer from Tampa and far more of a technocrat than an advocate, had droned on about the separation of powers and the importance of an independent judiciary. Now, it was time to pounce. Phillips glanced quickly at Skip Sullivan, the Governor's right hand, seated in the front row, then turned his attention to Maryanne Patterson.

"Ma'am, I have a question for you," the Chairman began, pausing for effect and to allow the cameras time to focus on him.

"How can you sit here with a straight face and suggest that the legislature not act when one of your very own is protecting the identity of a serial killer who's endangering the lives of every citizen of the State of Florida?"

Patterson was stunned. She stared blankly back and Phillips, trying desperately to come up with a response that would not be seen as directly defending Rian Coulter, yet not in agreement with Phillips.

"Excuse me?" was all that she could manage.

"What is the Bar's position on the attorney in Pensacola who has been arrested for obstructing justice by refusing to identify the killer?" Phillips challenged.

Patterson swallowed hard. "We, um, haven't taken a position and, I am, uh, not at liberty to discuss the matter," she responded weakly.

Several Democrats on the committee tried to intervene by asking Phillips for permission to speak, but the Chairman cut them off. The choreography had already been set.

"Mr. Chairman," J.T. Spencer said softly, almost unheard over the cacophony of the audience and the Democrats vying for the Chairman's attention.

"The Chair recognizes the bill sponsor, Senator Spencer," Phillips said, much to the disgust of the Democrats, who slumped in their chairs with their arms crossed.

As instructed, Spencer waited until the cameras all shifted his way and the room fell silent. He had been given a talking points memo that was on the desk before him, and he glanced at it briefly before he began to speak.

"Mr. Chairman, it seems to me that this is not a constitutional issue at all or even a battle between the branches of government. The issue here is whether the state has a duty and obligation to regulate the members of a profession that practices within its borders. We already regulate doctors, engineers, architects, and insurance agents. Why should attorneys be any different?" he said calmly. "The actions of the misguided attorney from my district and Ms. Patterson's response underscore the fact that the legal profession is obviously incapable of policing itself."

The voice of reason.

"Beautiful!" Arden Chambers exclaimed, watching the hearing on television from his office in the Capitol along with the Senate President and several lobbyists from various industries.

The bill passed the committee on a party line vote. Phillips's question and Spencer's statement were replayed dozens of times in news broadcasts, and Chambers would join them as a guest on several national talk shows in the days to come.

CHAPTER FIFTY

Rian and Sam entered the courtroom and took seats at the counsel table to the left, next to the jury box. Even though this was a preliminary hearing and there would be no jury, Rian always chose the counsel table nearest to the jury box out of habit. Craig and Beverly Coulter sat in the row of seats behind them, along with Abby, who was there to offer moral support. Since all court proceedings were open to the public, the room was filled with onlookers ranging from curious fellow lawyers, news media, and members of the general public. Mike Donovan was in the back of the room.

At the other counsel table, Allan Banning sat impatiently, rocking slowly back and forth in his chair and tapping his pen in the palm of his hand. Glenn Palmer was seated in the row behind Banning.

Events had moved quickly since Rian's highly publicized arrest three weeks before. The State Attorney finally settled on charging Rian with the crime of "refusing to assist a law enforcement officer in a criminal case or in the apprehending or securing of any person for a breach of the peace." The offense was a misdemeanor, but Banning was arguing that it should be increased to a felony because the breach of the peace Rian was allegedly interfering with was a series of murders.

Even without an enhancement of the charge, obstruction of justice was the type of crime that could cost Rian her license if she was convicted. She'd already been notified that the Florida Bar had opened an investigation, probably as a result of being made to look like idiots at the Senate hearing. They wouldn't hesitate to try to pull her ticket if she were found guilty of obstructing justice.

She and Sam decided to demand a speedy trial and a preliminary hearing to test whether there was even enough evidence to hold her for trial. It was a risky move that could either result in dismissal of the charges or unite public opinion against her.

Rian looked around the courtroom where she had tried so many cases and where she had always felt so comfortable and confident, feeling anything but at the moment. Today's decision wouldn't be made by a jury of citizens, but by Judge Axley, her least favorite judge in the circuit.

The door behind the bench opened, and everyone rose as Judge Clement Axley mounted the bench. The judge left everyone standing for several moments while he busied himself with papers at the bench, then told everyone to be seated. He looked up and surveyed the scene before him.

"I want it clearly understood that I will not tolerate outbursts of any kind during this proceeding. There will be no further warnings and, if any violations occur, I will clear the courtroom," he commanded. Looking at Banning, he asked if the State was ready to proceed.

"We are, Your Honor," said Banning, rising from his seat. "The defendant is charged with obstruction of justice under Section 843.06 and the State is seeking enhancement of the charge to a felony," he continued, pausing for effect, "due to the grave nature of the conduct." It was all Rian could do not to jump up and object. Sensing this, Sam placed his hand firmly on her forearm as if to hold her back.

"Judge, there is simply no legal basis for enhancing the charge," Sam said. "The legislature makes the laws, not Mr. Banning. Only they can enhance the penalty."

"Save it for argument, Counsel," Axley said impatiently. "Get on with it Mr. Banning."

Banning began with a long preliminary statement that summarized the Florida murders and the investigation to that point. The investigators from Birmingham were called to testify about the similarities between the killings there and the homicides in and around Pensacola. Palmer was then called to testify that Rian had refused to tell him who her clients had been in Birmingham and his suspicion that Barry Sellers's death hadn't been by accident, but that he was murdered, leading to the conclusion that a client of the Public Defender could be responsible for the killings. Sam had objected to this theory as speculation, but Judge Axley had allowed the testimony over his objection.

On cross-examination, Sam got Palmer to admit that he'd never directly asked Rian whether she knew the identity of the killer.

"So, can you testify under oath that Ms. Coulter actually knows the identity of the person who has committed these murders?" Sam asked.

"I do not know if she knows his actual identity," Palmer responded. "I do believe that she has information which, if divulged, would lead us to determine his identity."

In the back of the room, Donovan noted what would become tomorrow's headline in the *Herald*: Does She Know?

Satisfied with that answer, Sam concluded his cross-examination and turned back to the counsel table.

"Well, then, let's find out," Judge Axley said.

Sam turned back to face him. "I'm sorry, Your Honor. Did you say something?" he asked.

"I said let's find out. Ms. Coulter, please take the witness stand."

"What?" Sam said. "Judge, she's the defendant, and she has a right not to testify."

"We'll see about that, Counsel. Ms. Coulter?" Axley responded, gesturing Rian to the witness stand. Rian sat still, shaking her head slightly. Banning seemed equally surprised, though a smile began to cross his face.

"What the hell are you doing? You can't call witnesses and you can't take sides," Sam said to the judge.

Axley's gavel sounded like an explosion as he pounded it on the bench. "Watch your mouth, Mr. McKinney," he said icily. "I am running this hearing and another remark like that will land you in custody." He looked over Sam's shoulder at Rian, still sitting at the counsel table with her arms folded across her chest.

"Ms. Coulter, I won't ask you again. Please take the stand or I'll have the bailiff escort you." The deputy sheriff in the corner of the courtroom stiffened as though he was preparing for action.

They all stared uncomfortably at one another for several long moments before Rian slowly rose and walked past a seething Sam toward the witness stand. When she arrived, the judge told her to raise her hand and swear to tell the truth. She did, and as she settled into the chair, Banning started to speak, but Axley stopped him by holding up his hand.

"Sit down, Mr. Banning," he said. Banning looked confused, then slowly sat down.

"Ms. Coulter, I can appreciate the situation you are in," Axley began. "I also have an obligation to not only preside over this hearing, but to enforce the ethical rules and report violations of them to the Bar."

Rian stared back at the judge, unsure whether his statement called for a response on her part. He continued.

"It seems to me that the question that everyone is dancing around is the one that no one has directly asked of you. So, I'm going to do just that. Do you know the identity of the person who is responsible for these murders?"

Rian couldn't believe what was happening. She just sat there, unsure of how to respond.

"Objection!" Sam screamed. "Ms. Coulter exercises her constitutional rights under the Fifth Amendment."

"Overruled," Axley responded without taking his eyes off Rian.

"Your Honor . . ." Sam said, but Axley cut him off.

"Not another word, Counsel, or you're out of here."

Rian spoke before Sam could, choosing her words carefully. "I must refuse to answer that question on the grounds that the answer might tend to incriminate me," she said.

"I am not asking that you identify him, Ms. Coulter. I am simply asking if you know his identity. So I ask you again, do you know his identity? Yes or no," the judge said.

"To me it's the same thing," Rian said. "I will not answer that question on the same grounds."

Axley looked at her gravely. "Then you leave me no option but to find you in direct contempt of this court. I hereby remand you to the custody of the sheriff to be held without bond until you comply."

"*What*?" Sam said. "This is outrageous!"

"That will cost you a thousand dollars, Mr. McKinney, payable immediately. Bailiff, take Ms. Coulter into custody. We're adjourned." He pounded his gavel once and quickly left the bench.

CHAPTER FIFTY-ONE

Rian sat on the bed in her cell, a colorless, windowless, 10 x 10 room with a stainless steel sink and a matching commode bolted to the floor. Her bed was a rickety metal frame bolted to the wall covered with a thin, stained mattress that smelled like urine. She was dressed in the standard jail issue uniform; an orange jumpsuit with the words "Escambia County Jail" stenciled on the back and thin white shower shoes which Rian hated almost as bad as being barefoot in this place. There was another bed above her head but, for some reason, no one else occupied her cell. She was alone and for this, she was thankful.

Rian had been there four days. Following the preliminary hearing the previous Friday, she'd been taken from the courtroom to a holding cell in the courthouse. Two hours later, Judge Axley called everyone to the courtroom and asked Rian if she had changed her mind. When she responded that she had not, she was taken back to the holding cell.

This charade was repeated once more before Judge Axley left early for his weekend and Rian was taken to the county jail to spend hers. Before the day was out, Sam had filed a motion to recuse Judge Axley from the case, an emergency motion for rehearing, an appeal to the District Court of Appeal in Tallahassee, and a complaint against Judge Axley with the Judicial Qualifications Commission. Nothing happened over the weekend, and both Sam and Rian fully expected that she would be released on Monday but Judge Axley's office had stalled on setting a hearing on the motions. There was nothing but silence from the appellate court.

Rian's anger had grown exponentially since she arrived at the jail. The concrete block walls and tile over cement floors amplified even the smallest sound, so sleep was impossible even though she was exhausted. She'd refused to eat the crappy food and wasn't about to use the bathroom in full view of anyone who could see into the cell. That, combined with the inability to communicate with Sam about the case, left her feeling frustrated, helpless, and depressed.

"Coulter!" a voice said, and Rian looked up to see a guard opening her cell door. "Visitor," he said, cocking his head as an indication for her to leave the cell. Sam had left explicit instructions with the jail that she was to see no one but him. Rian got up and wordlessly followed the guard, enduring the hoots and howls from her neighbors. Most of the comments were vile, but one inmate, a former client of hers named Creamy, yelled, "Hey, Rian, you and me, dancin' to the Jailhouse Rock" while swiveling his hips and imitating Elvis. Rian had to smile at that.

The guard unlocked the interview room door and Rian stepped inside. Sam was already there and, although physical contact was strictly forbidden, she hugged him tightly. When she didn't hear the door close behind her, Rian turned to look at the guard, who was smiling slightly.

"Nothing conjugal now," he said with a wink and locked the door.

Sam eyed Rian closely, seeming concerned at her haggard appearance. Suddenly self-conscious, Rian quickly sat at the interview table.

"Well, where are we?" she asked.

"Have you eaten?" he asked. Rian's eyes flashed.

"Goddammit, Sam, I'll eat when I get out of this fucking hole. What's up with the motions?" she said angrily.

Sam brought her up to date. He'd enlisted the support of some high-powered appellate specialists in Tallahassee who were attempting to impress upon the District Court of Appeal the urgency of the matter. Judge Axley was still stalling, but Sam had been advised that all of the circuit judges planned to meet shortly to review the matter and, hopefully, convince Judge Axley to recuse himself.

Sam had also tried to ratchet up the pressure on the Judicial Qualifications Commission, but the governor appointed those members. Governor Chambers had appeared on several talk shows eager to comment on Rian's interference with justice, which, according to him, was all the more reason the legal profession should answer to the legislature. As to whether Rian should have been jailed for standing on ethical principles, the governor had replied that "sometimes you have to crack a few heads to achieve justice."

"Sam, I have got to get out of here," Rian said. He got up and walked around the table to her, wrapping his arms around her and holding her tightly. She responded, and they held each other for a while.

The guard knocked loudly at the door.

"Time!" he said and opened the door.

"I'll make it happen," Sam said and kissed Rian softly on the lips. She returned his kiss, smiled, and turned to leave. Suddenly, she stopped in the doorway and turned back to Sam with a determined look on her face.

"I want Axley's ass in my briefcase," she said. "And then I want Banning's." She turned and disappeared again into the bowels of the jail.

CHAPTER FIFTY-TWO

Terrell Carson glared down from the bench at the scene before him. Much as he would have liked to have banned the news media and closed his courtroom to the public, he knew that Florida law required open courts and allowed the news media, including cameras, at all proceedings except cases where sexually abused children were to testify. In his entire career, he'd never seen this much media coverage of a case over which he presided.

Carson was there because he and his fellow judges in the circuit had become increasingly concerned over the past week at the direction the case against Rian Coulter had taken in general and the actions of Chief Judge Axley in particular. They were all accustomed to Axley's idiosyncrasies and the fact that most of the attorneys who practiced before him considered him a tyrant, but the manner in which the judge had inserted himself into the case at the preliminary hearing concerned them. Many of them felt Axley was enthralled by the national media attention he was getting, which would undoubtedly increase the longer he kept Rian in jail. Either she would buckle under the pressure, which

Carson doubted, or Axley would continue his self appointed stand for justice. Either way, the political establishment and a fair share of the electorate would hail him as a hero.

The Governor had already indicated that a man with Axley's kind of backbone belonged on the Supreme Court. His fellow judges felt otherwise and that the entire judiciary in the state was being held up to ridicule. One judge claimed to have found the word "redneck" used in over fifteen news stories about the case.

Carson had taken the unusual step of organizing a meeting of all judges in the circuit, except for Axley, who voted unanimously to request that the judge recuse himself from the case. Carson had carried the letter signed by his fellow judges to Axley himself and asked him to step aside, unsure of what his reaction would be. After ranting about a "mutiny," Axley agreed and assigned the case to Carson, his point having been made.

The judge looked down at Rian, seated next to Sam at the counsel table, and was shocked at her appearance. He'd already met with Sam and Alan Banning in his chambers before court convened, but Rian didn't attend the meeting. She was dressed, as always, in a tailored business suit, but it hung limply from her as though it belonged to someone else. Her skin was pale and there were still traces of the bruising to the left side of her face from the accident.

Carson estimated that she'd lost more than twenty pounds since he'd last seen her. When their eyes met, her brilliant blue eyes flashed with a determination and anger that Carson had never seen.

"Gentlemen," he began with his deep rich voice resonating around the room, "I've reviewed the transcript from the previous hearing. Mr. Banning, we will not go through that testimony again but if there is anything in addition you want to present, I'll give you the opportunity."

Banning, seeming much less sure of himself than when Judge Axley had the case, wisely elected to tread lightly.

"No, Your Honor," he said. "The State of Florida stands by the previous testimony and believes that it has made a sufficient case."

The judge shifted his eyes to Sam. "Mr. McKinney?"

Sam, too, looked haggard and had slept little since Rian was arrested. Rather than launch into a tirade about the prosecution's tactics and the unfairness of the proceedings, he instead took a more professional tone.

"We've previously submitted our brief to you, Your Honor," he said, holding up a copy of the thick bound volume he'd delivered to Carson's chambers yesterday. "There is absolutely no legal basis for increasing the charge against Ms. Coulter to a felony. None. As for the evidence, the State has failed, miserably I might add, to demonstrate that my client has committed a crime. The case should be dismissed."

Personally, Carson thought the criminal case against Rian was weak at best, but the grand jury had indicted her. He would play this straight.

"Mr. Banning, I agree with Mr. McKinney. There is no basis to increase the penalty for the offense to a felony so that motion is denied." Banning didn't protest and sat silently.

"As to the charge itself," the judge continued, "the evidence that Ms. Coulter committed a crime is weak, to say the least. The purpose of this hearing is to determine whether there is sufficient cause to proceed to trial. I think it's close but I'm going to let the charge stand, for now." Banning breathed a sigh of relief.

But Carson wasn't finished.

"Mr. Banning, you'd better come up with something better than this or this case won't survive the defense's motion for directed verdict at trial," he said. Banning slumped in his chair but said nothing.

Turning to Rian, the judge said, "Ms. Coulter, as to the contempt charge, it is hereby dismissed. You are to be released from custody immediately." Glaring back at Banning one last time, Carson banged his gavel and said, "We're adjourned."

CHAPTER FIFTY-THREE

The meeting was held in the central conference room at the Sheriff's Office. Palmer sat at one end of the rectangular conference table with Sanchez to his right. Mike Donovan sat across from Sanchez, next to his editor, Emmett Bayer. Sam sat at the other end, next to Rian, who had reluctantly agreed to attend only after receiving written assurance from Palmer that anything she said during the meeting wouldn't be used against her in court later. Obviously missing was Alan Banning, whom Palmer had deliberately excluded.

Palmer had called the meeting for two reasons. An article had appeared in the *Birmingham Examiner* three days before, incorrectly reporting that Rian was succumbing to the pressure and would reveal the identity of the killer shortly. The "source" for the story was an unidentified member of the investigation, but in reality, the story had been planted at the insistence of Mayor Arrington and his minions who were taking full credit for the pressure being applied to Rian. Her license to practice law in Alabama had already been temporarily suspended and a complaint had been filed seeking to disbar her altogether.

Palmer rightfully believed that the story put Rian in significant danger. He was furious at the tactics used in Birmingham, but it had also given him an idea. That was the second purpose of the meeting.

Rian was clearly unhappy about being in the Sheriff's Office and sat with her arms folded across her chest, staring coldly at Palmer.

Palmer brought the Birmingham article up on the flat screen so that they could all see it. "There may be a silver lining in this," he said. "If he thinks Ms. Coulter is about to crack, he'll become desperate and have to come out into the open to silence her. He'll make mistakes, and that's our opportunity."

"You mean use her as bait," Sam shot back. "I don't like it. He's already after her."

"We don't know that for sure, and we can protect her," Palmer said.

Sam laughed at that. "You did one hell of a job with that before." Palmer could sense Sanchez bristling so he changed direction.

"Here's what I'm proposing," he continued. "We don't know if the guy has seen the article. We're pretty sure he's been reading Donovan's, though. The *Herald* will publish a similar story that Ms. Coulter is about to give him up. It'll force him into the open."

"We can leak details from allegedly confidential sources that give your location," Donovan added.

Sam was incredulous.

"Have you people lost your fucking minds?" he said, pushing his chair back as though he was about to leave. "If you think I'm going to allow you to risk her life so you can put her out there like a piece of cheese in a mousetrap, you're fucking crazy."

"We will have her under surveillance the entire time," Palmer added.

"Bullshit," Sam responded.

Palmer nodded to Sanchez, who got up and walked to the door. He opened it and a woman walked in who could easily have been Rian's twin sister, if she'd had one. Everyone's jaw dropped as she approached the conference table.

"Meet Officer Angela Foster," Palmer said, enjoying the moment. "She's a firearms expert, has SWAT experience, and holds a third degree black belt in martial arts."

The resemblance between the officer and Rian was amazing. Even Sam found himself looking back and forth between them.

Palmer continued. "Ms. Coulter, we will secretly move you out of town to a destination of your choosing. Officer Foster will move into your home and conduct herself as if she were you at all times."

Rian was no longer glaring at Palmer. She leaned forward with her elbows on the table, listening intently.

"The cabin," she said, turning to Sam. "I can go there."

"You're not seriously considering this," Sam said.

"Of course I am. Sam, the son of a bitch has already come after me once, and it's only a matter of time before he does it again," she said.

"Then I'm going with you," he said.

"Uh, Mr. McKinney, we don't think that's a good idea," Palmer interjected.

"What? Why?" Sam asked.

"To keep up the pretense, you need to be seen going in and out of Ms. Coulter's house, driving around town, conducting your normal activities. The subject needs to be convinced that Officer Foster is really Ms. Coulter. You must play your role."

"No way. I'm going with Rian," Sam said angrily.

"He's right, Sam," Rian said. "We're together all the time. It would look weird if you suddenly weren't around under the circumstances." The look on his face showed that Sam wasn't convinced.

"Besides," she continued, "folks in Tallahassee even have trouble finding the cabin. I don't think this guy knows about it or could find it even if he did."

Rian got up and stood next to Angela Foster. Everyone else smiled and shook their heads. Standing next to one another, it was nearly impossible to tell them apart. They were the exact same height and build. Foster had brown eyes naturally, but was wearing blue contact lenses so that her eyes were the same color as Rian's. She had cut and colored her hair to match Rian's exactly.

Rian put her arm around Foster's shoulder and hugged her slightly.

"I like it. It's time we played offense. Let's do this," she said to Palmer. Turning back to Foster, she said, "I hope you're not allergic to cats."

* * *

Rian and Sam headed to his Mercedes in the sheriff's parking lot. She got in first, but noticed something in the passenger seat before she sat down. It was a small box, elegantly wrapped, without a note or a card. Rian assumed it was a present from Sam, so she got in and opened it. Sam was still outside talking with Palmer. Inside the box was a blue velvet bag, the type that often contained jewelry, but this bag held something much heavier. She dumped the contents into her hand; thirty Eisenhower silver dollars.

Thirty pieces of silver.

She put them back into the bag and stared at it, a chill running all the way down her spine.

Sam got in the car and looked at the bag in Rian's hand.

"What's that?" he asked.

Rian handed him the bag.

"I guess this answers the question of whether he's read the article," she said.

CHAPTER FIFTY-FOUR

St. Teresa, a three-mile-long finger of sand forty miles south of Tallahassee on the eastern edge of the Apalachicola National Forest, was home to pine trees, palmetto thickets, and about fifty cottages. Most of the cottages were built in the 1930s by the upper crust of Tallahassee, Supreme Court justices, wealthy bankers, lawyers, and businessmen, and were passed down through these same families for generations.

Unlike their owners, the cottages were unpretentious, built more for comfort than for showing off. Most had large central rooms with high ceilings that opened onto screened porches, offering a spectacular view of Apalachee Bay and, beyond, the Gulf of Mexico. Access off the main highway was by St. Teresa Avenue, a bit of an oxymoron since the "avenue" was a hard packed dirt road covered in crushed oyster shells.

The cottages, identified only by the owner's last name on a hand painted sign stuck into the ground, were lined up one after the other, separated by a dense thicket of pine trees and palmetto bushes. There was a marina, open only in the summer, but most St. Teresa residents anchored their Boston Whalers in the shallow bay directly behind their houses.

The Coulter's cabin had been built by Rian's maternal grandfather, who owned the largest lumber mill and concrete company in Tallahassee. She spent every summer here as a child, wading through the wet sand at low tide with her plastic bucket picking up scallops, sleeping in the hammock on the back porch, and eating fresh fish over at Angelina's Restaurant in Crawfordville. Like the other residents, the Coulters had come down in the summer to escape the oppressive heat and pressures of the day. Rian guessed she was here for the same reason, though what she was escaping from was far from normal.

Although St. Teresa bustled with activity during the summer, at this time of year it was virtually deserted. A brisk October breeze greeted Rian as she parked her rental car next to the house and went inside.

The cabin was made of cypress logs hewn from the north Florida swamps by her grandfather's company. It smelled musty from being closed up for months, and she removed all of the Visqueen that her father had meticulously covered the furniture with before they left last spring.

The large, framed hurricane map was still on the wall over the couch, and Rian smiled as she noted the thumbtacks she'd placed on it as a little girl, marking the landfall of each hurricane that hit the Florida coastline. A few more had been added since her last visit.

There was a large flat screen television on the opposite wall, and Rian tried the remote. The reception was spotty at best, and she assumed there must be a dish antennae on the roof somewhere. The reception on her new iPhone was poor as well, only one bar, and she doubted that the Internet connection for her laptop would be much better. People came here to relax, not to work. Hopefully the reception would improve if she walked outside.

* * *

Officer Angela Foster settled into Rian's house and into Rian's life. Mannix, normally distrustful and uninterested in most people, took to her right away and Foster tried to simulate Rian's movements without interacting with too many people at the same time. She went on long solitary runs like Rian did, but refrained from going to the gym where someone who knew Rian might discover the charade.

Sam would come to Rian's house as he would normally, and Rian's new car would be seen parked at his house. They would appear briefly in public together where someone might catch a fleeting glimpse of them holding hands, but they didn't go out for dinner. This was understandable given the publicity, both good and bad, which surrounded Rian and the fact that photographers were lurking everywhere hoping to catch a candid shot of her.

Foster was wired for sound at all times and her movements tracked by a GPS device in her shoe when she wasn't under direct surveillance by law enforcement.

For his part, Sam played along. Although he'd expressed his doubts that this scheme would work, Foster had done her homework and mimicked Rian's movements exactly. She had even studied Rian's running style so that casual acquaintances would believe that the attractive, physically fit young woman with the baseball cap pulled low and dark sunglasses was Rian Coulter.

Foster and Sam kept up the charade, hoping the killer would make a move soon since Rian was so far away, unprotected.

Mike Donovan did his part, too. The *Herald* published articles daily, reporting the mounting pressure on Rian and that she was in negotiations to strike a plea bargain for immunity from prosecution in exchange for revealing the identity of the killer. It also falsely stated that Judge Carson was reconsidering his decision not to allow Rian's obstruction of justice charge to be increased to a felony. They'd had to let the judge in on that part since he likely would have reacted badly to such a false report and would've wanted someone's head on a platter.

Initially, Emmett Bayer and the *Herald* publisher had been against the idea of intentionally reporting false facts, claiming it violated their sense of journalistic integrity and ran counter to their natural distrust of law enforcement. Palmer had convinced them otherwise, particularly when he offered them the exclusive story when the killer was eventually caught.

CHAPTER FIFTY-FIVE

He watched her now more intently than ever, if only from a distance. He was careful, as always, but his caution was being severely challenged by his hatred of Rian Coulter.

Each time he saw her puttering around the house or relaxing in the back yard, his bloodlust returned. The racing of his heart, the rushing in his ears, was almost more than he could stand. He could feel that the end was getting near and that this would be the culmination of it all.

He hated her. He hated all women, of course, but he hated her more than all of the others combined. She was weak and spineless and would sell him out to save her own miserable ass. Then they would hunt him down like a dog. His father would apologize publicly and claim that he never knew this side of his son. Maybe he'd have just enough time to take the old man out before the end came.

As he watched her, he became aware of his arousal. This amused him, and he relived all of the others, one by one, his excitement building with each memory. Picturing Rian in his mind caused him to climax right there in his jeans. He closed his eyes and allowed his breathing to return to normal. When he opened them again, she was gone, back inside the house, he assumed.

Perhaps he should just simply walk up to the door, kick it in and take her like he always wanted to. No, he thought, he had to plan this carefully. She was formidable, not like the others who had been so easy to overpower. He had to have her, and he would, but he had to avoid her as well until it was time. The time was coming soon. Rian Coulter would die, but she would suffer first.

Besides, there was something he needed to do first.

CHAPTER FIFTY-SIX

"It's not working," Sam said, his frustration evident. Sam, Palmer, Sanchez, and Donovan were meeting again in the same conference room where the impersonation scheme had first been discussed. Officer Foster was there, too, having concealed herself on the floor of Sam's car leaving Rian's house so no one would follow her to the Sheriff's Office.

"We have to give it more time," Palmer replied.

Sam whirled his chair around and stood, pacing the floor as he spoke.

"With all due respect, Lieutenant, it's been a goddamn week. Rian's sitting her ass out in the middle of BFE all alone, exposed as hell even though she doesn't go anywhere. The plan isn't working," he said.

"We need more time," Palmer responded, his voice edgy but controlled. "It'll work if we just keep doing what we're doing."

"Shit," Sam said. "How long do we keep this up? Another week, a month, six months?" He threw his pen across the conference room table and it clattered to the floor.

Palmer was pissed. "You got a better idea, *Counselor*?" he asked sarcastically.

"If I might," Angela Foster interjected. "What if I become imminently predictable in my movements? You know, go on the same run in a secluded area for several days in a row? In the meantime, Mr. Donovan runs a story that I've cut my deal with the prosecution and that I will spill my guts on a certain day." She looked around the room. She had everyone's attention.

"Look, we know he's watching me, but he's cautious. If he thinks I'm about to spill, he'll panic and get more desperate than ever. We can provide him with the perfect location to make his move and take him down."

Palmer cut his eyes over to Donovan, who was nodding slightly.

"I like it. I think it'll work," he said.

"McKinney?" Palmer asked. Sam sat back down in his seat and let his breath out noisily.

"I'm for anything that ends this. The sooner, the better."

"Okay," Palmer said. "I like it, too. Foster, you take the same route at the same time every day, say 4:00, starting tomorrow. The light will be low then and the more secluded the route, the better. We'll let that go for three days."

He turned to Donovan. "You run with your article on Friday that Coulter's going to cut her deal in court on Monday morning. We'll assume he'll make his move sometime this weekend." All nodded in agreement.

* * *

Rian was sick of being cooped up like a caged bird. She thought it was ironic that a serial killer roamed the streets of Pensacola freely yet she was here, confined to this house now for a week.

She was under instructions not to go out to eat lest someone recognize her. If she went out to the store for provisions, she was supposed to wear a short blonde wig and speak in a Northern accent, just in case. They had even given her a false driver's license from Minnesota to help her be the tourist she was supposed to be.

Rian had tried it a couple of times and felt like an idiot. Instead, she sat and watched the sun set every afternoon, sipping from a bottle of single malt scotch her father had stashed away and subsisting on the frozen pizzas she'd brought with her.

Sam had told her of the latest plan they'd dreamed up. Rian saw the logic in it, but wondered what would happen if Monday came and Donny Ray hadn't made his move. She guessed that they'd cross that bridge when they came to it. She couldn't even let the rest of her family know she was here. She was lonely, bored, and frustrated.

She grabbed the bottle of scotch and headed out the back door to watch the sun set, again. As beautiful and peaceful as this place was, even the view was getting old.

* * *

He'd begun to notice a pattern. For several days now, she had done the same thing, at the same time each day. He hadn't known her to be so predictable, but perhaps this was the sign he'd been looking for. He'd continue to observe her, of course, but if the pattern continued, he would be ready to strike. The rest of his plan was ready and his body tingled with excitement.

Rian Coulter would soon be his.

CHAPTER FIFTY-SEVEN

Angela Foster cruised at a steady pace through downtown. Instead of heading up the large hill north of town as she typically did, for the past few days she had continued past the old historic cemetery and detoured through the park on one of the nature trails that laced through the trees.

"Entering the park now," she said breathlessly to the microphone attached to her sports bra. It was thick through here and, at this time of day, a bit dark and foreboding. A suitable place for an attack, she thought. Evidently others thought so as well, as she had the trail all to herself. She briefly wondered if the fiber optic camera embedded in the frame of her sunglasses had enough light to function.

Suddenly, as she slowed to make a left turn on the trail, the man burst from the bushes to her right. Even though she had anticipated it, the attack still caught her by surprise. He slammed into her right shoulder, causing Angela to lose her balance and fall to the left. He fell with his full weight on top of her, and she felt her left collarbone snap as she hit the ground.

Angela shook her attacker off and tried to get to her feet. A searing pain shot through her left arm which hung uselessly at her side. The attacker tried to kick her in the head, but she ducked the blow and struggled to her feet. He came at her again and was rewarded with a right foot to his face, which shattered his nose and momentarily dazed him. He turned to run away and met Sanchez, who was bearing down on him at full speed. Sanchez lowered his shoulder and pile-drived the man into to ground. Others arrived seconds later and the man was cuffed and hauled away.

"Jesus, Foster," Palmer said, smiling. "You could've saved a little for the rest of us."

She smiled and instinctively shrugged, wincing at the pain it caused.

"Motherfucker had it coming," she said.

CHAPTER FIFTY-EIGHT

The landline phone inside the cabin rang. Rian paused the music she was listening to on her phone and pulled the earbuds out of her ears. Confirming that it was the inside phone, she jumped out of her chair and ran inside to answer it.

"We got him," Sam said excitedly when she answered.

"What?" Rian asked.

"We caught the son of a bitch. He attacked Foster on one of her runs through the nature park. She kicked the shit out of him. It's over Rian, it's finally over."

Rian fought off the same elation.

"What's his name?" she asked.

"Huh?" Sam asked, confused by Rian's lack of excitement.

"Sam, did they identify him? What's his name?" she asked again.

"Hell, Rian, I don't even know. They took him to the hospital to fix the nose that Foster relocated. What difference does it make? They caught him," Sam said.

"Describe him," Rian said.

Sam thought for a moment. "I really didn't get a good look at him. His face was full of blood, and he was dressed all in black. Big fucker, but I can't say more beyond that."

"Did you see a tattoo or a scar on his right chest?" Rian asked.

"No, Rian," Sam said, getting irritated. "They didn't take his clothes off in the back of the squad car."

"Maybe I'm just being paranoid," she responded. "There'll be plenty of time for that later. What's the situation like there?"

"Madhouse," Sam said. "Place's going nuts."

She considered this and said, "Why don't you come get me then? I've had a few single malts and have no business trying to drive."

"I'll be there in three hours," Sam said.

Rian looked around the room that held so many memories from her childhood. It had now played witness to the end of the worst nightmare of her life. She sat on the couch and let the relief wash over her. Whether due to that or the alcohol, for the first time since the ordeal began, she let the tears flow freely.

CHAPTER FIFTY-NINE

Rian sat straight up on the couch, the empty glass still in her hand. She'd finished off the bottle of scotch and realized that she must have dozed off.

She looked at her watch and noted that Sam should have been there by now. She grabbed her cell phone off the coffee table, stepped out into the back yard to get a better signal, and dialed Sam's cell number. He didn't answer and the call went to voicemail.

Rather than leave a message, Rian disconnected the call and sent him a text message: *Where are you?* She waited a few moments to see if he responded quickly and, when he didn't, she went back inside the house to collect her belongings. It dawned on her that, if she went back with Sam tonight, she'd have to leave her rental car here.

Maybe we should stay here tonight and head back tomorrow.

She gathered the trash from the kitchen and walked out the front door to put the bag into the trunk of her rental car.

Sam's car was parked right next to hers.

"Sam?" she called, still a bit groggy from the scotch-induced sleep. "Sam? Are you here?" There was no response. Feeling a sense of urgency come over her, she dialed Sam's cell number again. Again, it went to voicemail.

She dropped the trash bag and walked over to Sam's car, finding it locked. She tried his cell again and noted a dim glow coming from his car. Sam's cell phone was in the cup holder.

Rian heard a noise that sounded as though it came from the back of the house and suddenly realized that she'd left the house wide open. She ran to the front door, slamming and locking it behind her. As she raced through the house to lock the back door, she heard the noise again coming from the direction of the guest house, a small studio apartment to the rear of the main house. She locked the porch doors and crouched behind the screen, listening intently and not taking her eyes off the guest house. It was completely dark, and several minutes passed without any sounds other than the breeze and the waves of the Gulf in the distance.

Just before Rian convinced herself that she was mistaken, she heard it again, a scraping noise, definitely coming from the guest house. There was no mistake this time.

There was someone in there.

Rian tried to clear her head and think. She never remembered her father ever having a firearm in the house and wouldn't even know where to look for one. There were knives in the kitchen, and she felt certain there was a baseball bat or a broomstick around somewhere. She considered making a run for her car, but dismissed the idea of leaving Sam behind, wherever he was at the moment. As she pondered this, she heard the unmistakable sound of Sam's car door closing. She raced to the front door and ran outside.

"Sam!" she screamed. "Where *are* you?"

Sensing danger, Rian turned to her right just in time to see a shadowy figure lunge at her, swinging his fist toward her neck. She tucked her chin and the blow caught her on the jaw, causing her to stagger backwards. Her knees buckled, but she recovered and didn't fall.

He came at her again, but she surprised him by cutting to her right and running around the side of the house. There were yard tools there if she could get to them. Just as she turned the corner of the house, he was on her again, tackling her from behind. Her foot caught the edge of a stepping stone and she went down hard, striking her knees on the concrete. Before she could react, the man was on her with all of his weight, stuffing a rag into her mouth and slipping some sort of canvas bag over her head. He bent her arms behind her and tied her wrists tightly to her ankles.

He picked her up, slung her over his shoulder, and carried her with ease. Soon, he stopped and she heard a door open. He stepped inside and dropped Rian rudely to the wooden floor, and she heard him leave through the same door. When she heard it close, she realized she was in the guest house.

Fighting panic and nausea from the oily rag in her mouth, Rian tried to assess her options. She was bound so tightly that she couldn't move and was starting to lose the feeling in her hands. The more she struggled to free herself, the tighter the rope seemed to be. She finally decided to conserve her strength and wait for a better option.

From across the room, she heard the scraping sound again, this time distinctly. She wasn't alone, but her attacker had left.

Who else is in here?

Minutes passed, and Rian had no idea how long she laid there. Her hands were completely numb and her shoulders and knees cried out in pain. It was difficult for her to breathe with the bag on her head, and she stifled several waves of nausea caused by the rag in her mouth. The scraping from across the room continued but Rian couldn't determine what was making the sound.

Eventually, she heard the door open again and someone entered the room. The light in the room went on and the bag was pulled off of her head. She was face to face with the scraping noise from across the room.

Judge Clement Axley.

The judge was bound in the same manner as Rian, with a similar rag in his mouth. He'd obviously been beaten as his face was swollen and red. Blood oozed from a wound on the side of his head. When he saw Rian, his eyes blazed with a mixture of hatred and fear.

Donny Ray Cooper stood between them, staring down at them and smiling. He squatted, his face inches from Rian's.

"Hello, Counselor," he said, smiling.

He raised her on her knees facing Judge Axley, who still lay on his side.

"Let's call court to order, shall we?" Donny Ray said, snatching the judge up by the rope that bound his hands and feet. The judge's scream was muffled by the rag in his mouth and he was breathing heavily.

Donny Ray sat on the floor between them, forming a triangle so that each could see the other.

"Word has it that the judge here threatened to throw you in jail and keep you there if you didn't give him my name. That true, Counselor?" he asked.

Rian couldn't answer because the rag was still in her mouth. Donny Ray reached over and yanked it out.

"Look, Donny Ray," Rian said hoarsely, "you need to know that I've written everything down. If anything happens to me, they'll find it and know it was you." It was a lie, but Rian now wished she had done exactly that. Now Donny Ray's identity would die with her.

Donny Ray slapped her hard across the face, knocking her over onto her side again.

"Wrong answer," he said. "How 'bout you, Your Honor?" he said, turning to look at the judge. "Anything you want to say in your own defense?" he asked. The judge tried to speak, but still had a rag stuffed in his mouth. Donny Ray left this in place.

He sat Rian upright again and squatted next to Judge Axley.

"Last chance, Your Excellency. No?" he asked. He pulled an ice pick from his back pocket and placed it in the judge's left ear.

"Trial's over. Verdict; guilty. Sentence; death," he said and shoved the ice pick through Axley's ear and into his brain. The judge's eyes flew open, then rolled back into his head. His body convulsed for a few seconds, then went limp and he fell on his side, dead.

The horror of what she'd just seen was too much for Rian and she vomited all over the floor.

Donny Ray made a face and shook his head.

"Now look what you did," he said. "I have something special planned for you, too, Counselor, but we'll have to do it outside." He kicked her over onto her side and picked her up by her bindings like a suitcase and carried her outside, dropping her to the ground about fifty feet away.

"You always were a pretentious little prick, Donny Ray," Rian said, knowing those were likely the last words she would ever say.

Donny Ray took off his belt and dropped down, putting his knee in Rian's back and forcing the breath from her lungs with his weight. He looped the belt around her neck and began to pull back, cutting off her air and strangling her. As she gasped for air, he leaned forward.

"You obnoxious bitch. You should've kept your fucking mouth shut," he whispered in her ear. "The animals are gonna pick your bones apart before anybody finds you."

Rian was starting to lose consciousness as Donny Ray tightened his belt around her neck. There was no peace, no bright light, no comfortable feeling. Her last thoughts were of Sam and her family. She would miss them all terribly.

Suddenly there was an explosion and Donny Ray's grip tightened, then the belt around her neck went slack. He rolled off her, and she was vaguely aware of a warm and thick liquid pouring over her head and down her back. The sides of her vision field were closing rapidly, and she knew she would die momentarily. She was aware of someone standing over her, but couldn't see clearly enough to tell who it was before the blackness overtook her and she faded away.

CHAPTER SIXTY

Angela Sellers looked down at the bodies that lay before her. Donny Ray's head was missing, but she put one more shotgun blast into his chest, just for good measure. Rian was covered in Donny Ray's blood and brain matter, and Angela couldn't tell whether she was alive or dead.

She reached into Rian's pocket and retrieved her cell phone, holding it up to see if there was sufficient signal intensity. She punched in 9-1-1 and waited for the operator to answer and ask what the emergency was. She dropped the phone next to the bodies and made her way back through the palmetto thicket where she'd been for days, patiently waiting for the opportunity that presented itself tonight.

As she did, she passed Sam McKinney, lying face-down in the bushes next to the house. He still wasn't moving, so she knelt next to him and felt for a pulse, which she readily found. Sam would live, although he would have a concussion from the blow she delivered with the butt of her shotgun.

Angela knew that Barry wouldn't approve of her taking another life like she'd just done. She also knew that, if she hadn't intervened, Donny Ray Cooper would have escaped again and there would never be justice for those whom he had killed, one of whom was Barry. She felt no guilt, no remorse, and no sorrow for Donny Ray or Judge Axley. God would judge her one day, but not this day.

She did have some regret about Rian Coulter, whom Barry had always liked and spoken highly of. She'd been instrumental in Barry's quick promotions in the Public Defender's Office. On the other hand, Rian had protected Barry's murderer, and Angela wasn't certain she could forgive her for that.

As she sat there in the palmettos watching Donny Ray choke the life out of Rian, Angela had wrestled with the decision whether to save her or let Donny Ray kill her first. It was actually Barry himself who intervened, waking Angela from her stupor.

"Angela!" he'd said to her. "She's one of our own. Help her." She'd done what Barry had asked, though she was now sorry she hadn't acted in time.

CHAPTER SIXTY-ONE

When the details of Donny Ray's crimes and Rian's actions were finally revealed, public opinion quickly and decidedly shifted in her favor. News talk shows kept the story alive for weeks, and everyone from Fox News to Nancy Grace to MSNBC hailed her as a heroine. Even Sarah Palin, as different politically from Rian Coulter as two women could be, proclaimed her the "ultimate hockey mom." The Florida Bar closed its investigation and even went so far as to praise Rian for "preserving the integrity of the Bar."

Governor Arden Chambers viewed all of the accolades with disgust. He was, above all, a political pragmatist and so, at his direction, Senate Bill 119 was withdrawn by its sponsor, Senator J.T. Spencer, who then promptly announced his resignation from the Senate.

Mike Donovan was nominated for the Pulitzer Prize for investigative reporting. He didn't win, but his nomination was a significant achievement for a small newspaper such as the *Herald.*

Glenn Palmer received his captain's bars shortly after receiving the highest honor bestowed by the Florida Department of Law Enforcement. He proudly pinned Sergeant stripes on Sgt. Emil Sanchez.

CHAPTER SIXTY-TWO

Sam carried his coffee over the foot bridge and sat on a bench overlooking Boston Harbor.

Six weeks spent recuperating on Cape Cod, far from the Gulf Coast and everything associated with it had healed his injuries and begun the repair of his soul. The headaches were much less frequent now, and his vision had nearly returned to normal.

As the wind from the ocean whipped around him, Sam sipped his coffee and let his mind drift back to the days seemingly so long ago when he and Rian would sleep in on Saturday mornings, then stroll through the farmer's market sipping coffee and arguing over which bistro they would go to for lunch. He would forever carry guilt over his inability to be there to save Rian back in St. Teresa.

Sam glanced at his watch, noting that his flight to Pensacola was leaving in two hours. He felt conflicted. Part of him never wanted to go back there but to stay in this vibrant city and start a new life.

He turned to the woman seated next to him.

"Would you like some?" he asked, extending his coffee cup.

CHAPTER SIXTY-THREE

"No, thanks," Rian said, smiling at him.

Donny Ray Cooper had inflicted serious injuries on her. Her physical injuries had improved, but Sam wasn't so sure about the psychological ones. Rian claimed that she was fine, but she hadn't witnessed the night terrors that gripped her repeatedly like Sam had.

Despite all of the accolades that had come her way over the past several weeks, Rian seemed adrift to Sam. She resigned from the Public Defender's Office and seemingly had no real plan to move on with her career. She constantly wondered who had taken off Donny Ray Cooper's head and, in turn, saved her life, and felt frustrated that she couldn't focus in on the person she saw, or thought she saw, that night.

Rian wrapped her arm around Sam's and rested her head on his shoulder. They sat together in silence for a long while, listening to the seagulls overhead and watching the sailboats whip through the harbor.

"I like it here," Sam said eventually. "We could make this work."

Rian sighed. "I like it here, too," she said. Then, standing but not letting go of his hand, she turned back to look at Sam.

"Come on," she said. "Let's go home."

Thanks so much for reading *The Judas Dilemma.* I hope that you enjoyed it.

As an independent author, my success depends upon readers like you to spread the word. If you enjoyed the book, please tell your friends. Whether you liked it or not, your feedback is very important to me. If you have a moment please post an honest review at www.amazon.com. You can also reach me through my website at www.robertheathbooks.com.

I hope so see you again soon with my next book, *Scapegoat.*

Sincerely,

Robert Heath

ABOUT THE AUTHOR

Robert Heath is a former state court prosecutor and criminal defense lawyer and is now a nationally certified civil trial attorney. *The Judas Dilemma* is his first novel. He lives in Pensacola, Florida with his wife, Debbie, and two Cavalier King Charles Spaniels, Atti and Boo Radley, who rule the roost.

He is currently at work on his next novel of suspense.

CPSIA information can be obtained at www.ICGtesting.com
Printed in the USA
LVOW07s1719200116

471540LV00003B/757/P